GREAT PARTY! SORRY ABOUT THE MURDER

D.B. ELROGG

A MILO RATHKEY MYSTERY

Great Party! Sorry About The Murder
A Milo Rathkey Mystery

Copyright © 2017 Alyce Goldberg, Harvey Goldberg

All Rights Reserved

ISBN 978-0-9998200-0-1 (Paperback)
ISBN 978-0-6920544-5-1 (eBook)
ISBN 979-8-9856252-3-3 (Hardcover)

No part of this publication may be used, reproduced in any manner, or published in any form or by any means, electronic, mechanical, photocopying, recording or otherwise, without the prior written permission of the publisher, except brief quotations to be used in the production of critical articles and reviews.

If you wish to contact the authors, you may email them at: authors@dbelrogg.com

This is a work of fiction. All characters and incidents are totally from the minds of the authors and any resemblance to actual persons, living or dead, or incidents past and present are purely coincidental.

Cover Art by Drew Proffitt

Dedicated to Annie the Cat
They also serve who only sleep on the keyboard

SPECIAL THANKS TO

JODY EVANS
STAN JOHNSON
DOUG OSELL
NICK GOLDBERG
PIPER GOLDBERG
DREW PROFFITT

1

If Milo Rathkey had seen the blow coming, he would have done a better job of ducking. The sucker punch to the side of his head sent the scruffy, barrel-chested detective sprawling off the short retaining wall and onto the ice and snow-covered parking lot. A steel-toed work boot slammed into his midsection. Barely breathing, he drove upward with his fist, hammering his assailant in the groin. The man groaned and doubled over. Milo sprang up, pummeled him with uppercuts to the face until he dropped to the ground. Enraged to the point of feeling no pain, Milo had to restrain himself. Blood poured out of his assailant's nose and mouth, and one eye was swelling shut. The bloody face belonged to Chet Duncan, the cheating husband he had been tailing, obviously not well.

Crawling to the end of the short retaining wall, Chet tried to stem the blood flow from his nose with the sleeve of his shirt. He grabbed the wall and struggled to his feet.

Milo, wincing at the sharp pain in his own ribs, was relieved to see the man keeping the wall between them.

Chet was reduced to a pathetic wail. "Why have you been following me?"

Milo, ignoring Chet, scanned the ground for his cell phone.

Chet shivered. It was cold—Duluth-Minnesota-in-December cold—and he had bolted from his motel room without a jacket. The fight was out of him, but the anger returned. "You're working for that bitch wife of mine. I've seen you before! You're going to pay for this! Damn it! You assaulted me!"

"Idiot!" Rathkey muttered, slowly bending to retrieve his phone, thinking he was getting sloppy if a dope like Chet could pick him out.

Shifting toward his car, Milo continued to keep an eye on Chet as the man floundered against the cold, steady Lake Superior wind. He fell twice to the hard-packed snow until he finally disappeared into his rustic love shack. At this point, Chet was no longer Milo's problem.

Rathkey finished the frigid, solitary walk back to his car, questioning why he didn't have a nubile young secretary to console him. Once inside, he unearthed an old, crumpled Kleenex box and used the three remaining dusty tissues to blot the blood off his knuckles and the side of his hand. He touched his ribs and sucked air. They were at least bruised. He hoped not cracked or broken. Either way, he knew he was in for at least a couple of weeks of pain. His hand located the Costco-sized bottle of Extra Strength Excedrin in the glove compartment. After twisting the safety cap and washing two down with what was left of his morning coffee, Milo eased his car seat back to take pressure off his midsection.

Between calming shallow breaths, Milo grumbled about how he hated following wayward spouses to pay the bills.

He thought he had set up the surveillance well. The morning was so bone-chilling cold, Milo couldn't stay in the car to operate his camera-cell phone surveillance unit without running the defroster, something he was afraid would give him away. Looking back on it, the car would have been the better option, at least less painful. He checked the phone and the camera, both had recorded Chet slipping into the cabin with his secretary, as well as the assault on Milo. The process had been messy, but the video was clear.

The strong, Lake Superior winds were permeating his 2004 Honda Accord. He needed heat and needed it fast. Turning the key, the Accord groaned but failed to start. A sense of dread came over him.

"Oh, not now!" he said to himself, bemoaning the fact he hadn't had the car serviced in a long while, and the battery was old. He would get only one or maybe two more cranks before it was dead. This was always tricky. He pumped the gas gently so as not to flood the engine, turned the key, and the Accord was alive again.

As he waited for the heat to encircle him, he took the time to call his friend, police Lt. Ernie Gramm.

"Hey Milo, what's up?" Gramm answered.

"Ernie, I just got punched by a guy I was tailing. I think I broke his nose. I'm just telling you in case he files a complaint. Consider this a prior complaint."

Gramm was confused. "Are you all right? Are you filing a real complaint?"

Hearing the surprise in his friend's voice, Milo sought to allay any confusion. "Yeah, I'm okay, and I'll only file a complaint if he does."

"You do remember I'm a homicide detective."

"It coulda been a homicide. I was mad enough."

Gramm sighed and figured he would point out the obvious to Milo one more time. "Chasing husbands is beneath you, and if he spotted you, you're getting sloppy."

Gramm wasn't telling him anything he didn't already know, but he was in no mood for a lecture. "Yeah, I know."

"Do you need a doctor or a hospital?"

"Naw, he only got in one good kick."

"One good kick? Milo you're over forty years old and shouldn't be thinking of only one kick as a good thing. At least go home and take it easy."

"I would, but I have to go downtown to a will reading of all things."

"Who died?" Gramm asked.

"Nobody, I just broke his nose," Rathkey cracked.

"No, not your fight, dumb ass, the will reading. Who died?"

"Oh, John McKnight."

"The real estate guy? Why are you mentioned in his will?"

"My mom used to cook for him. I grew up in his house. He was a good guy. I always liked his collection of mystery books. I'm thinking he left me one or two."

"Good. You can read them while you heal. Hey Milo, hang on for a minute." Gramm paused, and Milo could tell he was dealing with somebody named Robin who had come into his office. A few seconds later, Gramm came back to the phone. "You know Milo, I still think you should go to the emergency room to get checked out."

"Naw, I'm okay. Besides, I would need insurance for that."

Exasperation was getting the better of Gramm. He had known Milo for more than fifteen years and worked with him when Milo was a police detective in Brainerd. He was a pro and damn smart. "You need to quit this silly-ass private eye work and take the job as consultant here. You can help me with the tough cases, and it comes with insurance."

"Yeah, I know, but I got tired of people murdering people when I was a cop—remember?" Milo repeated his standard line, which even he doubted these days. Instead, he was beginning to realize leaving the force had more to do with his divorce than strangers murdering other strangers.

"So, getting punched by a cheating husband is better?"

"Ernie, my friend, you have a point, and my ribs are agreeing with you right now."

"Think about it. I gotta go. I'll alert Herb about your possible assault case."

Rathkey thanked him, and the line went dead. Because of the pain in his ribs, Milo's breathing was shallow, so the car seat went back another notch. Running his fingers through his black, curly hair, he felt a bump beginning to grow on the side of his head where Chet had punched him. Milo glanced at the clock. There was no time to go home and clean up. He would have to go to the will reading like this. John was a popular guy. He hoped there would be a lot of people there, and he wouldn't be noticed.

The Excedrin was at last beginning to take effect. He adjusted the seat upward, carefully pulled on his gloves, and put the car into drive. His tires crunched on the snow-covered parking lot as he headed for the scenic two-lane highway that led to the non-touristy four-lane back to town. Both highways hugged Lake Superior, which wasn't as much a large lake, as a small ocean. Glancing to his left as he drove, Milo could still see some open water, but the ice was winning the battle.

As he hit the outskirts of Duluth, his phone interrupted the quiet. "Milo Rathkey," he answered.

An angry female voice screeched, "You son of a bitch! You're fired!"

Recognizing the voice, Milo sighed, not wanting to deal with this. "You can't fire me Mrs. Duncan. You already paid me. The job is done. I have the evidence, if you care."

"I don't care. My husband called, and said you attacked him for no reason!" she shouted.

"For no reason?"

"He's going to the police!"

"He assaulted me first, and I recorded it! So, along with assault, he will also be charged with making a false report."

"Go to hell! You hurt him! You're fired!" she shouted one more time and hung up.

Oh Lord, they're both idiots, he thought.

§

Gloomy gray skies were the norm for Duluth in the winter, but the events of this day made it seem even drearier, if that was possible. Milo's stomach was letting him know it was empty, but there was little he could do about it now. He had gotten one bite of Ilene's delicious cheese-filled breakfast bagel before the attack.

Up ahead he spotted a parking ramp. Milo hated parking ramps; it was like paying for car day-care. Going around the block a second time, he heard the bells from Old Central High. He was late but was sure he wouldn't be missed in the crowd.

He was prepared to go around the block a third time when a new, bright-red Mercedes flashed its back-up lights. Waiting as the driver checked her mirror, fixed her lipstick, and did other vehicular cosmetology, he reached over and put a handful of Excedrin in his pocket for later. After a couple of minutes, she pulled out, and Milo pulled in.

He was pleased to see there was still forty-five minutes on the meter and didn't bother to feed it. Late, and a half a block away, Rathkey pulled up the collar on his old overcoat and hunched his shoulders against the forbidding cold.

Moving as quickly as his ribs would allow, he entered the Algood Building, home to the offices of Haney, Jenson, and Hamft.

The welcoming rush of steamy hot air hit him in the face the instant he opened the door. The Algood Building had once been the home to the city's power brokers, where deals were made and broken. The younger crowd had abandoned it for the new builds, glitzy glass and chrome.

Haney, Jenson, and Hamft, however, still resided in the wood and marble of a different era.

Rathkey brushed as much salt and sand off his clothes as possible. He noticed a white stain on his trouser leg, but there was nothing he could do about it now. As he moved toward the elevators, his overshoes began to squeak on the marble floor. He considered taking them off, but his ribs didn't want to move any more than they had to. The elevator arrived with a thud, and Milo entered it alone.

He hadn't been in regular contact with John McKnight for more than twenty years other than the occasional birthday card or holiday greeting. He was surprised when John called a month ago, asking him to visit. As they talked, John seemed to know quite a bit about Milo, his years as a military policeman in the Navy and his time being a cop in Brainerd. Both men touched only briefly on the losses in their lives—Milo's divorce and Laura McKnight's death. The visit was comfortable, and they agreed to keep in touch.

Milo regretted that second conversation wouldn't be happening now.

The old elevator creaked to a stop on the sixth floor and slowly opened. With galoshes squeaking away, he saw the double glass doors of Haney, Jenson, and Hampft.

"Can I help you sir?" the receptionist asked, wondering if this disheveled man was in the right place.

"I am here for the McKnight's will reading." "Your name sir?"

"Milo Rathkey."

She looked at a paper and smiled.

"Have a seat, sir. Mr. Haney will be with you shortly."

Milo scanned the nearly empty reception area. He figured they must have started already. Debating whether sitting or standing would be less painful, he opted to stand.

A tall, pleasant looking man in a well-tailored suit and conservative blue tie looked up from his paper. "Well, hello there, Mr. Rathkey. We meet at last."

The two creases between Milo's eyebrows etched deeper, a sign he was in thought—or confused. The tall man's familiarity took him by surprise. Milo didn't like surprises. He didn't return the smile. "Do I know you?"

"No, you don't. I'm John's son, Sutherland McKnight."

His mind questioned briefly why John's son would not be included in the other room but then centered on the man's name. Sutherland, an unusual first name, but one Milo had heard once before more than thirty years ago. In fact, the last time he heard the name Sutherland, this thin, fair-haired man standing in front of him had not yet been born. Milo remembered sitting in the library, telling John about his plans to join the Navy when John surprised him with the news that Laura was expecting. "It's a boy," John had said. "We are going to name him Sutherland. It's a family name on Laura's side."

Milo took off his gloves, and, as they shook hands, he smiled at the memory. Sutherland was the male version of his mother.

"I'm sorry about your father," Milo offered. "I reconnected with him a while ago. I didn't realize he was ill."

"He wasn't. He had a heart attack; it was sudden and unexpected."

Sutherland suggested they sit down, but Milo declined, saying he had a few aches and pains that made standing more comfortable. "I hope you weren't waiting for me."

It was Sutherland's turn to look confused. "Of course we waited. You have to be here."

Milo was again taken off guard. "Why?"

Sutherland sensed the problem. "Did my father ever mention his will to you?"

"No, not at all."

Sutherland said almost to himself as much as he said it to Milo, "Well, I guess he thought he had a lot of time to bring it up."

Before Rathkey could respond, a man in his late fifties, early sixties approached them and led them into a traditional, wood-dominated conference room. "I'm Richard Haney, John McKnight's attorney," the man explained. "Of course, I know you, Sutherland, and I assume that you, sir, are Milo Rathkey. Would either of you gentlemen like some refreshments before we begin?"

Sutherland took only a bottle of water, while Rathkey poured himself some coffee, loaded it with cream, grabbed several muffins, and topped them with butter.

Reacting to the stares, Milo offered, "My breakfast got away from me." He thought about his airborne bagel.

"Your hand is bleeding," Sutherland said.

Rathkey looked at the side of his left hand which he had used to stop his fall earlier. "Hmm, you're right." He grabbed a couple more napkins and held them to his hand where they stuck.

Bringing his food back to the conference table, he asked, "Where is everyone else?"

Haney looked up from his file in surprise as he informed Milo that they would be the only two. Noticing the napkins attached to Milo's hand, and blotches of blood seeping through, he asked, "Mr. Rathkey, do you need some first aid? We do have a first aid kit."

Milo again looked at his hand. "Yeah, I could use a couple of Band-Aids, some sharp ice got the better of me this morning," he said as an excuse.

Haney disappeared and came back with a box of Band-Aids and some antiseptic. Milo took a few minutes to doctor himself before cautiously sitting down. He had looked around for a waste basket, but finding none, shoved the Band-Aid wrappers and bloodied napkins into his coat pocket, not the Excedrin pocket.

Haney sat at the head of the table, with Sutherland to his left and Rathkey to his right. The room was so massive that the threesome huddled at one end of the huge table seemed almost silly. Milo leaned back as far as possible in the comfortable high-backed chair, taking pressure off his ribs while checking out portraits of long-dead partners that decorated the walls.

Haney clasped his hands on his folder. "Mr. Rathkey, before we start, could I see some identification. It's just procedure."

Thinking Haney could have asked for this while he was standing, Milo winced as he took out his wallet and handed the lawyer his driver's license. Haney glanced at it and handed it back.

"Before we start, do either of you have any questions?"

"Well, I'm not so sure why I am here," Rathkey said.

Haney looked surprised and glanced at Sutherland who sat back in his chair, smiled, and said, "I am afraid my father failed to have a key discussion with Mr. Rathkey."

"Well, this is certainly going to be fun," Haney said, smiling, something he rarely got an opportunity to do.

Milo had no idea what was going on and scratched his head, noticing that the welt was still growing. The furrows between Milo's eyebrows deepened yet again. Haney opened the file containing the will and began to read.

"I, John McKnight, being of sound mind and body do hereby bequeath the following: To my son, Sutherland McKnight, I leave my business, McKnight Enterprises, in the hope he continues to see it grow. I also leave him half of my personal wealth in stocks, bonds, and other investments, amounting to fifteen million dollars."

Sutherland nodded.

Milo thought if he'd been handed fifteen million dollars, he'd be doing back flips. He took another sip of coffee. It was free.

"To Milo Rathkey," Haney continued, *"who grew up in my house, and whom I have always considered to be an important part of my extended family, I leave the other half of my fortune."*

"What!" Milo choked on his coffee and started coughing which didn't help his ribs. There were no backflips.

Haney continued unfazed.

"In addition, I leave my beloved estate, Lakesong, to both my son Sutherland and to Milo Rathkey to be shared equally and enjoyed by both."

Milo, no longer coughing, was silent, almost in a state of shock.

"Lakesong is special to me, and was, even before I bought it. It is too large an estate for Sutherland to enjoy by himself, and I fear it will simply become a burden. Both of you grew up there. Although you don't have experiences together, you both have fond memories of Lakesong. I hope those memories help to bond you. Also, I am pairing the two of you because I believe that Sutherland, you lead a structured but uneventful life, and Milo, your life is sometimes too chaotic. I feel that in time you two will even each other out and this will be a productive partnership. I am only sad I will not be there to watch it unfold."

"There are other minor bequests to staff and charities, but that, gentlemen is the meat of the will," Haney said, closing the folder. He stood up and addressed them both, "I think you two need to talk. The conference room is yours for as long as you need it."

Rathkey remained silent. Normally, Milo was quick at assessing a situation, but what he had heard confounded him. After several minutes, he mumbled, "What the hell just happened here?"

"In a nut shell, you received fifteen million dollars and half of Lakesong from my father."

Milo remained confused. "Why would he do that?"

"I wish he would have had a chance to explain his thinking but let me try. He viewed you as family. Even though you weren't there, he kept track of you, and he mentioned you often."

"I still don't get this. Why would he give me all this money? You're his son."

"I have a considerable amount of money from my mother. My father left me his business, and, quite frankly, I am surprised that he gave me any of his money at all."

Milo stared at this young man who was okay at losing half his home and fifteen million dollars.

Who was this guy?

"This is crazy. I mean, I know John liked me. I liked him! But I'm still wondering…"

"The short, pragmatic answer is he needed to know that someone would love his estate. I love parts of it, but I suspect not the parts you like."

"I love the library!"

Sutherland smiled. "There you go. It was my father's pride and joy. But I do not love it, at least not the way he did. You have cracked the case, detective. You have solved the mystery. This could be all about that dusty old library."

Rathkey tried to take a deep breath and change positions in the chair, but his ribs refused.

"Are you in pain?" Sutherland asked.

Trying to downplay the results of a middle-aged man still getting into fist fights, Milo quickly bushed it aside. "It was an active morning."

Finishing his coffee, taking time to think, he glanced again at Sutherland McKnight. "So, I get fifteen million dollars and half a house because I love the library? That's crazy."

"Crazy possibly, but my father's love of that house goes back to his childhood, even before he owned it. My mother used to kiddingly call it my father's 'other' relationship."

"Why?"

"I don't know. Another mystery for you to solve perhaps."

Rathkey nodded. After a brief pause, he added, "So, this is real?"

"Yes. Why don't we go down to the café on the ground floor and continue this conversation. I'm getting hungry."

Rathkey said nothing and took several minutes to stand up.

2

Sutherland looked up at the menu which was above the cash register. "Let's order first, then talk." Almost to himself he mentioned, "I seem to remember this place has an acceptable mixed green salad with a raspberry vinaigrette, or a trendy avocado dressing."

Rathkey's face did not hide his disdain. "I know I have trendy written all over me, but I'm looking for some serious food." Walking up to the disinterested woman at the register, Milo ordered two hamburgers, French fries, and a Diet Coke. After several minutes of negotiation over hamburger toppings, Milo believed he had won out with ketchup and mustard only.

"That'll be twenty-four ninety-seven," the woman chirped.

Milo stared at the woman in stunned silence. "Are you kidding?"

Sutherland, realizing this bill might be out of Milo's usual lunch price point, offered to pick it up.

"I'm not going to argue," Milo said taking a glass and filling it full of Diet Coke before heading to the table against the wall. He heard Sutherland order a mixed green salad with avocado dressing and garlic hummus on the side. Rathkey reached into his coat pocket for more Excedrin, making a small pile of pills on the table. Taking two from the pile, he washed them down with his drink, as he sat down with great care, in case his ribs might be broken. Closing his eyes, trying to relax, he wondered how John, a man who loved his steak, raised a son who preferred hummus.

Rathkey shifted his body several times in the chair, searching for the least painful position as Sutherland joined him and placed the yellow order-number marker on the table. It was a bright number twelve which Rathkey thought strange because there were only three other people in the café.

He also noticed that Sutherland was again drinking bottled water. This was Duluth, Minnesota, home of Lake Superior. There was more fresh water in this city than anywhere else on the face of the Earth! Rathkey made a mental note to ask Sutherland—at some point—why he drank water from some swamp in Florida.

Sutherland, who lived in the land of healthy, looked at the small pile of pills on the table. "Vitamins?" he asked.

"Excedrin. Extra strength."

"Excedrin and Diet Coke?"

"Absolutely, I'll be good as new in a few minutes," Rathkey challenged. "It cures just about everything and makes me feel good at the same time."

"I use turmeric and ginger," Sutherland said, as his salad arrived.

"Sounds like two strippers."

Sutherland laughed, knowing he would never look at turmeric and ginger in the same way again.

Realizing that his companion was waiting to eat until the hamburgers arrived, Rathkey told Sutherland to dig in. As Sutherland spread his first fork full of hummus on pita, Rathkey announced, "If you had been a girl, your name would have been Susan."

"What?" Sutherland asked, laughing and drooling a bit of hummus.

"Sorry. It was back when I was leaving for the Navy. Your father told me that your mother was expecting you, and you were going to be a boy. But if you had been a girl, you would be Susan," Milo said with a smile.

Leaning back with a big grin, Sutherland kidded, "At least it has a nick name. Sutherland is…Sutherland."

"You're right…Sue."

"Let's not be making that a running joke."

Rathkey again noticed how much Sutherland resembled his mother, especially when he laughed. It was a full-throated, head back, robust laugh, which seemed out of place on petite Laura McKnight but at home on the younger man sitting opposite him.

Milo's hamburgers came with tomato and lettuce and pickles which he removed with disdain. "I ordered just mustard and ketchup. What's with all the rest of this stuff?"

Remembering the message in the will, Milo grumbled, "Maybe John was right. Even my twenty-four-dollar hamburgers are chaotic."

Sutherland looked down at his plate. "Following that logic, because I got what I ordered, my life is, as my father stated, too uneventful." If nothing else, Milo Rathkey was entertaining. Sutherland could not remember going anywhere with a bloody hand and a bodily injury that needed a pocket full of Excedrin.

"So, your father never explained that line in the will about my life being chaotic and yours uneventful?" Milo asked.

Sutherland thought for a moment, "Not really, but let's look at it this way. You've clearly been in some…physical altercation. The worst I did this morning was drip water on my tie, but I think we're making too much of that. I think this is really about the future of Lakesong."

As Sutherland once again talked of John's love of the estate, Milo took the time to assess his companion. The stocky detective had spent half a life time reading people. He saw a guy who, apart from enjoying salads, was an okay sort. He seemed to have gotten the confidence and kindness of John and the acceptance of his mother.

Taking a break from his burger marathon, Milo asked, "So, how is this going to work?"

"Well, to begin with, you move into Lakesong."

Milo thought of the last time he moved into Lakesong. He was eight, his father had been killed, and he was the cook's son. "This is your home, Sutherland. How are you okay with some stranger co-owning your home?"

"This concept is new to you, but my father and I had long talks about it. I admit, I thought it was more than a little strange to begin with, but I understand what my father wanted. He knew that no one would buy Lakesong to live in.

Even if he gave it away, the upkeep would be prohibitive unless one had a lot of money. He did not want it to be destroyed and replaced by some monstrosity."

Either logic or Excedrin seemed to be working on Rathkey, "So, that's where I come in?"

"Yes, there are now two of us who want only the best for Lakesong. I think my dad was playing the odds. At least one of us will continue to live there, and he made sure you had enough money if that person was going to be you. He has extended Lakesong for at least one more generation."

In a strange way, it made sense, but it begged one more question. "Why don't you just get married and fill the house up with kids?" Milo asked.

"Now why didn't I think of that?"

"Too chaotic for you?"

"I was engaged for several years, but the relationship faded away. She wanted to be married, but not necessarily to me. She got her wish. She was married, but is now divorcing a financier from Portugal. Right now, for me, the *wife-and-kid's solution* seems far away."

"Better you break up before you got married. Trust me, I know. I was married when I was a cop, but she left me. It's tough being a cop's wife, long hours and danger."

"I'm sorry. That's too bad. Do you have any kids?"

"No, we had a dog. He ran away."

"Oh, that's too bad. Did you ever get him back?"

"Yeah, he was caught by the dog catcher."

"That's good...right?"

"No. That's bad. My wife left me and married the dog catcher."

Sutherland tried to stifle a laugh. "She left you for the dog catcher?"

Rathkey grinned. "That's okay, you can laugh. I see the humor in it myself—now."

Sutherland said, as an apology, "I guess it's the fact that the guy is a dog catcher that makes it funny."

"That's why I tell it that way, but for the record, *the dog catcher* is really a Crow Wing County Animal Control Officer."

"You're right, that's not as funny."

"None of it was funny at the time. I write it off to dog catchers having better hours and dogs not shooting back." With that Rathkey began his second hamburger.

Sutherland recalled his father's description of Milo as a highly-decorated detective—one who always solved his cases. Looking at this disheveled, hurting, hungry man sitting opposite him, he found that description hard to believe.

Milo prided himself as a person who could always steer a conversation back on topic. "So, my moving into Lakesong, how will that work?"

Sutherland took another bite of his salad. "Well, first we get a moving van to bring your things to the house."

"Forget that! I can get all of it in my car."

"You don't have furniture?"

"Naw. It all stays with the apartment. So which bedroom do I get? I used to sleep in one of the back bedrooms on the second floor."

"I figure we use the house like a duplex, you on the first floor and me on the second. It's how I have been living in the house since I was a teen. I have done renovations up there to suit my taste, but the first floor is exactly how you remember it because my father never changed a thing."

"You're giving me the master bedroom?" Rathkey was surprised.

"Sure. If you don't mind. You also get my father's office. It's quite nice if you like dark oak. I like my more modern rooms, and I don't want to move downstairs. Oh, and that dreary library is all yours. My father said you would want to use the library extensively."

Milo thought this sounded ideal, better than he could have imagined, but there was no easy way to ask the next question. "What about John's things?" he asked.

Sutherland sat back, as this matter-of-fact conversation had taken an emotional turn. "My father and I talked about the details, but I never thought it would happen so soon. He wanted most of his personal things given away to charity. I have to admit, it was difficult…took me longer than I expected, but…it's done. The master bedroom area has been refurbished. I have removed my father's papers from the office and put them upstairs. I will get to them later."

"Nobody is prepared for the loss of a dad," Milo spoke from experience. "It shocked me when I heard about John's death. We had just talked a couple of weeks before, and I got the idea that he wanted to stay in touch. I went to the funeral but got there late," Milo said, remembering another stake-out that ran long.

Sutherland looked distressed. "I am so sorry I didn't contact you to let you know about John's passing. I should have asked you to speak at the funeral or something. In my defense, it happened so suddenly, I was in shock for most of that time."

"No, no, no, don't apologize. You shouldn't have contacted me. You didn't even know me."

Sutherland brushed aside Milo's kind reasoning. "But I knew this day was going to happen, so clearly, you were important to him. But like I said, I wasn't operating at my usual efficiency."

"So, when should this happen—my moving in?"

Sutherland shrugged. "Anytime."

Milo leaned back and thought about sitting tonight in that great paneled, book-lined, library, a place he had loved as a child. "If this is real, I can move in this afternoon. I have to meet some people after this, but I could pick up my stuff and head over to your house around five this evening."

"Our house," Sutherland corrected. "You can move in today? Wow, that is fast. I guess this is real. You know my father showed me some pictures of you when you lived in the house. Would you like those in the bedroom?"

Milo was touched that John had kept pictures of him from so long ago, but avoided the direct question and made light of the whole matter. "Where did he find pictures that old?"

"In the vault."

Milo began, "You have a…." then stopped and rephrased as he saw Sutherland shaking his head. "We have a vault?"

"We do, but that's a discussion for another time. I will tell Martha to expect you for dinner. We usually eat dinner at seven in what I call the family room, you know, the small dining room off the kitchen."

Milo acknowledged the small dining room and asked about this person named Martha. Sutherland explained she was their personal chef, and an excellent cook.

"I look forward to eating Martha's cooking. John always had good taste when it came to who prepared his groceries," Milo teased, thinking of his mother.

Sutherland laughed, getting the joke about Milo's mother having been the cook. "Oh, I think you and Martha will get along fine. On another note, there is a front gate code. Why don't you put it in your phone."

"Let me guess—26643," Rathkey said, smiling.

"How would you know that? Has it always been the same?"

"Yeah, it was just something that was easy to remember."

"How is 26643 easy to remember?"

Rathkey's cell phone rang, interrupting his explanation. Sutherland nodded for him to answer it, putting further discussion of the code mystery on hold.

"Yeah?" Milo asked the caller.

"Milo, it's Ed Patupick. I got a chance to check my security tapes, and I think you are going to like this."

Patupick was the close friend of Rathkey's, who set him up with the dash-cam, phone-camera combo. As luck would have it, Ed's electronics store was opposite a liquor store robbery Milo was investigating.

"That's great, Ed! I'll be right over."

He hung up and explained to Sutherland, "My next appointment."

Sutherland stood up. "Not a problem. I've arranged to have my afternoon free, so I will be at the house when you arrive."

"Great." They shook hands, and on the way out the door, Rathkey wondered if he had dreamed this entire thing. If so, he was going to be pissed when he woke up.

§

Sutherland drove his Porsche 911 Turbo S Cabriolet back to Lakesong, parking it in the garage next to the Bentley. He ran up the steps to the main house and stopped by the kitchen where Martha was getting started on dinner. "Well, I met the man," he informed Martha.

Martha put down her chopping knife, looked at the tall man in front of her, took a deep breath, and asked as calmly as she could, "And?"

"I like him," Sutherland said, sampling a newly chopped carrot stick.

Letting the pilfering of her food go for the minute, she asked the most important question. "Does that mean you are going to keep the house?"

"It does," Sutherland said, pushing his luck and taking a piece of celery too.

Martha smiled and took a deep breath for the second time that day. When her parents were killed in a traffic accident on the Miller Trunk highway, she left her job as a sous chef in Minneapolis to raise her two younger brothers and sister. Becoming John McKnight's personal chef had been a life saver as it also came with the caretaker's cottage. She and her three younger siblings moved in a month after their parent's funeral. With John's recent death, she had been worried her situation might have to change.

"Good, I hate moving," she quipped, not betraying the fear that had gripped her since John's death.

"So do I," Sutherland added, reaching for another piece of carrot only to have his hand gently slapped.

"How would you know?"

Sutherland smiled. "You have a point there. What do I know about moving?" *More of that uneventful life my father referred to in the will.*

Martha handed him the carrot stick he had tried to sneak away with earlier, and he left her to continue her food magic.

Walking through the hearth room and family room, he sat down in the two-story gallery, a grand, glass-domed room which let in whatever sunlight Duluth could muster in the winter.

Sutherland's thoughts were interrupted by a loud, sharp meow which emanated from a high branch in a Guiana chestnut tree to Sutherland's right. He glanced up and saw the green eyes of the 'calico monster,' Annie, staring back at him. He interpreted her meow as if she were saying, "This is my room. Why are you here?"

"My fine cat, like me, you too are in for changes. You are going to have to share your house—and this room—with someone new, a man named Milo Rathkey."

He thought about what he knew of Milo from his dad, and what he experienced of the man today—his bloodied hand, aching body, and clothing in need of a good press—and challenged the cat, "How well do YOU deal with chaos?"

After standing up and stretching, she gave him a silent meow, a sign that she felt herself above it all. At least that's what his father said it meant, and he was an expert of sort, having had a number of calico cats named Annie.

Annie had been right to question Sutherland's appearance in the room as this was not one of his normal haunts. Sitting down in one of the cushioned rattan sofas, he reflected on how this was his mother's favorite area, and a place he could always find her. She always said this room with its greenery, white marble floor, and colorful furniture gave a respite from the gray dreariness of winter.

Sutherland smiled as he remembered riding his tricycle in and around the plants and clumps of trees while his mother sat on one of the sofas and read. In the evening, his father would join them and play before supper. Those were happy times.

He had not sat in this room nor thought about his childhood for many years. Sutherland now had a clearer realization that he was not the only boy to grow up here. His mother, who died when he was ten, had known Milo Rathkey as a boy.

Today had been filled with out-of-the-ordinary events, not the least of which was the meeting of a stranger to him, who was not a stranger to the house, or the people that he loved.

3

"Damn it!" Milo cursed staring at the parking ticket neatly tucked under his windshield wiper. *I could have parked in the ramp for a week for what this is going to cost me,* he thought to himself as he grabbed the ticket off the windshield and glared at the twenty-five-dollar fine. He stuffed ticket in his pocket with the Band-Aid wrappers and the bloody napkin.

Easing himself into the Honda, Milo turned the key several times before the car started, sat back in the seat to take a deep breath, and stared straight ahead. It all seemed real…but was it?

He needed to call someone to help clear his mind, so he could determine if this was legit. As people filtered through his brain like an old-fashioned Rolodex, there was only one person who fit all the criteria he needed right now. Milo called Saul Feinberg and hoped the lawyer was not in court.

Great Party! Sorry About The Murder

Feinberg answered on the second ring and immediately asked if Milo was coming over later that afternoon. He added that Milo's check was waiting.

Milo, ignoring the pleasantries, got right to the point. "I have a problem. I need some advice."

Saul, unaccustomed to the uncertainty in Milo's voice, was somewhat taken aback and said, "Really? Sure. What's up?"

Milo took another deep breath. "Okay, this is going to sound crazy. I'm not drunk. I'm not on drugs—except for Excedrin—but I might be hallucinating or the victim of a huge mistake."

"Wow, you have my full attention."

"Remember I told you I was going to John McKnight's will reading?"

"Yeah."

"They say John left me fifteen million dollars and half of his estate. I mean it was like they were giving me a ham sandwich…here take it, do you want lettuce?"

Saul was silent.

"Saul? Saul? Are you there?"

"I'm here, but when this gets around to being a problem, ring a bell or something."

"Saul, this is a problem! I don't know if it's real. It makes no sense. People do not drop that kind of money in other people's laps—especially my lap."

"Did he have any children?"

"Yeah, one, a son. He now owns the other half of the estate. I kid you not."

"Okay, he's obviously going to contest that will. I agree—that's a problem"

"No, no. He's not. In fact, he seems almost happy about it. I know, it makes no sense which is why I need you to find out what's going on."

Feinberg puzzled over what he had just heard, agreed with Milo that this was not the norm. "First, who's the lawyer handing the will?"

"Haney of Haney, blah blah, and blah blah."

"Haney, Jenson, and Hampft," Feinberg filled in. "I know Richard Haney quite well. Trust me, he is not a practical jokester. If what you tell me is true, you, my friend, are a very rich man."

"It all appeared to be true, but now I'm doubting any of it happened. Maybe I'm having an episode. Tell him you're my attorney. Just get a sense of what the hell is going on. I expect a call at any minute telling me it's…I don't know what it is."

Not used to Milo being even a calm hysteric, Saul placated him. "Okay, I'll call him. Richard already thinks I'm a kook, so this will only cement his opinion of me. I will deal with your problem. Please visualize my fingers doing air quotes around the word *problem*. Getting back to reality, what about my real problem, the robbery case? Have you found anything out?"

Milo condensed the conversation with Ed Patupick and told Saul it sounded optimistic. He added he was heading over there now. After they hung up, Milo felt a lot better.

Saul Feinberg, the heir to the Feinberg pastrami fortune, as Milo referred to it, was young, liberal, and bent on fighting injustice.

His office was a large Mercedes Van which he parked behind the courthouse. He said it was less intimidating and more accessible for his poorer clients. Milo was attracted to the free parking as he could pull up next to the van.

Handing this over to Saul allowed Milo to continue with his life as if nothing had changed because, in reality, nothing had changed. He still had a parking ticket he couldn't afford, a car that barely started, and an appointment with Ed Patupick.

From Wi-Fi Routers to laptop computers, Ed's shop was full of expensive electronics but devoid of customers. It was always this way. So much so that Milo often accused Ed of running a money-laundering scheme for the mob. It was a joke Ed never seemed to get and always denied it as if Milo was serious. He defended himself by saying that he made a lot of money setting up home theatres and high-end surveillance systems.

Walking to the back office, Milo thought that the sight of his tall, hawk-like friend bent over his small laptop was comical: Ichabod Crane checking his email.

Without looking up, Ed called out, "You're walking funny."

"Your camera setup didn't protect me from getting punched and kicked in the ribs this morning."

Ed challenged with his usual dry delivery, "Your protection was not in the specs. It was operator error."

Patupick ran his fingers through his shoulder length, stringy, black hair which hadn't seen a comb or brush in a while. "Come over here and look at this," he said, motioning to his computer. "This video from my security camera begins seconds before the robbery. As you can see, it's dated and time-coded in the lower left, and I can testify that both are accurate. I set the time to the Naval Observatory."

"I would expect no less," Milo agreed with a tinge of playful sarcasm that he knew Ed wouldn't get.

A minute into the video, Milo saw a short, hefty male back out of the liquor store, gun in hand, and run down the street out of range of the camera. Seconds later, as the cops pulled up, Feinberg's client, a hooded fifteen-year-old boy, came jogging past.

"Wow! This does it, Ed. The kid was in the wrong place at the wrong time." They watched as the cops grabbed the kid and put him in the back of the squad car.

In an overly dramatic manner, hand over his heart, Ed crowed, "I am overjoyed to once again be the super hero who comes to the aid of the people."

"I was sort of thinking that was my role in all this."

"Not to worry...you can be my sidekick."

Milo winced at the words 'sidekick' as he pocketed the thumb drive with the video, thanked Ed, and left the still-empty store. He stood in the doorway to shield himself from the biting wind blowing down Second Avenue as he found Saul's number on speed dial.

Saul picked up immediately, and Milo started by saying he had the goods. "The video caught the real thief and your client, who was clearly just jogging by after the robbery."

"Perfect!"

"You got anything for me?"

"Oh yeah, I talked with Haney. You, my friend, are, as I said before, a very rich man. It is legit, and there will be no contesting of the will. There is no problem or mistake here, so may I be the first to welcome you to a much higher tax bracket."

Milo was silent.

"Are you there, Milo?"

"Yeah, I guess this is going to happen," Milo mumbled, hiding his unease.

"Yes, it is! You got handed millions of dollars. This is a good thing! You should be celebrating! What is your problem?" Saul asked, not hiding his exasperation.

"I don't know. I've never been rich. My family's never been rich. I don't know how to be rich."

"Oh Lord! That's a shrink problem. I'm a lawyer. Speaking of that, you will need a financial guy. May I suggest my guy, Creedence Durant?"

"Oh great. I need a shrink, a lawyer, and a now a financial guy. Too much…too soon. All I know is that I'm moving."

"When?"

"Now…today…later. Sutherland McKnight expects me tonight. I guess if this is legit, I'm doing it."

"Wait! What about my evidence?" Saul demanded.

Milo patted his coat pocket. "The thumb drive is in my pocket with my Band-Aid wrappers and parking ticket. I can I get it to you tomorrow."

Ignoring the contents of Milo's pocket, Saul asked that Milo make it early in the morning. "It's too late in the day to get him out now, but I want this kid out of jail and home where he belongs as soon as possible."

§

Milo's office and apartment were above Ilene's Bakery on First Avenue East. Ilene was his landlord and friend. He first rented the place ten years ago when he left the Brainerd Police Force. In fact, he blamed the tasty location for the ten or so pounds he had gained since then. Nobody made cream puffs like Ilene, and Milo was a sucker for cream puffs.

Today, however, he needed some coffee, or so he told himself, until he entered the bakery and a million sweet smells assaulted his nose.

Ilene's white blond spikes had a purple streak today, and her sleeves were rolled up to reveal her fully tatted left arm. She was at least forty but looked younger. Maybe it was her style or maybe her manner. She took no crap or prisoners but always had a fondness for Milo. "Not much happening today, Milo?"

"I wouldn't say that," he said as he sat down by one of the five small tables that lined the wall opposite the counter.

"You do look beat. Coffee?"

He rubbed his eyes with the palms of his hands and pushed his fingers through his curly hair and over the lump he received this morning. Looking up, he answered, "Coffee would be good."

Ilene poured out two cups, walked over to the table, and sat down in a familiar manner. Her thin frame fit easily into the chair which was up against the wall. "So, what's happening?"

"Would you like it chronologically or just the big chunks?" Milo asked, stirring his coffee and adding more than a sufficient amount of cream.

"I've got time. The going-home rush hasn't started yet, so give it to me from the beginning."

"Well," he said, taking a large gulp that felt warm and soothing, "this morning I got punched by some guy I was tailing."

"So what," Ilene countered. "I mean that happens to me every day. I'm making some specialty five grain bread, and—wham—I get punched."

"I come in here for the coffee and the sarcasm."

"And the cream puffs."

"Oh yeah, the cream puffs. Can't forget those." Milo's gaze wandered over to the glass refrigerated case that held his lovely cream puffs.

"Pay attention!" Ilene chastised as she snapped her fingers in Milo's direction, "I can see the results of the fight: that welt on your head, that bandaged hand, and…anything else?"

Leaning back and pressing his ribs with the palm of his hand, Milo assessed the pain level. "I think the ribs are just bruised. At least I hope so."

"That will slow you down for a while. So, when's the last time you took your beloved Excedrin?"

"Around noon, I think, so I'm good until around three or four."

Knowing there was no future in urging Milo to see a doctor, Ilene moved the conversation forward. "So, after the pummeling, did you go see that lawyer, and more important, did you get anything?"

"Yes, you might say I did." It amazed him that she remembered the will reading. He had only mentioned it once, a week ago.

"Well, don't make me guess. What'd you get?"

Milo debated the specifics in his mind. *Exactly what should I say?*

There was an embarrassment about telling a hard-working person like Ilene he was rich through no effort of his own. "Well, I got some money, and half a house."

"Half a house, that's nice. Who has the other half?"

"John McKnight's son, Sutherland. We're going to share the house."

Ilene stared at him with her eyes squinting, trying to figure out what exactly Milo was talking about. "Where is this house?"

Milo lowered his eyes and concentrated on his now empty coffee cup. "On London Road. They call it Lakesong."

"Sweet Jesus!" she exclaimed as she reached out and grabbed Milo's hand. "Are you telling me you got half of that estate?"

Milo looked up and nodded his head.

"I don't know about you, but I need more coffee."

Milo eased himself up. "I know what you mean, I'll get it." He headed for the coffee pot behind the counter.

Ilene turned and asked, "Can you afford to live there?"

Milo grabbed the coffee pot and returned to the table. "Yeah, he gave me some money."

Ilene grabbed three packets of Splenda, tapped them repeatedly on the table, ripped them open, tapped them some more and finally poured the contents into her coffee. As Milo watched her usual sugar ceremony, something that usually drove him crazy, he realized how important Ilene's friendship had been over the past ten years. He was afraid this might spoil it.

"So, I guess you'll be leaving me?" Ilene said in her landlord voice.

"Just the apartment, I'll keep the office and pay for both of course. I'm sorry."

Exasperated, she sat back and put both hands on the table. "Sorry for what?"

"I don't know. I'm just sorry. I guess everything's changing."

"Things change. That's life. The first thing that's changing is I expect your rent—on time—and the second is no more free cream puffs."

Her response made Milo feel much better. Maybe nothing had changed except Milo wouldn't live upstairs anymore, and Ilene might make a profit on her cream puffs.

"No more free cream puffs? How cruel!" Milo feigned. "What about my morning pastries?"

"Actually," Ilene said, shaking her finger at him, "I think you're covered on that score. One of my best customers, Martha Gibbson, is the chef at Lakesong. Nice lady by the way. She actually pays."

Ilene thought for a second about what she had said. "Jesus, Milo, you have a chef!"

"Yeah, I guess, whatever." Milo's gaze went back to the cream puff case. He wanted a cream puff more than anything.

Ilene followed his gaze, stood up, grabbed the coffee pot and announced, "Okay, one last free cream puff for old time sake."

Milo did not refuse.

As Milo savored the cream puff, the first wave of the going-home crowd, the high school kids, arrived in pods, looking for their sugar fix. Ilene rolled her eyes and said glancing at the kids, "My public awaits."

Milo watched them for a while, but when they were replaced by yet another pod, he swallowed the final gulp of coffee, waved goodbye to Ilene, and exited the shop.

Turning left, he opened the door that for several years had read **RAT KEY INVESTIGATIONS.** The missing *H* had faded and was not noticed anymore. With care, he walked up the well-worn wooden steps to the inner door, unlocked it, and gave it a hard push because it often stuck.

His office, with the familiar dusty smell, cheap wooden desk, two mismatched filing cabinets, and two green, faux-leather chairs had not changed. The only thing that had changed was Milo.

He sat in his creaky old chair and turned on his computer. It was the only fairly-new item in the room, set up by Ed Patupick, with many programs that were indispensable to his investigating work.

Milo could have accessed his email on his smart phone earlier, but he hated typing replies on the little keyboard. Email was answered on his computer. There was one email from Harry Reinakie, the Cadillac King of Duluth, demanding Milo continue following Heidi, his trophy wife of five years.

Milo sighed. Harry was one of his best customers. Heidi wasn't cheating. As far as Milo could figure out, she had never cheated, but Harry, who was no prize in the looks department, always suspected her. She had been his best sales person and was much younger than Harry.

Great Party! Sorry About The Murder

"All right Harry," Milo said to himself, "I'll follow her one more time." At least he doubted Heidi would slug him as she picked up her dry cleaning.

He moved on to his incoming credit card receipts, something Ed had set up for him so clients could pay with plastic. Harry had already paid the three hundred dollars which Milo always demanded up front.

The three hundred was more or less a half a day's work. He sent Harry an email in the affirmative and added the surveillance of Heidi to his calendar. She usually left the house about ten-thirty.

Milo's plan for the day had included a computer search for two missing husbands, but that was before his life had been turned upside down. Now it would have to wait until tomorrow.

Turning off the computer, Milo got up and wandered into his studio apartment in the back room. Looking around, he realized he would never sleep here again. After ten years, it seemed odd to be leaving it. It wasn't home, but it was comfortable.

He pulled up his shirt and cringed at the large purple blotch on his side, but after gingerly pressing the area, was convinced the ribs were not broken. With that decided, Milo moved into the bathroom.

Looking at his image in the bathroom mirror, it was clear he could use a little cleaning up. The cuts and scrapes stung as he removed the Band-Aids and washed his hands.

Without bending, Milo tried to wash his face. The water felt good, but he managed to splash more on his shirt than his face. He was a mess.

After patching himself up, and painstakingly changing his shirt and pants, he checked his image again. It looked more presentable for his new residence. Two more Excedrin and he would be good for most of the evening.

Milo pulled out his barely-used suitcase which was new when he and his now ex-wife went on their honeymoon. Most of his clothes fit into it, and the rest he tossed into a black garbage bag—not elegant, but practical.

Protecting his still sore ribs, he slid his suitcase and black bag down the steps managing to get both into the trunk. Milo edged into the Honda, took a deep breath, and headed for Lakesong.

§

London Road is a tree-lined street that at one time featured more millionaires per square mile than any other place in the country. That was the turn of the last century when lumber and fur barons showed their wealth by creating huge estates on the shores of Lake Superior. Some of the mansions were gone, some had become museums, but Lakesong, one of the smaller estates, lived on. Rathkey punched in the code, and the gates silently opened.

Sutherland was working out in his second-floor gym when he heard the beep and saw the red light on the intercom panel. It was the front gate opening.

He stopped pedaling and took a deep breath. Knowing this day was going to happen, he still couldn't deny a feeling of disquiet. After all, he had only met Milo Rathkey for ninety minutes this morning, but at the same time the Excedrin popping detective knew the code to the front gate, and why it was the code to the front gate. What else did this man know?

Hopping off the exercise bike, Sutherland headed down the stairs to the front door as Milo arrived. He yanked open one of the leaded glass-and-mahogany double doors proclaiming with a grin, "Welcome back to Lakesong!"

Milo walked up the granite steps into the foyer taking in Sutherland's natty spandex bicycle outfit. "That's a good look for you, but a bit chilly don't you think?" He added, "should I bring my stuff in the front door?"

What is it about this guy? No one teases me about my workout clothes! They are the uniform of the avid bike rider.

In answer to where Milo should put his stuff, he told him to pull his car into the garage, and they would unload it from there.

The cat came down from her tree in the gallery to rub up against Milo's leg.

"Annie!" Rathkey exclaimed. "Long time, no see."

The cat immediately began to purr.

"You know the cat?"

"Of course, I met her a couple of months ago, and I also knew her great, great, great grandmother, who, by the way, was also named Annie."

"You do know that none of the Annie cats are related. When one died, my dad would get another from the shelter."

"I do, but he always insisted on maintaining that mystique." Glancing back at the double front doors, Milo added, "Look, let me pull into the garage, so I can get this stuff stowed before my Excedrin wears off."

Milo went back out and drove over to the garage where Sutherland had already opened one of five garage doors. As he pulled his Honda in between the Bentley and the Rolls, he said to himself. "Yeah, sure, my car fits right in between these two luxury models."

It only took one trip to unload the car. The master bedroom was huge with its king-sized poster bed, over-stuffed chairs, large fireplace, and three massive windows that overlooked the grounds and Lake Superior.

Milo looked around, puzzling as to where to put the contents of his suitcase. Sutherland stood in front of the fireplace and drew Milo's attention to the two doors on either side. "The door to the left leads to a dressing room outfitted for women's clothing. The room on the right has built-ins made for men's clothes."

Without hesitation, Milo rolled his suitcase to the right leaving the black garbage bag for Sutherland.

"Nice luggage," Sutherland said, hoisting the bag over his shoulder.

"It's a matching set. I have many more pieces on a roll back at my apartment," Milo joked as he opened the door to the dressing room and exclaimed, "This room is bigger than my apartment."

Sutherland dropped the bag and left Milo to get settled, saying that he would see Milo later that evening at dinner.

Standing in the dressing room, Milo realized that his problem hadn't been solved. There was still no place to put his clothes. Straight ahead was a sink.

Check, good place to shave.

Glancing to the left he saw a separate room with a toilet and a bidet.

Good to know where the toilet is. I may need a user manual for that other puppy.

Walking to the right, through a wide, arched opening, he finally found the closet. It wasn't just a walk-in closet. People could dance in there.

Milo minded his ribs as he began to put his clothes away. There were places to hang up his pants, and an entire section for ties of which he had only one.

His five shirts could either be hung, or, if they were folded, each one could go into its own drawer. There were dozens of drawers. Milo laughed.

A ladder led to still more storage cubes, and he had no idea what went up there. None of this was modular, the kind that people had installed. This had been crafted and carved to match everything else in the house. This was a gentlemen's dressing room.

Milo finished putting his clothes away taking up almost none of the closet space. He hoped his clothes were not insulting the room.

Despite the size of the dressing room and closet, he had yet to find a shower.

There's got to be a shower in here somewhere.

He backtracked into the dressing room, opened the only door he could find, and saw the bathtub in clear sight.

Could the shower be far behind?

A large elevated planter loomed in the middle of the room populated by large philodendrons, peace lilies, two Yucana trees, and too many flowers and ferns for Milo's taste. Giving it a wide berth, questioning why it was even there, he spied what looked like a shower. So many dials and knobs, none of which said hot and cold.

I need another damn user's manual.

Milo knew he could stand a nap, but what he wanted was a drink. He wound his way back, through his bedroom and the gallery into the area he knew as the family room. The bar was still in the far corner.

He made himself a vodka gimlet and sat down. He tried to put his feet up on the coffee table, but his ribs complained. Annie joined him, jumping up onto the arm of the chair. Milo petted her for a bit. She then playfully bit him on his unbandaged hand and jumped down. It was her way of saying, "Welcome to Lakesong."

As Annie made her retreat, a young woman wearing a bright red chef's coat with black slacks peeked into the room. "You must be the legendary Milo Rathkey."

"I don't remember any legends with me in it, but please feel free to make one up," Milo said, standing to meet her. Shaking her hand, he added, "You must be the legendary chef, Martha, who buys pastries from Ilene."

"I do," She seemed surprised. "I take that as a request for breakfast. In the meantime, dinner is salad, chicken and dumplings, steamed asparagus, and an apple crisp for dessert."

"Sounds delicious," Milo said.

Sutherland entered the family room which was an informal dining and sitting room with the bar, a large fireplace, and a comfortable sitting area around a large TV.

As Martha retreated into the kitchen, Sutherland invited Milo to join him at the small dining table. Rathkey noticed he had changed from the bicycle getup into a dark blue sweater and gray slacks.

Milo suspected that his own plaid shirt and slightly worn pants, which were fine for picking up takeout, might need an upgrade.

Martha came in with a bottle of Riesling, showed it to Sutherland and Rathkey, and poured each man a glass.

Sutherland raised his glass and said, "To new beginnings, as strange as they may be."

"They couldn't be stranger," Milo agreed. He began the conversation by asking about the ladder in the dressing room closet.

"It's for boxes of gentlemen's shoes," Sutherland explained. "That's what goes up there. You have to remember it was installed at the turn of the last century when gentlemen wore a lot of shoes."

"I don't a have a lot of shoes."

"Then stay off the ladder," Sutherland joked.

Milo sighed and nodded his head in agreement.

"Now you tell me something," demanded Sutherland. "What's the secret of the gate code? You said 26643 was easy to remember. How is that?"

"First, take out your phone."

Sutherland was dubious but did as instructed.

"Now look at the key pad. What does 26643 spell?"

Sutherland stared at the keypad for several seconds before hitting his forehead with his palm. "I should have guessed: Annie!"

"All these years you never figured that out?"

"What was with my father and the name Annie?"

"I don't know. He never told me, but for six hundred bucks a day I could try to find out."

"Whoa, that's pretty steep."

"Yeah, but you're paying for the best," Milo quipped.

"I think we should let it rest for now."

"Your choice," Milo said, eyeing Martha's entrance with the salads. Sutherland dug right in, but Rathkey picked around the lettuce looking for something that resembled the iceberg variety.

He leaned across the table and whispered to Sutherland, "Can I tell her I don't like mixed greens. It's like eating your lawn."

"I wouldn't," Sutherland advised. "She has knives." Turning toward the kitchen, he yelled, "Hey, Martha! Milo hates mixed greens salad!"

Rathkey looked shocked, his eyes wide. "Don't tell her that! I'll never be able to eat here again. I just got here."

Martha strode in with hands on hips staring at Milo, holding back a smile. "Well then, Mr. Rathkey you need to open up your mouth, or are you," She said, glancing back at Sutherland, "going to do all the talking for him?"

Sutherland shrugged, putting Milo on the spot. "Well, yeah, I…I only like iceberg lettuce."

"Ahh, one of those people," Martha said, turning and going back to the kitchen. Seconds later, she returned with an iceberg wedge, blue cheese and bacon. "How about this? I call it a John McKnight special, but I warn you, you will have to share with the cat."

"Is that blue cheese and bacon?" Milo asked, surrendering the mixed green salad for the iceberg wedge. "Thank you!"

"Please, you need to let me know what you like and what you hate."

As predicted, Annie appeared, rubbing up against Milo, receiving a small chunk of bacon in return.

"The tradition continues. Bacon is shared," Sutherland said, laughing.

Annie purred in agreement.

4

Rathkey awoke the next morning to quiet darkness, and the scent of freshly polished wood. Panic clutched at his chest. Where the hell was he? Sunlight should be pouring through the holes and cracks in his bedroom shade, but the room was tomb dark. He reached for his phone but slammed his hand into a side table that was not supposed to be there. Cursing, he raised himself into an upright position. Though his ribs ached, and head pounded, the panic in his brain was clearing. He was in John McKnight's bedroom.

He eased out of bed and stumbled in the darkness not knowing where to find a light switch. "Goddamn it!" he yelled, stubbing his toe on something hard.

His left hand found a wall and he shuffled along, slapping it, trying find some light. He touched a heavy cloth which he hoped was a window covering. Jerking it back, a sliver of light crept in at last.

Holy crap, I need a night light.

Great Party! Sorry About The Murder

His eye caught a large remote control on the night stand. "Damn! I forgot about that!" Now that he could see, he fumbled with the remote, turning on the fan, the TV and the lights. Finally, he saw the button labeled *Drapes*, pushed it and watched as the floor to ceiling drapes parted. "What the...I'm living in a goddamn fun house!"

It was only a few minutes past dawn. Looking out the window he saw the rising sun reflecting off a wall of billowing fog, painting the high, rich vapor with oranges and yellows. Rathkey had seen the rolling tsunami of what locals call sea smoke many times before, but never so close and never out his own bedroom window.

Showering, shaving and dressing as quickly as his recent injuries would allow, he left the bedroom and headed across the gallery.

Annie came down from her tree and fell in behind him, meowing all the way. She knew an easy mark when she saw one, and this one was headed to breakfast.

Upon entering the kitchen, Martha greeted him with a quick, "Morning, Mr. Rathkey. There are no mixed green salads for breakfast."

"Good to know, Martha. Thank you."

"Mr. McKnight is in the morning room," Martha said, pointing beyond the hearth room toward the corner bank of windows. The morning room got its name from the ceiling to floor windows that surrounded three sides and allowed in the rising sun.

As he walked past the hearth room with its massive stone fireplace, Rathkey thought that heat would have felt comfortable on the cold bathroom floor this morning. For the moment, Annie abandoned a chance at breakfast for the warmth of the fire.

Before sitting down, Rathkey stared at the white, snow-covered ground, the trees, and beyond them, the magnificence of Lake Superior.

"Good morning," Sutherland said, looking up, following Rathkey's gaze. "It is nice, isn't it?"

"It beats a view of First Avenue!" Rathkey poured himself a cup of coffee from the side table. "It's so cold out there and so warm in here; it doesn't even seem drafty. Which reminds me, that bathroom tile is pretty chilly in the morning."

Sutherland looked up. "Oops," he laughed.

"What? Oops? What does oops mean?"

"Well, I may have forgotten to tell you, the bathroom floor is heated, but you need to set the timer."

"Where's the timer?"

"Behind a panel near the bathtub."

"Are there any other *oopses*?"

Sutherland sighed. "I imagine there will be a few…none life-threatening."

Martha walked in from the kitchen. "Mr. McKnight likes a variety of vegetable smoothies for breakfast, but I took the liberty of surmising that a man who likes his iceberg lettuce might also like pancakes, sausage, bacon, potatoes, and various assorted pastries."

Rathkey's eyes lit up. "You would be correct." Milo proceeded to eat far more than he should considering the growing tire around his middle. He knew that, sooner rather than later, he would have to begin to exercise. But for today, the pain in his ribs told him that the lumberjack breakfast would go unchallenged.

Annie, who did not worry about her weight, managed to score several small pieces of bacon from Milo before strolling back to the fire. Midway through his feast, Milo pulled a small bottle of Excedrin from his pocket and washed two pills down with orange juice.

"Still taking your miracle drug?"

"The ribs are better today, but still not great."

The next few minutes were filled with the sounds of Milo's eating and Sutherland's ruffling of the paper. Milo kept looking out the windows at the big lake, watching the mountain of sea smoke wane until it was only a hill.

Flipping through several sections of the paper on the table, looking for the sports page, Rathkey realized that none of this paper looked familiar. "No sports page?"

"No, sorry, this is the Wall Street Journal," Sutherland said. "No sports page. I have a guy who delivers it. Do you want me to call and have him add the Duluth Trib?"

"Yeah, that would be great." Milo was used to reading other people's Duluth News Tribune when customers would leave them at Ilene's. Getting a paper without jelly and coffee stains would be a new experience.

"Are you going to want any more breakfast, Mr. Rathkey?" Martha asked.

"Only if I plan to explode. Thank you very much, Martha. It was wonderful!"

"If you have any special requests, write them out and leave them on the island. I am in and out a lot during the day. I live in the cottage on the grounds and cook breakfast and dinner, but can do lunch if necessary."

As Martha returned to the kitchen, Rathkey remembered the spacious three-bedroom, two-fireplace cottage that used to house the caretaker couple, Olaf Henderson and his wife. Olaf had been a favorite of Rathkey's.

"So, I guess we no longer have a caretaker?" Rathkey said to Sutherland.

"Not since Olaf and his wife retired. Were they around back in your time?" Sutherland asked putting down his paper.

"You're making my time seem like 1850," Milo chided. "Of course they were around! I helped Olaf mow the lawn and weed on weekends and during the summer. Not that I liked doing that stuff. I just liked Olaf, his stories, and the riding lawn mower."

"Despite your extensive lawn mowing experience, we now have a service that comes in twice a week."

"Good to know. Who pays for all this stuff?"

"Until yesterday, I did," Sutherland announced with a chuckle. "Now, *we* do."

Milo considered himself a cash and carry guy. No cash, no carry. Now he seemed to be racking up bills for services of which he was not aware. Lawn care? He never owned a lawn. Milo didn't know how any of this was going to work. His forehead began to crease again. "Do I pay you or what?"

Sutherland put down his paper and responded as though he had never thought about it. "That's a good question." For the next few minutes Sutherland filled Milo in on the family history of the position of house manager who took care of the day-to-day running of the place.

"The last one retired around the same time that my dad reduced his work load at the office, so he took over the household finances. I think we should probably go back to the house manager plan. That way neither of us has to worry about the daily running of this place."

"Is there really that much to do?"

"You'll be surprised. To keep the house and grounds running smoothly, there is some type of regular upkeep every day, such as maid service, pool service, grass cutting in the summer, snow plowing in the winter; you get the idea. Then there are the scheduled repairs and the unscheduled repairs… things break."

As Sutherland kept listing the chores, Milo was getting the idea that a house manager was a great idea. None of the maintenance things interested him at all.

"Oh, and I forgot about the cars. Mr. Anderson comes in and maintains the cars," Sutherland added.

On-site car repair was something Milo could get behind. "Can he service my car?"

"Certainly."

"It's in bad shape. I need a new battery, a new starter and who knows what else. When does he work on them, because I can't just leave my car."

"He comes in two days a week. You could leave your car and take the Bentley."

Rathkey choked on his coffee. "The Bentley? Really? I think it might be tough to do undercover work in a Bentley."

"Well there's the old Lincoln Limo, the Rolls, the SUV, or rent a car."

Milo stared at Sutherland. *Rent a car! How the hell can I afford a rental car?*

Knowing that Sutherland had never been broke in his life, Rathkey dialed the outrage down a bit, "I have three hundred and thirty bucks between my checking account and my pocket change. That is not enough for me to rent a car or pay for all these services. I know John left me a lot of money, but I don't have it yet. Does it just magically appear if I need to pay a house manager or need to rent a car?"

"Well, I don't want to tell you what to do, but...."

"Stop!" Rathkey held up his hand, "Tell me what to do. I don't have a clue here. Is it magic?"

"Well, first you must get a financial planner."

"You're the second person to mention a financial planner to me. What do they do?"

Sutherland explained about investments, interest, various accounts, and taxes, all of which could be handled by a financial planner. Rathkey's eyes glazed over midway through.

"How do I actually get…" Rathkey began to question, but Martha interrupted him. "If there's nothing else, I will be leaving now, Gentlemen." Martha headed to the basement stairs behind the kitchen.

Rathkey recalled the tunnels in the basement that led to the outbuildings including Martha's cottage which he mentioned to Sutherland.

"Yes, the tunnels are still operative," Sutherland said. "Martha leaves every morning about this time to make sure her family gets off to school."

"Family?"

"Her brothers and sister. Their parents were killed in a traffic accident. She is their guardian."

"Wow, that's rough."

A piercing buzzer caused Milo to jump and look in the direction of the wall intercom. It was modern, had both red and green lights, and many more buttons than the old one that Rathkey knew as a boy.

"That red blinking light means someone's at the front gate," Sutherland explained, looking at Rathkey, who shrugged his shoulders as if to say I'm not expecting anyone. Sutherland got up and pressed the red intercom button.

"Yes?"

"Courier with a delivery for a Mr. Milo Rathkey." Sutherland pushed the *Open Gate* button.

Milo asked if the buzzer could be toned down a bit, but before Sutherland could answer, Milo's phone interrupted. Sutherland got up and gestured that he would go to the front door.

The phone alert was a text from Saul Feinberg reminding him to come over first thing. Texting back in the affirmative, he also checked the time on his phone. It was seven forty-five; he had time.

"Well, news travels fast," Sutherland said, holding a large white envelope which he handed to Milo.

Milo took the envelope, ripped it open, and held up an engraved invitation. He was perplexed. "It seems I have been invited to a New Year's Eve party…someone named Bonner. I don't know anyone named Bonner. Why would they invite me?"

"They invited you because you co-own Lakesong. That makes you a neighbor. Besides, I called Mary Alice Bonner yesterday and told her about you, so she's curious. Mary Alice holds parties and runs much of the social scene in this neck of the woods."

Rathkey sipped his coffee. "First off, it seems news travels fast because you spread it. Second, as much as I love being a curiosity—I'm not much for parties."

"Look at it as a business meeting. I could introduce you to two or three financial planners. You might find one you like."

Looking at it that way seemed logical, but hand-delivered invites to a society lady's New Year's Eve bash still made Milo uneasy. "I bet this is a formal affair. Right?"

"Well, not a tux, but at least a nice suit. Not to be insensitive, but do you have any nice suits?"

Rathkey liked his clothes; they were inexpensive, comfortable, and durable—what clothes should be. However, he knew they would not be appreciated in certain circles. He had a suit he bought years ago, but like his shirts, it was a little tight. "Okay, if I need clothes, what do you suggest?"

"I think you go to N&J Clothiers and get outfitted. You know, a nice suit, a tie, shoes, belt, no salt or blood stains, the usual. Try not to get beat up on your way there—oh and a new overcoat," Sutherland joked, taking another bite of toast.

"I fell."

"Yeah, yeah, yeah, you fell. Right."

"N&J is too expensive! I have three hundred and thirty dollars, or did you miss that point?" Rathkey protested.

Sutherland sipped his smoothie, "You can afford it."

"On paper maybe, but once again, the money is not yet in my pocket. Why are you having trouble grasping that?"

Sutherland stared. "Don't you have a credit card?"

"Yeah, but it's for emergencies."

"Well, this could be an emergency. It will be two to three thousand."

Rathkey grimaced. "My remaining balance is just a tad under three thousand. In fact, it's a tad under three hundred."

Sutherland was having trouble understanding Rathkey's situation. In his world, a working professional always had multiple accounts and would have money or credit from somewhere. Milo was a working professional, but he had zero investments. "I tell you what, I will call N&J and tell them what you need. They can charge it to my account."

Milo could afford his prior lifestyle, but at the moment, he couldn't afford what was becoming his current lifestyle. This party was in Sutherland's world. If he wanted Milo to go, he could pay for it. Milo accepted the offer. "That will be helpful, thanks."

"When should I tell the people at N&J to expect you?"

Milo checked the calendar on his phone. "I have a busy morning. How about midafternoon?"

"I'm curious. What exactly do you do? I mean this morning for instance, what will you be doing? I go to my office and run things, you know, have meetings, and talk to employees and clients who buy houses and office buildings. What do you do?"

"Well, this morning I'll meet with attorney Saul Feinberg, give him the evidence that he needs to get his falsely-accused, teenage client out of jail, and then I will follow Heidi Reinakie for a couple of hours while she does her shopping."

"The Cadillac Dealer's wife? The guy on those endless television commercials?"

"That's the guy, Hollering Harry. If you need a deal on a new Cadillac let me know, I have an in."

"Should you be telling me your client's name?"

"This client I can tell you. I have been following Heidi for five years because Harry is worried she may be cheating. The world knows Harry is worried she may be cheating. She's not. Harry needs help."

"Have you told him that?"

"Many times. But Harry wants to spend the money, and until yesterday, I needed the money."

"Sounds exciting, but if you only follow her for a couple of hours per day, how do you know she isn't cheating the rest of the time?"

"It's Friday. Heidi goes to the nail place, gets coffee at the Sweet Shop with a lady friend, and then she goes home. When this first started, I followed her for days. Now, I just check in from time to time."

Sutherland laughed. "Your day is certainly different from mine. It seems like you know a lot of characters. This lawyer, Saul Feinberg, is he the guy who works out of his van?"

"That's him. He's smart, does mostly pro bono. If you're ever charged with a felony, make a trip to that van. He parks it behind the courthouse."

"The district attorney, who plays tennis at the club, is not a fan."

"I would imagine not. Saul has put a huge dent in the DA's conviction record."

Sutherland looked at his watch and said, "I've got to go. I have an eight thirty meeting."

"See you tonight." After years of eating takeout, Milo was looking forward to Martha's cooking.

Putting on his coat and galoshes, Sutherland called from the hallway. "Do you know how to program your car for the garage door? If not, there are door openers hanging up on the far wall of the garage."

"Sure, no problem," Rathkey lied.

5

The St. Louis County Courthouse was one of those depression-built stone structures that looked as though it could survive a direct nuclear hit. It sat in a circle with other county buildings and Duluth City Hall. City workers were busy taking down the Christmas decorations which had served the civic center as the only relief from the grays of winter.

Rathkey, on his way to visit Feinberg, ignored the circle and headed to the back of the courthouse. Only one vehicle sat in that parking lot this morning—Saul Feinberg's large white Mercedes customized van. Milo pulled up next to it, got out, and knocked on the van door.

Saul pushed open the van's side panel and smiled. "Right on time Milo, come on in."

The interior of the van was customized to be an unintimidating law office with a small desk, several chairs, and bookshelves. Rathkey was always surprised at the van's roominess.

Feinberg was a friend. It was an odd pairing. He was younger—in his thirties—but he was smart and Rathkey admired and appreciated smart. He also admired Feinberg's neatly trimmed beard. How did he keep it that way? Feinberg was especially excited this morning to see what Milo had on the thumb drive. "If this video is what you describe, I think we can get the kid out this morning."

Rooting around the old Band-Aid wrappers, napkins and the ever-present Excedrin bottle, Rathkey eventually pulled the thumb drive out of his pocket and turned it over to Feinberg who plugged it into his computer.

The video came up quickly, and the smile on Feinberg's face became wider and wider. He jumped up and yelled, "Yes! Great work Milo! Fabulous! Wow!"

Milo smiled a bit at Feinberg's over-the-top reaction, "Yeah, I thought you'd like it."

Feinberg sat down. "Give me a second," he said, pointing to Milo's weakness—a box of Ilene's pastries. "I've got the judge's number on speed dial."

Ilene's sugar-laden delights would have been Milo's morning repast, but that was before Martha's lumberjack breakfast.

Feinberg was still on hold for the judge, so Milo carefully sat down and checked his phone. There was only one email—Harry, reminding him to tail Heidi. His to-do list showed meeting with Feinberg, tailing Heidi, lunch with Gramm, and computer searches for two deadbeat husbands. He added N&J Clothiers to the mix. His day was packed.

Feinberg talked to the judge who conferenced-in the district attorney, and a hearing was set for ten. "This kid will be home for lunch." Feinberg raised his arms above his head in a triumphant Rocky imitation.

Saul did enjoy his victories. Trying to bring the barrister back down to earth, Milo brought up an obvious point, "Maybe you should call his mother. She probably needs to know."

Feinberg crinkled his face like he was experiencing real pain, not just forgetfulness. "What is wrong with me?" Picking up his phone and checking on the number, he made a quick two-minute phone call to the happy mother. Hanging up the phone, Feinberg sat back grinning and pronounced with gusto, "Now that's the way to start the day!" He couldn't resist looking at the video one more time.

"So, I suppose you are going to hold another of your, *The cops are racists,* news conferences, right?" Milo chided.

Feinberg, who had no sense of humor when it came to civil liberties, countered, "How could the cops have missed this? Give 'em a running black kid, and they go no further."

"These could just be lazy cops, not necessarily racist cops," Milo defended his past profession.

The two had debated this topic before, but neither had the time for it now. As Feinberg pulled out his checkbook, he somewhat acquiesced. "True, and some of the blame goes to the DA's office, and I hope there is huge unhappiness there this morning." Looking up he quipped, "Oh, by the way, do I make this out to you or the Children of the Poor?"

"I am the Children of the Poor until I get the McKnight money."

"You've got to meet with those financial planners and rooms of lawyers in designer suits, soon," Feinberg mocked.

"Speaking of designer suits," Milo said, ignoring Feinberg's own well-tailored suit, "I am going this afternoon to get new clothes for somebody's New Year's Eve party."

"The Mary Alice Bonner gala?"

Taken back, Milo said he thought that that was the name on the invitation.

Feinberg wrote out the check. "Well, if it's Mary Alice, the upper crust wants to take a look at you. Before you know it, you'll be the heading up the Old Republican League for Decency and Thrift."

Milo shrugged. "I doubt it. It's just a party. Wait, how do you know about it? Were you invited? Are you going?"

"Yes, to all of your questions. One doesn't miss a Mary Alice Bonner party."

"Why?"

Saul sat back in his chair, with his hands behind his head. "You haven't met her. She's one special lady. Everyone loves Mary Alice Bonner. It simply can't be helped."

"Really? I can't wait to meet her, but if she's that great, and this party is so special, why did I get an invitation?"

Leaning forward with his hands on the desk, Feinberg continued as if Milo were a child. "You're rich. Have you forgotten?"

Milo sat back. "So, that's the price of admission?"

"There are artsy people but pretty much, it's the moneyed. That's why I will be there. I'm not loved. I'm rich," Feinberg explained, handing Milo his check.

Milo used his smart phone to scan the check into his account.

Feinberg stared. "This is new. Since when do you do that check thing on the phone? You rich guys are all alike."

Ignoring the gibe, Milo explained, "Patupick set it up for me. It saves me a trip to the bank. By the way, I'm meeting Gramm for lunch over at Gustafson's. Wanna join us?"

"Nope. After I spring the kid, I have another court session, and I have to prepare."

As the two shook hands, Feinberg asked, "You're still going to be my investigator, right?"

"Of course," Rathkey said, wondering if that was true.

§

It took Milo only twenty minutes to get up to Woodland Hills and the sprawling ranch house of Harry Reinakie. He stopped at the end of the block.

Heidi was younger than Harry by about ten years, and a looker. Last time Milo tailed her, he remembered her long blond curls cascading over the collar of a white fur jacket that must have set Harry back a tidy sum. His day dreaming was interrupted by the white Cadillac SUV pulling out of the garage.

He hoped her Fridays hadn't changed, mani-pedi, coffee with a girlfriend, and home. Milo had a busy day and didn't need Heidi screwing it up.

Following a safe distance behind Heidi, he parked a couple of rows down from the nail place. She got out of her car, wrapped the same white fur jacket around her, and strode into Hu's Nail Emporium.

Great Party! Sorry About The Murder

Milo knew Cindy Hu. She was a customer who had Milo do background checks on prospective employees. Milo sat back and sighed. He knew it would be at least an hour before Heidi reappeared.

Poor Harry. He will never believe this stunner chose him.

Milo found it hard to believe too. His thoughts of Heidi were interrupted. It was Earl Sanderson calling from the Sanderson Detective Agency in Minneapolis.

"Rathkey here."

"Milo, you busy?"

"Tailing someone, but I've got time. Whatcha got?"

"I need a photo of a guy named Ray Rajack—real name Bert Sunberg. We need confirmation that Ray is really Bert."

Milo felt his ribs. "Is he violent?" Milo asked, not relishing a confrontation until he healed from the last one.

"Naw…shouldn't be. All we need is a photo, like I said. You don't even have to confront him."

Milo knew he could fit this in, and Sanderson paid well. He got the particulars. The guy worked nights selling appliances at Best Bargain on Burning Tree off the Miller Trunk Highway. Sanderson was pretty sure he was working today.

This type of work was usually easy. The only downside was that Ray might not be working, and Milo would have to go back tomorrow.

Going through a mental inventory of all of his equipment, Milo settled on the knit cap with a hidden video camera. He could grab a still from the video and send it to Minneapolis. He wondered where he would be if Ed Patupick hadn't set him up with all these toys.

Bright red seemed to be the nail color of the week, Milo noticed as Heidi got back into her car and drove away. There was no coffee with a friend today; instead Milo followed her to the grocery store and the dry cleaners before she headed home.

Harry wanted her followed all afternoon, but Heidi rarely came out of the house twice in the same day. Besides, Milo had a full day, and Gustafson's meatloaf sandwich was calling. He told himself he needed the extra protein to heal.

§

Police Detective Ernie Gramm looked through his office window out onto the central bullpen where most of the sergeants sat. Even though several months had passed since his old partner, Sgt. Bill Jablonski, had retired, his absence from the bullpen was jarring.

At Jablonski's desk sat a young woman named Robin White. She was a member of the Ojibway Tribe, and had done three years as an Anishinaabe Reservation patrolman where her father was chief. She joined the Air Force as an MP to get more policing experience, and now she had made Sergeant in the Duluth Police Department.

While Gramm still missed Jablonski, he had to admit White came with some useful skills such as being able to touch type, knowing her way around computers, and having young legs when chasing suspects became necessary.

Gramm smiled as he watched White adjust the rubber band on her pony tail in counterpoint to how Jablonski would rub his bald, shiny head.

Great Party! Sorry About The Murder

The Christmas holiday had been fun with the grandchildren, all excited, waiting for Santa. Today was also the first day in a long time with no open cases. Leaning back and drinking his coffee, he knew that some of the case clearing was due to the speed with which Sgt. White could operate.

He got up, leaned out of his office door, and asked her what she was doing for lunch. She looked up and smiled, "I was going to get a sandwich at the cafeteria."

"I tell you what, I am having lunch with an old friend, a private detective. I think it would be good if you got to know him. Do you want to come along? I'm buying."

"I'm in!"

§

Duluth is perched on a giant hill that plunges into Lake Superior. Half a block from the restaurant, Rathkey saw a free parking spot. It required tricky parallel parking on the steep terrain, but it was free. Free was still good. The streets were kept clear, but the tough part today was going to be climbing over the snow banks to get to the sidewalk.

"I should have moved to Miami," he mumbled to himself as he climbed up and over the knee-high snow mound. It was time for more Excedrin.

Gustafson's Restaurant was a few blocks away from the courthouse and catered to cops, lawyers, and reporters in its noisy cluttered interior. Nick and Nicola Christos, a Greek couple, had owned the restaurant for as long as Rathkey could remember. He always wondered if there ever was a Gustafson, or if this savvy couple gave it a Scandinavian name to fit in the area. At least half of the Duluth population was Scandinavian of some type or at least pretended to be.

As he opened the door, his senses were assailed by noise, heat, and wonderful, welcoming smells. The place was packed with people talking at high volume. Nick waved at him from behind the counter and then shouted, "Who are you looking for?"

"Ernie," Milo shouted over the conversations and the clinking of dishes.

"In the back, third booth from the wall," Nick shouted and waved his arm in that direction.

Rathkey found Gramm already downing a bowl of split pea soup. He was sitting next to a pretty young woman who was eating a salad. Rathkey thought that Gramm had gotten even jowlier since he last saw him.

The Lieutenant looked up and smiled. "Hey Milo, the meatloaf sandwich is on special." It was his joke. Milo always ordered the meatloaf sandwich. "And this is Sgt. Robin White, my new partner."

Sgt. White offered her hand, and Milo shook it as he sat down. "I'm Milo Rathkey."

Her eyes opened wide. "*The* Milo Rathkey?"

Milo looked puzzled as did Gramm. "Well, I'm the only Milo Rathkey I know."

"Were you a cop in Brainerd?"

Not knowing how she would know, or where she was going with this question, he nodded. She would have been in grade school when he worked in Brainerd.

Sitting back and smiling, she announced, "You worked with my father, Dennis. He's still the chief of the Anishinaabe

Reservation Police Department over in Leech Lake. This is not the first time we've met."

Milo took a closer look, remembering the Chief and his shy, little, tag-along daughter. He too smiled. "Oh, my God, you're Robin! How can you be a sergeant? You were just a little kid."

"Wow, I feel like a stranger at old home week," Gramm interjected.

Ignoring Gramm, Milo asked White, "So, how is your dad?"

"Oh, he's fine, talking about retirement, but I will believe it when I see it," she said, rolling her eyes.

The two briefly talked about old times, and cases that Milo and Robin's father had worked together.

"The usual, Milo?" Pat—the overworked waitress—asked as she came up to the table, pad in hand.

"You know Pat, one day I am going to change my order," Milo said.

"Yeah, but not this day. Hot meatloaf sandwich, mash potatoes, green beans, extra gravy and Diet Coke." She wrote it down and shouted to Nick over the din of the restaurant, "It's Milo, the usual."

"I stopped in at Ilene's this morning," Gramm said to Rathkey. "She told me you can afford to pick up the check today."

Milo shook his head feeling somewhat uncomfortable with the news being out. "If you want the world to know something, just tell Ilene! I hope you brought your wallet because I don't have the money yet."

Looking back and forth between the two men, Sgt. White waited for an explanation.

Gramm continued to eat his soup, so Milo responded, "I've recently come into some money."

"As in yesterday," Gramm added.

"Well congratulations. Did you win the lottery?" White asked.

"Well, in a way. I was remembered in a will."

Gramm laughed, "He thought he was getting some books, but got half of a house and a still-undisclosed amount of the money. Are you going to disclose it?"

"In a word, no," Rathkey said, not wanting to discuss it.

"Wow! That much, huh?" Gramm exclaimed.

Pat came by the table dropping off Milo's Diet Coke and moved on. Milo pulled out his Excedrin and washed them down. Translating Gramm's disapproving look, Milo explained to Robin, "It's a work-related injury. I'm fine, just sore ribs." Transitioning back to Gramm, Milo added, "Your boys in armed robbery are in for a surprise."

Gramm put down his bowl and glared at Rathkey. "What did you do now?"

"Their jobs. That liquor store robbery on First Street… they were too lazy to go across the street and get the surveillance tapes from Patupick's place. It shows the Howard kid was just jogging past, like he said."

"So, does it show the thief?" Gramm asked.

"Yeah, older guy, gray hair," Rathkey said.

"This is going to upset a few people. I'm glad it's not my problem."

Again confused, White asked Rathkey, "Why are you involved?"

"Saul Feinberg is the kid's attorney, and he retained my services to sort it out."

Staring at Milo as though the stare might make more of an impact, Gramm explained to Sgt. White, "I keep offering Milo a job as our consultant. I'm hoping he takes us up on it."

Milo glanced over at White and mumbled, "Tell the Lieutenant, I'm thinking about it."

"After yesterday morning's fiasco, I figured you'd snap it up," Gramm said.

Rathkey grimaced.

Becoming accustomed to being out of the loop with these two, White chimed in. "What happened yesterday morning?"

"Milo got his ass kicked," Gramm said, finishing up his soup.

"One lucky punch, then I broke the guy's nose. Oh, did he file charges?"

"Not that I've heard," Gramm answered, shaking his head.

"Good, now all I have to do is heal," Milo, touching his ribs.

The plates of food arrived balanced precariously up and down Pat's arms. "Gee, who has the meatloaf sandwich?"

"No meatloaf here. We all ordered salads," Rathkey kidded.

"Right," Pat said, placing the gravy laden plate in front of him, handing Gramm his pastrami on rye, and Sgt. White her turkey club. They ate in silence, interspersed with brief conversations on the day's minutia.

Gramm moved the conversation back to rumors about Rathkey. "So, if I got it right, you are moving to London Road?"

"Already done, the place came furnished," Rathkey said.

"I'll bet and not from Furniture Palace!" Gramm laughed. "So, let's get to the important stuff, the Sunday night poker game. It's supposed to be at your place this week."

"I know, it just moves a little down the hill to London Road, but nothing else changes. Wait, I lied. The chairs are probably a little more comfortable. I haven't checked."

"I bet they match too," Gramm said. "Not that your eclectic clutter of crap wasn't charming. I particularly liked the folding chairs, especially the one held together with duct tape. I assume they did not make the trip to London Road with you?"

"They stay with the old apartment, part of the décor." Turning to White, he asked, "Do you play poker?"

"Not much anymore," she said, "I'm into video games these days."

Gramm shook his head and muttered, "Who are we gonna get to replace Jablonski?"

"I'll ask Sutherland. He's a good guy. Maybe he plays poker," Rathkey offered.

Gramm looked at a loss. "Who's he?"

"Oh yeah, he owns the other half of that house on London Road." Checking his phone, Milo said, "It's almost two. I got to go. See you on Sunday."

Gramm turned to White. "Did that make any sense to you?"

"He's your friend," White said, looking at the dessert menu.

§

Rathkey hated buying clothes and usually spent no more than a few minutes to find his favorite pants and shirts. He knew N&J didn't work that way. Some mope was going to measure him all over, and he would have to try on everything twice.

As he walked in the door, Milo was met by an older man with a tape measure around his neck. "Hello Mr. Rathkey. Mr. McKnight said you would be paying us a visit."

Feeling a bit like a smart ass in a place where he was not comfortable, Milo asked, "How do you know I'm Rathkey?"

"Mr. McKnight told us you would be in around two, and it's now two. In addition, Mr. McKnight gave a brief description of you."

"I'd love to hear that description," Milo muttered.

The salesman moved past the remark. "Shall we begin?"

One suit, two pairs of pants, two pairs of shoes, various shirts and ties, three sweaters, plus one overcoat later, Milo left the store empty handed. N&J delivered.

It was after four, and Duluth was getting dark. Remembering the Minneapolis job, he headed over the hill to Best Bargain to take a picture of Ray Rajack. With the knit cap's hidden camera recording, he found the appliance department.

Lucking out, Milo saw a salesman with a *RAY R* badge trying to sell a washer to an older couple. Minutes later, Milo had his video and headed back to the car to transmit it to Minneapolis.

After transmission, he sat for a bit staring at the darkness. He could go back to his office, where he didn't want to be, and start the computer search for his clients, or go to Lakesong for another of Martha's dinners.

I should bring the damn computer home! I've got an office there, why not use it?

He fired up the Honda, turned on the heat full blast, and headed back down the hill to his old office.

§

Arriving at Lakesong shortly after seven, his laptop and docking station in tow, Milo apologized to Martha for being late and dropped the computer off in his office.

Sutherland was already working on a salad in the family room, but Milo was thirsty and gratefully took a gimlet from Martha. He sipped it and asked, "Why are yours better than mine?"

Martha smiled and went back to the kitchen. Milo didn't even care what was on the menu. Whatever it was, it would be good. He sipped his gimlet and sat down.

Sutherland looked up. "Did you the get the clothes?"

"I did, and thank you," Milo said, sitting back, closing his eyes. His days were getting far too busy.

After a satisfying dinner, Milo went to his home office and set up the computer. Two troubleshooting calls to Ed Patupick, and it was done.

Milo opened the programs, inputted the information on both missing husbands and let the programs do their work. By morning, Milo would have leads on people who match their descriptions and lifestyles.

He knew that he had moved more than his computer over to Lakesong. He would tell Ilene to rent the apartment and office to somebody else. Thinking it might be difficult, he would give her several months' notice.

With the computer humming away, Milo slipped into the library and pulled down *The Murder of Roger Ackroyd*, one of his favorite Christie's. While he read, Annie, always a fan of murder and mayhem, curled up by the fireplace.

"You and my father are the same person aren't you?"

Rathkey, caught by surprise, looked up to see Sutherland smiling. He hadn't heard him come into the library. "What?"

"You and my father—you're the same person. My father would sit by that fireplace and read into the night."

"It's a great way to end an evening. Didn't you join him?"

"When I was younger, and had to read novels for school, I would sit here. But as I got older, I realized I didn't like fiction, and this is a fiction library," Sutherland explained. "Also, I don't particularly like deep leather chairs, fireplaces, or purring cats."

At that, Annie looked up and gave Sutherland a feline stare. She meowed once and went back to sleep.

"I always loved this room," Milo said.

Sitting down in the opposite leather chair, Sutherland asked why.

"Even as a kid I loved to read mysteries. Your father and I would talk in here about the characters and their motives.

John already knew the story of course, but I would try to guess who did it, explaining my reasoning to your dad. In a way, he was my best teacher."

Sutherland sighed. "You are like the older brother I never knew. My father and I rarely connected on books. We had sailing and business in common."

"Sailing and business, huh? Not me. You know, being in the Navy for six years, I should love sailing, but to be honest, the Navy taught me more about poker."

"Well, you and I have poker in common then. I love poker."

"You're in luck. It's my turn to host the traveling weekly poker game on Sunday night, and we need a fifth."

Not having been part of a regular poker game since college, Sutherland enthusiastically accepted. "Deal me in. Who's we?"

"Ernie Gramm, Saul Feinberg, myself, and George Shaffer."

Sutherland crinkled his forehead. "Should I know Gramm and Shaffer?"

"I don't know. I'll introduce you. The game was going to be at my old apartment, but I assume it can be here."

"Absolutely! We can play in the billiard room. You know, there is that poker table against the far wall. If we give her advance notice, Martha can prepare some snacks."

"Do we have cards and poker chips? I could always use mine, but the plastic would clash with the place."

Sutherland was slow to respond while trying to do a quick mental inventory. "We have beautiful, inlaid, hand painted, wooden chips somewhere in the billiard room, I'll find them. How much do we play for?"

"Nickel, dime, quarter."

"Sounds good. Sunday night, you say? I will mark it on my calendar." Sutherland got up to leave. "I'm gone. All of these burning logs, and sleeping cats are making me sneeze."

Rathkey waved him off and went back to his book. As Annie repositioned herself from the chair to the rug by the hearth, he stopped to look around, and for a moment, he was a boy again in his favorite chair.

He sighed. "Thanks John…for bringing me home."

6

N&J Fine Men's Clothiers delivered Milo's wardrobe as promised, early Saturday morning. Rathkey stared at the expensive looking clothing hanging in his nearly empty closet. He knew he would wear the black suit tonight, but when would he wear any of the other clothes?

The clothes had not only been delivered, but they had come with a tailor who had insisted that Milo try them on to make sure the fit was perfect.

He hated trying on clothes; they never fit, and he demanded to know what the tailor was going to do when they didn't fit this time.

To his credit, the tailor had been up for it. "Fix them," he said, glancingbent over his glasses.

"Do you have a sewing machine in your back pocket?"

"In the car for special clients," the man had said, pointing toward the door, "but I don't think it will be necessary."

It wasn't. They fit. His clothes were ready for this first New Year's Eve party, but was he?

He spent the rest of the day reading in the library after deciding against getting a haircut. It was a benefit of curly hair—even when long, it looked tidy. After showering, he put on each item of his new ensemble, and had to admit, he liked what he saw even better than he did this morning.

The suit was well tailored and hid his growing spare tire. He had never had a suit fit so well, but then he never had the money to buy something like this. Even the new shoes were comfortable.

Milo had always been at ease with who he was, and he sometimes had disdain for those with more means. Now he was one of them. This would take some figuring out. How far would he stray from his norm?

As he bent to tie his shoes, the ribs told him that he wasn't living a totally civil lifestyle. He downed two more Excedrin and put two more in his pocket, just in case.

Rathkey entered the gallery. Annie's long, plaintive cry and enthusiastic rubbing against his pant leg left Milo unsure if his new ensemble met with the cat's approval. Cat hair on a black suit did not meet with Sutherland's approval who handed Milo a lint roller. "I came prepared," he said with self-congratulations.

Sutherland was dressed in a somewhat similar suit, and Rathkey figured it was the uniform for the night. He noted that it looked far better on Sutherland's tall, thin frame than on his shorter squat one, but he still felt classy in his new suit.

"I thought we would take the Bentley," Sutherland said.

Rathkey laughed. "You're determined to get my butt into that Bentley."

"According to Mr. Anderson, it needs to be driven. Consider it car maintenance. Oh, by the way, he made a special trip to replace your battery and tuned up your car."

"I'm glad Mr. Anderson finally got to work on a classic car," Milo quipped as they walked into the garage.

"Speaking of classics, get a load of that baby," Sutherland said, pointing to a vintage Vespa parked near the SUV.

"I can't believe it's still here. I used to putt around with that thing as a kid!"

Sutherland smiled. "Me too." They looked at each other in silent agreement—the Vespa would ride again come spring.

Sutherland drove and Rathkey asked why they had a mechanic but not a driver. Sutherland expounded with a short history of family chauffeurs, first for his mother, and then for John. He summed it up with the present situation. "I love to drive, but not fix."

"Good point."

The party was only a few estates down from Lakesong. The drive was short. Sutherland pulled onto the grounds of the *whale* as he called the house. The home of James Bonner, real estate magnet, was a modern, massive, white stucco mansion nestled among the old Jacobean Revival, and Tudor style estates along London Road. No steep roof, gables, balusters, or parapets to be found here.

The whale stood out like a sore thumb, or a middle finger, which Bonner didn't mind extending to his neighbors. Sutherland explained that Bonner had torn down a beautiful manor house to build this McMansion.

There were seven cars ahead of them waiting to pull under the front portico. A host of hustling valets helped the guests out of their cars and into the house. It took only minutes before Sutherland pulled up and the Bentley was whisked away to parts unknown.

Two pretty young ladies greeted them, and took their overcoats, handing them each a numbered silver coin. Rathkey followed Sutherland's lead and put the coin in his suit pocket. It mingled with his extra Excedrin.

The noise of the party grew louder as they left the foyer and headed to the main gallery. Rathkey looked around and agreed with Sutherland, the house was cold and sterile, more like an ultra-modern art museum than a home.

Bright, white, long, and wide, the gallery seemed to stretch the length of Bonner's expansive house. Massive paintings and photographs littered the walls. Rows of shiny black benches held the middle of the floor broken in spots by unusual sculptures.

It was not Rathkey's style, but he was sure someone had spent a fortune on this avant-garde show. Interspersed between the sculptures and benches were people chatting and laughing. Rathkey was always bad at estimating crowds, and he figured this one at about twenty-five. It was closer to seventy-five. Still, the people hardly filled the space.

Checking out the uplit paintings of spots and splatters, Rathkey asked Sutherland, "Are these any good?"

"Well, art is in the eye of the beholder, but most of these are crap. Mr. Bonner bought most of this stuff. His wife, Mary Alice, has her own collection elsewhere in the house. She has a much better eye."

As if on cue, a stunning blond woman dressed in a form fitting, black, cut velvet, Vera Wang dress strolled toward them, her hand outstretched. "Sutherland, so good of you to come," she said, shaking his hand and giving him a friendly hug.

"I would never miss one of your parties Mary Alice," he pronounced. "They are always the highlight of the season." Looking around, Sutherland commented, "I see James has added some new art works to the walls."

She rolled her eyes and sighed. "James thinks they make him look like a patron of the arts. He says it's good for business." She glanced at Milo for the first time, extended her hand, and asked the question she already knew the answer to. "Have we met?"

Milo remembered scoffing at Feinberg's description of Mary Alice being a special lady everyone loved. Staring at her gleaming blond hair, toned curvaceous body, and inviting smile, Milo felt that Feinberg had underplayed her. In addition to all her other attributes, Mary Alice had deep blue eyes. Milo was a sucker for deep blue eyes. Hers locked onto his. He found them to be so spectacular he couldn't stop staring.

He managed to shake her hand and respond with some semblance of dignity. "I'm Milo Rathkey"

"Ahh yes. You moved into Lakesong." Without dropping her gaze, she smiled and asked in a polite yet sassy manner, "Are you a close friend of the family, or have you found a skeleton hiding in the McKnight closet?" Smiling at Sutherland she added, "Lakesong has so many closets, and I suspect so many skeletons."

Laughing at her irreverent style, but still entranced by the lady, Milo countered, "It's a long story, but that skeleton idea isn't a bad theory. "

"I'm so glad you're here. You and I will get together soon. You intrigue me. I want to hear your story, every… little…detail."

She played her part as the Queen of London Road well and wasn't ashamed of it. There was something about her that was charming, funny, and sexy—a presence which endeared her to Rathkey immediately. It was only a brief encounter, but he thought that she might be one of those rare people who actually listened after asking a question. When she spoke to Milo, it was as though he was the only person in the room. Milo was smitten.

"Come with me," she said as she enclosed Milo's arm under hers with casual intimacy. "You must meet my husband James, but I must warn you, he's not a nice person."

Rathkey noticed that Sutherland did not accompany them. He took off in the opposite direction. Milo was on his own.

She moved him over to a tall, thick, bellowing man with a patchy beard and thinning red hair, standing in the middle of what appeared to be an argument. He was berating a short man with a slight build and an unfortunate holiday-inspired red and green bow tie. The shorter man looked nervous and distressed. Rathkey could see people edging away as the argument grew louder.

In Milo's world, an argument this heated would end in a fist fight. He had no idea what would happen here.

"Christmas is over Roger, no presents for you. Your silly idea is as stupid as your awful bow tie."

The smaller man, though embarrassed, was trying to be civil. "Well, James when you invited me to this party, I thought it was to finalize our agreement."

"I didn't invite you, my wife did," the tall man sneered.

Mary Alice turned to Rathkey and whispered as if to set the record straight, "That's not true, I don't even know the poor man." She tried to get her husband's attention, but he ignored her and continued his tirade.

"We're done here, Roger, you bore me."

The little man persisted. "You said you wanted to buy the properties…my plan."

"Your plan is stupid, trust me. I wouldn't spend a dime on it. Take my advice and burn down the whole block, including that wreck of a furniture store. Enjoy the party, Roger. Bring home a doggy bag to your unfortunate wife and kids. My treat." This last comment amused the large red hulk as he let out a loud guffaw at the retreating victim.

Mary Alice leaned into Milo. "I told you he's not a nice man."

Milo met her eyes, admiring her ability not to hide the obvious, and said with defiance, "Bring him on!"

She smiled. "I think I'm going to like you Milo Rathkey." Turning to her husband in a louder voice, "James, James, I would like you to meet Milo Rathkey, our new neighbor."

Noticing his wife, Bonner barked, "What? What do you want?"

Mary Alice's smooth-as-silk demeanor never changed. "This is our new neighbor, Milo Rathkey."

Bonner turned and stepped into Milo's personal space, towering over him. Milo had run into this kind of man before. Always bigger than anyone else, he used his physical presence to intimidate.

"Why would I want to meet you, Mr. Rathkey?"

"Don't have a clue," Milo countered, not backing down an inch.

Bonner smiled a wicked smile. "Neighbor? How are you my neighbor?"

Mary Alice cut in. "He now lives in Lakesong."

"Did McKnight's stupid kid sell that wreck of a house to you?"

This overbearing putz insulted me, John, and Sutherland in one question. What a gem!

Milo leaned into Bonner's space, letting him know there was a force pushing back. "Do you really care?"

"I don't!"

Milo didn't like him. "Good talk," he cracked, aware that Mary Alice's arm was still wrapped in his.

Bonner stood, arms folded, staring down at Milo. His manner was malevolent, but inside his head there were questions. He wanted to know more about this new neighbor. Without another word, Bonner marched off looking for a new victim.

Ignoring her husband's rude and insulting manner, Mary Alice continued as if nothing happened. She loosened her grip on Milo's arm and instead took his hand, "Let me introduce you to a much friendlier group." Guiding Milo along again, she explained, "This party caters not only to business people but artists as well. Do you prefer painters, musicians, writers, what?"

Milo shrugged. "I have never really thought about it."

Mary Alice reached out her other hand and snagged a short man with a pronounced red birth mark on his left cheek. "Jules, I want you to meet Milo Rathkey. Milo recently moved into Lakesong with Sutherland McKnight."

"I thought Sutherland was straight," Jules said smiling.

Mary Alice rolled her eyes and laughed. "Oh, Jules, it's not romantic, only financial. Everything is sex with you."

Jules shook Milo's hand and said, "Lakesong already has a magnificent art collection, however, I could still help you mix it up a little."

"I don't think I've ever noticed the artwork," Milo admitted.

"Oh my, you need me to give you an art tour of your own home," Jules offered.

"Is that what you do?"

"Some say I sell paintings. I prefer to say I facilitate art's movement through the great houses of Duluth, the Twin Cities, and the upper Midwest. You may want to change up some of the old masterpieces with more modern masterpieces."

Knowing he was unprepared to discuss masterpieces of any era, Milo took a slight left turn and pointed to the numerous works of art surrounding the gallery. "So, what do you think of this collection?"

Mary Alice laughed as though she and Jules had discussed this many times, and now Milo could be party to the fun joke between them. "Go ahead Jules, tell him what you think."

Jules peeked around, presumably to make sure James Bonner was not nearby. Satisfying himself on that score, he over-enunciated, "It's hideous! James has some guy in Chicago who sells him this crap at three times the going rate. I could do that for only twice the going rate," he whispered, then roared at his own joke.

Jules amused Milo, but he didn't see an art lesson in his future. Although, when he got home, Milo thought he might look at the paintings on the walls—or not.

"I use Jules to find paintings for my private collection," Mary Alice said as a tall man with an athlete's build came up and offered her a fresh drink.

Dropping Milo's hand, she took the drink and introduced the man as Brad Nelson, explaining that he owned a competing real estate company to her husband's. Rathkey shook his hand. They exchanged pleasantries and then Nelson guided Mary Alice away. As she departed, she turned to Rathkey. "We will chat, soon."

The warm companionship that she exuded faded with her retreating figure. He missed her, and felt alone even as he stood next to Jules. Echoing Milo's thoughts, Jules stated, "She is delightful, isn't she?" He was not expecting an answer.

Turning back to Milo, Jules said, "I am going to take a giant leap and guess that you are not in the arts. Yet, I don't get a business vibe off of you either. What do you do for a living, Mr. Rathkey?"

Eyeing the bar, Milo stated, "Currently, I am a very thirsty private investigator."

"Oh my! Mary Alice's guest list is getting more intriguing every year. Well, if I ever need a PI, I'll look you up."

"And if Sutherland and I ever decide to update the art collection at Lakesong, I'll give you a call."

"First you need to notice what's already there," Jules said laughing as he moved on to talk with other people.

As he surveyed the room, Milo wondered how many people here were like Jules, mixing business with pleasure. Since Milo was not looking for any new clients, the next up activity was a drink.

There were bars in all the corners of the room, and a dance band was setting up at the far end. Waiters were walking through the ever-growing crowd with trays of hors-d'oeuvres, most including a member of the mollusk family or eggs of Russian sturgeon. Milo sighed. There wasn't a tiny wiener in a bun to be had.

"Champagne sir?" a waiter asked while holding a tray of tall glasses.

"I prefer Vodka."

"I suggest you go to one of the bars, sir. They will fix you up," the man said, and moved on.

Milo took his advice. Avoiding small circles of chatterers, he moved to the least busy of four bars and ordered his favorite, a vodka gimlet.

"Certainly sir," the bartender said, "What vodka would you prefer?"

"Stolies if you've got it."

"Stolichnaya, the pride of Latvia. On the rocks?"

"Yes, please."

The bartender mixed a tall gimlet and handed it to Milo who, after taking a sip, was pleased with the result. He walked about the room not talking to anyone, observing the eclectic crowd.

The lovely Mrs. Bonner was holding court in a closed group of people, standing next to that Nelson fellow, picking a piece of lint from his coat. As friendly as Mary Alice seemed to be, years of tracking errant spouses told Milo that there was an excessive degree of familiarity between those two.

His surmise was rewarded when Nelson's hand rested on the small of her back only to be jerked away at Mary Alice's annoyed glance.

Milo looked for the brutish, obnoxious husband, but he was nowhere to be found. This party was getting interesting. Even more interesting was the fact that Milo had a mild dislike for Brad Nelson. Jealously perhaps? Feelings he had not experienced in a long time.

His thoughts were interrupted by Sutherland who appeared out of the crowd with a thirtyish man in a trendy, tight, Italian, blue, shiny suit. "Milo, I would like you to meet Paul Taylor."

They shook hands as Sutherland explained, "Paul is a financial planner. He can help you invest your money. I need a drink but go ahead and chat."

Taylor flashed a blinding number of white teeth. "So, you have a windfall to invest."

The image of a leopard taking down a gazelle appeared in Milo's mind. He didn't like the part he played in the image. "I was thinking of putting it under my mattress. Do you have something better?"

Taylor was hampered by youth and a total lack of humor. "I don't understand. Why would you put it under the mattress?"

"Just kidding." Milo turned his attention back to his gimlet.

"Well, we should get together soonest." Taylor handed Milo his card. "We have to get that money making money. No pain no gain. No risk, no reward."

"I'm a low risk kind of guy." The unread card joined the Excedrin and the coat check coin in his pocket.

"Oh no, no." Taylor wagged his finger in Milo's face. "It takes boldness to make money these days, my friend. Hit one out of the park. Pitch a perfect game, so to speak. We need to set up a meeting."

"Soonest," Milo echoed and avoided more conversation by putting two or three groups between himself and Mr. Baseball.

Well, there's one guy I don't need to check out. I could have been clichéd to death.

Emerging from the crowd, Milo heard a familiar voice, "Milo Rathkey in an expensive suit. Am I hallucinating?"

Milo turned around to see the smiling face of Saul Feinberg. Making an exaggerated pose Rathkey explained, "I'm the real deal—from the cover of GQ to your local neighborhood party."

Feinberg was wearing a tapered Italian suit that only the long and lean can get away with. A style much like that cliché-loving financial guy wore, except Saul's looked classy.

"Well, I don't remember seeing that suit in the courtroom."

"It's part of my 'other life' collection. So, what do you think?" Saul gestured out to the party. "Have you met the hostess yet?"

"Yes, I have, and I am willing to chuck it all and run away with her to some remote island in the Pacific."

"Ah yes, we all have those fantasies."

"Tell me Saul, why is a woman like her with a man like him?" Milo nodded at Bonner, who had reappeared and was now in a mild argument with yet another man.

"Yeah, I know what you mean. It doesn't figure at all. It all happened when I was young, but as the story goes, Mary Alice's father was wealthy, even for this crowd, but then lost his money. James Bonner, who was at that time more charming than he is now, came along with oodles of bucks. Still, their marriage set tongues wagging."

Milo followed Feinberg to the bar where the latter ordered a vodka martini. They stood sipping their drinks for a few minutes as Feinberg pointed out various people, groups, and sub groups, filling Milo in on who was whom.

Milo could see, by how people were dressed, whether they fit into the artist groups or the business groups. The artists were all well-dressed but in much brighter colors than the business people.

For the most part there was no co-mingling, except for Jules and of course Mary Alice. Both were working the room.

"Don't move. I am going to find Creedence Durant to talk to you about your finances."

"I hope he's better than the guy Sutherland just introduced me to."

Left alone, Milo wandered the hall sipping his gimlet, being ignored by everyone but not looking to engage. To his left, a scary looking woman with purple hair and a purple feathered boa was talking art alongside a friendly, ample looking man in a somewhat worn suit. The poor man was working up a sweat dodging her feathers.

"I think the artist is brilliant!" she proclaimed with a swish. "I see the gift of the existentialist. The color portrays the intellectual expression of profound anxiety about the fate of all humanity."

After a brief pause, the man said, "I see black circles."

Undeterred, the woman turned to Rathkey. "And you? What do you see?"

"I don't know anything about art, but I see black circles too," Milo admitted.

The woman gave them both a look of exasperation. She wanted more insight from them. It didn't come. With feathers flying, she flounced away.

"It's just black circles. What makes it art?" Milo asked in a puzzled tone to the stranger.

"You ask the right question. I'm Creedence Durant by the way," the man said, shaking Milo's hand.

Milo laughed. "You're the person Saul Feinberg is hunting for. He wants me to talk to you. I'm Milo Rathkey."

It was Durant's turn to be puzzled. Creedence adjusted his glasses, something he seemed to do unconsciously. "Okay, Mr. Rathkey, you found me…talk."

Milo smiled. He wasn't pitching Milo. Milo had to pitch him. Clever man. "I just moved in down the block. I'm a private detective."

Adjusting his glasses once again, Creedence remembered the odd phone call from Saul Feinberg about a PI friend. This friend had come into a lot of money and needed help. This must be that guy. "Well, serendipity strikes again."

"Strike as in baseball? I just met a financial guy named Paul something or other who put me in a coma with one baseball reference after another. Are you all like that?"

Creedence laughed louder than he meant to, but few noticed as the noise had now increased with the growing crowd drowning out his loud guffaws. "No, it wasn't a baseball reference, but I know who you are talking about. Mr. Taylor is enthusiastic, and some people like that."

"So, what do you suggest I do with my money, besides hit it out of the park?"

Again, an inappropriate guffaw left the portly man's lips. "Hmm, well, do you want to risk it and try to make money or keep and spend it?"

"Definitely keep it and spend it."

"Well, I could set you up with a zero-balance account if you have enough money. That pays your everyday expenses but still makes some interest. The rest we put in safe investments such as certificates of deposit which are insured and T-Bills. You don't make much interest, but you don't lose either. Oh, and we'll have to do some things to ease the tax load."

Milo was impressed. Creedence Durant, the man with a rock-star name was unpretentious and listened. Creedence was Milo's guy! "Sounds good."

A little taken aback, Durant asked, "So, we're in business? When would you like to get started?"

"As soon as possible. John McKnight's lawyers have the money, and I don't."

"How much are we talking?"

"The will said fifteen million."

Creedence pushed his glasses up the bridge of his nose. "Well, Mr. Rathkey this could be the beginning of a beautiful friendship."

"No, no, I get to play Bogie."

"For fifteen million, you can play Ingrid Bergman as well." This time they both laughed. Mr. Baseball would not have understood.

Having set up a meeting for the following Monday, Rathkey and Durant separated and began to remingle.

So, this must be what Sutherland meant when he talked about finding new clients at a party. Maybe I should be asking people if they trust their spouse.

As Rathkey laughed to himself, he spotted Sutherland looking every inch the young successful executive on the rise. His animated conversation had the attention of three other business types, all of whom were nodding in agreement. He was holding court. This was his kingdom, his environment. Milo was impressed.

Drifting through the crowd with no clear destination, Milo passed Mary Alice who grabbed his arm and said in a hushed tone, "You and Creedence Durant seemed to hit it off over there."

"We did. I like him. He's my new financial planner."

She smiled that you're-the-only-person-in-the-room smile again. "Good choice. He's not flashy or trendy, so he doesn't get much big business." She hesitated, and then added, "Except for yourself and me. Come, meet my son."

Mary Alice adroitly maneuvered through the ever-growing throng of people. The gallery was now full, as people were arriving fashionably late. Rathkey was in need of another gimlet, but given a choice between alcohol and Mary Alice, he chose the latter.

She led him to a blond-haired young man who shared his mother's thin nose and high cheek bones. "Richard, this is our new neighbor Milo Rathkey. Milo, this is my son, Richard, who recently graduated from the University of Minnesota School of Business."

If Milo had not made a point to catch Richard's hand, their handshake would have been a slapstick comedy routine. Richard's eyes avoided both Milo's and his mother's. Rathkey did not know if he lacked social skills or if there was a problem.

Being polite for Mary Alice, Milo said, "Congratulations."

Richard stopped searching the room, and looked stumped. "I'm sorry, congratulations for what?"

Milo moved from politeness to mild sarcasm. "You graduated."

"Oh yeah, right. Glad to be finished."

"Richard, what are you looking for?" Mary Alice scolded.

"I'm looking for Father. I need to talk to him."

Milo began to wince but caught himself. The thought of needing to talk to the James Bonner he met was similar to needing a root canal, but he didn't know the relationship between father and son. "Are you going to work for your father?"

"Why do you ask?" Richard seemed stunned but recovered and smiled. "Who knows? Oh, he's over there by his office. Good to meet you, Mr. Rathkey. I'm sorry if I appear preoccupied, but I'm…on a deadline. Mom, great party. Don't worry. It's all okay."

As Richard charged over to where his father was standing, Mary Alice looked concerned. "I am afraid I don't know what that's about."

"Maybe a job?"

"I doubt it. Richard will not work for his father, and I have no idea what that deadline thing is about. Why he would seek James out on New Year's Eve is beyond me."

Mary Alice seemed lost in thought for a few seconds as she watched her retreating son. Regrouping, she turned to Milo and said with a smile, "It's time to party, and your glass is empty. Let's get you another drink."

Rathkey allowed himself to be led to the bar by the Mary Alice Express. This time there was a long line and Mary Alice, being the hostess, offered to buck it, but Milo turned her down. "I'll wait," he told her. She tilted her head to the side. "Wow, a believer in fair play over privilege, how unique. We'll talk." She touched his arm and, unfortunately for Milo, glided away into the crowd.

A pretty brunette wearing a tight red dress with almost no back fabric eased in line ahead of Milo. He didn't mind. After enjoying a moment of mentally undressing her, he glanced up at the paintings. This time there were wheels, wagon wheels, in different colors parading across the canvas. Were wagon wheels existential too?

Raised voices in a heated argument pulled Milo's attention away from the painting and onto the crowd. Turning, he realized it was his host James Bonner again, and the tall man who Mary Alice thought was way too linty.

Perhaps Bonner had caught on to the man's intimacies with his wife. This was quite a party! After hearing a phrase or two, Rathkey realized the beef was not personal, it was again about business, but it was still a fight.

"Get away from me, or I will squash you!" Bonner yelled, invading the man's space.

Nelson pushed him back while shouting, "We had deal for that land, and you reneged."

Unlike Nelson, Bonner barely moved. "That's the best you can do? You're powerless."

Nelson, who thought himself fit, was embarrassed that he couldn't move the loathsome Bonner. "I'll sue!" was all he could come up with.

"Go right ahead," Bonner challenged. "You've got no contract!"

For the first time, Nelson realized that the party had stopped and almost everyone was looking at them. He lowered his voice. "You son of a bitch. It was your word, which I now realize is worthless."

"You bore me. I'm through with this conversation, and I'm not buying your worthless land." Bonner turned and walked away, laughing.

"This isn't over. I will have the last say," Nelson said to Bonner and the crowd, in a last-ditch effort to appear the winner.

Bonner kept walking and laughing.

"James Bonner, our delightful host, evil and ruthless. Whom will he skewer next?"

Glancing to his right, Rathkey saw the cherub face of Creedence smiling at him.

"Does he always scream at guests in his home?"

Creedence shrugged. "He does what he wants to do, and Lord help anyone in his way."

Saul Feinberg joined them, making a rather dark joke. "Anyone who offs that guy, I'll defend."

"They couldn't find an impartial jury," Creedence added to the joke. "I think the Bonner murderers are standing in line."

Lightening up a bit, Feinberg chided Creedence for finding Milo without his help.

"Oh, Milo and I go way back. At least forty-five minutes, maybe an hour."

"He's my financial guy," Milo said with pride.

"This happened without me? I'm crushed," Saul complained.

The three made small talk until they reached the bartender. Milo sipped his new gimlet. Two was usually his limit and these were large. The band was about ready to play so Saul, a party animal, went in search of a dance partner.

Creedence started in the other direction, having spied the buffet table. "I need food."

"Sounds good," Rathkey said. "I need to put anything in my stomach besides vodka."

Not being the first to notice the food, they queued up, plates in hand. Unlike the hors d' oeuvres, this spread was down to earth, and Milo had to resist the temptation to pile his plate high.

He opted for medium rare prime rib, baked potato, and asparagus. Creedence had no problem piling his plate high, hiding his first choices under mountains of second and third choices.

At that point, the band let loose at ear piercing volume, at least it seemed that way to Milo. He liked music but not this loud.

Creedence shouted that he was going to find a place to sit down. Milo nodded but said he was looking for someplace quieter. They parted company.

Looking around, he saw a young woman open the doors to a room off the gallery not far from where he stood. She seemed to know where she was going, and since where she was going was away from the band, Milo decided to join her.

The room—a library—like the rest of the house, was ultramodern with white shelves full of well-dusted books. He looked around for a place to set his plate.

The young woman came to his rescue. "These chairs over here, closer to the French doors, are much more comfortable, and I always appreciate a table when trying to eat from a buffet."

Milo smiled still balancing his plate and his drink. "Thank you," he said, heading in her direction. "I've taken refuge from the band."

"It is rather loud," she agreed carrying a martini and a plate full of hors d' oeuvres balanced on top. Rathkey admired her ability to balance drink and food, and sit down.

"I'm Milo Rathkey. I live down the block."

"I don't think I know you. I'm Agnes Larson, Mr. Bonner's administrative assistant. I work here," she said, tucking her wavy blond hair behind her ear.

"Aha, I thought you were walking around as if you knew this place." Milo began to cut his prime rib, and looked at her plate. "You know there's real food out there."

"I know, but I enjoy the caviar, and oysters, and all of the rest of these hors d' oeuvres. They are such a treat."

"Go for it," Milo said, attacking his prime rib.

Where would someone so young develop a taste for caviar? I don't know anyone who really likes that stuff.

"What do you do, Mr. Rathkey?"

"I'm a private detective."

She stopped a cracker with caviar halfway to her mouth. "Really? Whom are you investigating?"

Milo laughed. "I'm just a guest. I'm new to the neighborhood…just moved into Lakesong."

Agnes narrowed her brown eyes for a brief moment. "The McKnight estate," she thought out loud. "Ahh, might you have received the special hand-delivered invitation?"

At Milo's nod and smile she continued, "I was wondering who you were. Mrs. Bonner wanted you here tonight. You may not know it, but you are the one being investigated," she giggled. "Mrs. Bonner enjoys knowing everything that goes on in her environment."

Milo leaned back and took a sip of his gimlet. "Mrs. Bonner did make contact. She has been a very charming hostess."

"Oh, she is that." Agnes held up her drink in toast fashion and said, "To our hostess."

Milo clinked his glass with hers. As they savored their cocktails, Rathkey revised his 'so young' assessment of Agnes. He now thought she was in her early thirties.

Still holding her glass, Agnes said, "This is another of my treats at these parties, I usually have only one dirty martini."

"Why only one? I'm on my second gimlet."

"Because I never know when my boss will want me to work."

"Tonight?" Rathkey was surprised. "I thought only cops and ambulance drivers worked on New Year's Eve."

Agnes looked amused. "Mr. Bonner will work tonight, Sunday night, any night. When he wants to work, we work. However, Happy New Year to me; a few minutes ago, Mrs. Bonner told me to enjoy the party. She would see to it that there would be no working tonight. I so appreciate that. To celebrate, I'm on my second dirty martini."

Milo toasted her and thought that from what he saw this evening, working with that man had to be hell. "I hope he pays well."

She laughed. "He has to or no one would work for him."

"I believe that, I mean I just met the man, but he's a bully. He yelled at two or three of his guests that I saw, and I wonder if he's yelling at someone now. I can only hope he doesn't yell at you."

"Mr. Bonner can be dismissive, but the aggressive yelling is for people he does business with." She took a slow and calculated sip of her martini and admitted, "You're right in your assessment though. He is a bully."

"Why do you work for him?"

"The pay is more than double what I would make elsewhere, and he gave my sister a job as his bookkeeper, after her divorce."

"Is your sister at this party?"

Tears welled up in her eyes, and she turned her head, "No, no she's not here. She was...she died days before Thanksgiving."

"Sorry to hear that." Rathkey never knew quite what to say to the grieving, except he hated the phrase, *Sorry for your loss.*

Agnes continued, trying not to get emotional. "It was a hit and run driver. She was crossing First Street."

Rathkey's unease was abated by Sutherland opening the library door and for a few seconds, allowing the blaring music to penetrate the room. "Creedence was right," he said, closing the door and sealing the music out. "He thought you were heading this way."

Milo was glad for the interruption. "I found this private dining room and a pleasant dinner companion. Sutherland meet Miss…"

"Larson." Sutherland interrupted shaking Agnes' hand. "And a Happy New Year to you, Agnes."

As if he had discovered a new species, Milo proclaimed, "She likes caviar!"

Sutherland looked at Rathkey as if he were a new species and then turned his attention back to Agnes. "Did you try the Beluga?"

"Of course, I love it! I am about to indulge in the Gold Osetra."

"I'm having the prime rib," Rathkey interrupted. "The Iowa prime rib, not the Nebraska prime rib."

He was ignored.

"Mr. Rathkey and I were seeking refuge from the band. It's too loud."

"Amped too high to cover bad musicianship," Sutherland explained

Agnes nodded. "So true. You should show them a thing or two."

"Wait, what?"

"Mr. McKnight plays a mean guitar. He's known for it."

"You are a man of many surprises," Milo conceded to Sutherland. "So, what brings you in here?"

"I was checking on you, but it is obvious you are fine."

With no warning, the house shook amid loud explosions. Milo looked alarmed, but Agnes touched his arm and said, "It's the fireworks. Mary Alice always has fireworks over the lake at midnight on New Year's Eve."

Sutherland offered Agnes his jacket and led the trio through the French doors onto the balcony to check out the show. Despite the frigid temperature, guests were crowding the balcony to the left that led down to the garden.

The fireworks were fabulous, and, thankfully, short. Mother Nature even added to the excitement with large fluffy flakes of snow collecting on the ground.

Re-entering the toasty library, Agnes returned Sutherland's jacket and announced that it was time for her to go home. Sutherland offered to give her a ride, but she refused.

"I have a regular Lyft driver I use, and I told him I would be calling shortly after midnight. I don't want to disappoint him," she said, walking to the phone which sat on a side table in the library.

"Do all of these houses have land lines?" Rathkey asked. "I guess cell phones have not come to London Road."

Before Sutherland could answer, Agnes said, "Mr. Bonner is paranoid about cell phones because he read somewhere they can be easily tapped. He forbids any of his employees to use them at work. Mine is never on in this house or the office." She picked up the receiver and pushed one of the unlit buttons.

Sutherland added, "Besides, cells have connection problems here. Have you tried using your cell phone in our house?"

"Yeah, it worked fine."

"Well, you'll find it's spotty. It's great in the breakfast room, but awful in the library. That's why we still have a land line…"

Sutherland's discourse on cell phones was cut off when they both noticed the look on Agnes' face. She had replaced the receiver and appeared stunned. Her face was pale, her eyes glazed as she mumbled, "Bonner. Murder."

"Bonner's been murdered?" Sutherland questioned, rushing to Agnes' side as she seemed unsteady.

Rathkey, who doubted that Bonner had been murdered, also moved to the stricken woman.

"There was no light…he was on the phone…I picked it up," she said, almost to herself.

"Oh, I see. So someone threatened him?" Sutherland guessed.

Agnes came out of her fog. "What?" she asked, looking at Sutherland.

"You said you heard a threat?" Sutherland repeated.

"I didn't mean to…to overhear…he was on the phone, and he said it."

"Who said what?" Rathkey asked unclear about what Agnes was saying.

Agnes stared at Milo. He could see that she was no longer the relaxed, caviar-loving dinner companion. "It was a man's voice…he…he…"

"Sit down and relax for a minute; you've had a shock," Sutherland offered.

Agnes allowed herself to be guided to a nearby chair. Sutherland fetched her martini and told her to take a sip. Color came back to her face and, smiling at Sutherland, she thanked him.

Milo, not wanting to agitate her anymore, dropped his questioning about the phone conversation and moved on to, in his mind, the next logical step. "Maybe one of us should go check on Bonner."

"Oh no!" Agnes protested. "If he knows I heard him on the phone, he'll fire me. The light on the phone was off. Maybe it's broken. I couldn't have known, but he hates when people snoop on his business."

"You can go if you want to," Sutherland said to Rathkey. "I steer clear of him."

Agnes pleaded. "Please don't tell him I listened to him on the phone! Please!"

Rathkey was quick to ease her fear. "I won't tell him about the phone. I will be vague."

He left the library after getting directions to Bonner's office. It was on the same floor off the gallery. Unfortunately, Rathkey had to walk past the band to get to the hallway. His ears took a serious beating, but his eyes were entertained by Feinberg dancing with the woman in the backless red dress.

Knocking would be polite, but Rathkey had no intention of being polite to this clod. He opened the door, only to be brushed aside by a frantically exiting Richard. Milo cursed, his ribs not needing the contact.

"I don't know what they will do!" Richard moaned.

"What the hell?" Rathkey demanded.

Richard looked shocked as if he hadn't seen Rathkey standing there until now. "I'm dead," he whispered, as he hurried away but not in the direction of the party.

Too much drama, Rathkey thought, as he walked in straightening out his jacket.

The study was as modern as the rest of the house. White and devoid of charm, it presented a cold, stark atmosphere. Bonner was sitting behind a Lucite-topped desk whose only features were three computer screens and a phone.

Looking up at Rathkey, Bonner shouted, "What the hell do you want? It's one damn interruption after another."

Milo stared and wondered why he was there. Why would anyone help this man? "I heard that someone threatened to kill you."

Bonner laughed, shaking his head. "People threaten me all the time. Are you talking something specific or the general crowd out there, most of whom would like to see me dead."

Glaring at Milo in his intimidating manner he added, "And why, may I ask, do you give a damn?"

Ignoring the tone, and the question, Milo asked again, wanting to make this interaction as short as possible, "So, you're okay?"

Bonner pulled a Glock 9mm from an open drawer.

Milo stepped back as the gun was being pointed at him, "Is that loaded?" Milo asked, more calmly than he felt.

Bonner put the gun on the desk . "Are you a cop?"

"Used to be."

"Well, it used to be unloaded, but not anymore. Now get the hell out of my office."

Rathkey turned around, walked out and returned to the library.

Screw him!

"So, is Bonner okay?" Sutherland asked.

"Belligerent, insulting, but in good health—unfortunately."

Sutherland shook his head at what an abomination Bonner was, as Agnes asked in a frightened tone, "Did you tell him I was the one who overheard him?"

"I told him nothing."

"We are driving Agnes home."

"And what about Mr. Lyft?"

"He's been paid and gets to go to bed earlier than expected," Sutherland explained. "He's happy, we're happy, Bonner's happy. Happy New Year!"

The trio said their goodbyes to Mary Alice and climbed into the Bentley. Like most destinations in Duluth, it was a short ride to Agnes' house.

As they pulled up to her 1950's Lakeside bungalow, Agnes, who had been lost in thought, thanked them and went inside.

Sutherland pulled away, and Rathkey asked, "You play the guitar?"

"Since I was nine. I'm pretty good. I played in a couple of bands in high school and college. You may get a concert one of these days. *Stairway to Heaven* should be around your time, right?"

"Around the time I was born! I'm not that old!"

D.B. Elrogg

As they pulled into the garage, Sutherland asked, "Do you think that threat was real?"

"Don't know. Don't care."

7

James Bonner was quite pleased with himself, and the evening's events. The night was almost Shakespearean. Little Lund was disposed of, and Nelson the Ninny may have met his ruin. *Fool around with my wife will you.* It was a wonderful way to start the New Year. Although he couldn't hear any noise in his sound proof office, he thought the party should finally be winding down and felt no need to say goodbye to anyone. Mary Alice took care of that. That's why he married her. Besides, he had money to make and people to make miserable.

Interruptions irritated him. Richard the Unready, as he enjoyed calling his weak son, barged in sniveling about needing money again. Bonner chuckled to himself. The two plans for his supposed prodigy were on schedule. The added bonus of the second plan, a job for Richard, would be a kick in the gut for his loving wife. He couldn't wait to see that.

D.B. Elrogg

Insomnia had its advantages, one of them being able to work well into the early morning hours without losing time to sleep. A smile that never met his eyes stayed on his lips as he perused the three computer screens in front of him. One of his screens held the latest worldwide stock market returns. The middle screen was full of his latest real estate research, and the last screen held information about Milo Rathkey. Bonner read with interest about his new neighbor, a former cop, now a private detective, and an asshole. He hadn't flinched when Bonner reached for his gun. Most did, except for a couple of *crazies* he kept on the payroll. Bonner had not yet decided on how to proceed with Rathkey—hire him, con him, or ignore him. It was up in the air.

The door opened one more time, and he looked up. "I'm busy go away." He went back to his computer and the Tokyo Stock Exchange.

The intruder did not go away. The noise level kept increasing. His declaration that he needed to be left alone was met with even more babble. He was vaguely aware of yet another threat. Without looking up, he went to his go-to bag of insults, cut short by a single shot.

With half his skull, brain matter, and copious amounts of blood on the far wall, James Bonner heard and felt nothing.

His head, now clear of all thought, bounced several times on the blood-stained Lucite desk top. After a number of minutes, the intruder set the gun—Bonner's gun—back down on the desk and left. The computer screen beeped, James Bonner had made several thousand dollars in his completed stock deal.

It no longer mattered.

8

"Poverty is like punishment for a crime you didn't commit." Leroy Thompson thought about this quote often. He heard it somewhere years ago, maybe in juvie. He never read Eli Khamarov or even knew who he was, but Leroy liked the quote. It appealed to his sense of injustice at being born poor, and he used it as an excuse for conning rich people every chance he got.

Leroy was getting hot in his leather coat and puffer jacket—the latter worn under the coat to give the illusion of size and muscle where there was none.

A sleeping Stan Shultz stirred in the passenger's seat, grunted, and went back to soft snoring. Stan, being a couple of years older and much stronger, was a necessary commodity in Leroy's scams and had been since the two had met in juvenile hall. He protected Leroy. Stan fit the bill then. He still did.

Looking across tree-lined London Road at the Bonner Estate, Leroy scowled. He shoved his small hands into the large, oversized pockets in his long, leather coat feeling nothing but empty space where Richard Bonner's money should have been. Ten minutes ago, he texted the kid to come out and pay last night's poker debt but got no response. A chunk of the money from young Bonner would go to crime boss, Morrie Wolf, who expected it early Monday morning. Morrie did not do late.

It was now six-thirty Sunday morning. The kid was still a no-show. Reaching for his phone to text again when he heard the first siren. Stan bolted straight up. More sirens. The gates to the Bonner estate began to open as one, then two, then three squealing cop cars sped through them, followed by two quiet unmarked cars. One lonely ambulance brought up the rear. This was an unexpected event. Leroy instinctively slid down in his seat behind the wheel so as not to be seen.

What the hell is going on? I need my money! Damn, where's my money?

§

Milo awoke, being pawed on the left shoulder by Annie, who wanted her morning bacon. "What?" he blurted in a haze. Her reply came in the form of a silent meow, a stern warning that a more vocal admonishment could be on the way.

Milo was still tired. He was not a party guy, never had been, and that party last night was late and exhausting. New people, new territory, new clothes, just new. Some of this *new* was to Milo's liking. He always loved this house even though his current place in it was unfamiliar. There needed to be a balance. Today, the fashionable Milo needed to reconnect with the comfortable Milo, and nothing said old Milo better than his ancient kakis, comfy flannel shirt, and worn Nikes. Balance having been established, Annie led the way to breakfast, looking back from time to time as if thinking Milo too dim to follow.

"Good Morning Martha," he said, in a cheery tone. "I hope you have bacon. This cat could get angry if she doesn't get her bacon. I have already been lectured."

"Good morning to you. She may give you a lecture, but not me. She knows who cooks the bacon."

Rathkey poured his coffee and joined Sutherland at the table. Martha followed him, carrying the cat's coveted plate of bacon along with Milo's French toast. He was so hungry he almost failed to notice Sutherland's equally dressed down look of jeans and a University of Minnesota sweatshirt.

After exchanging good mornings, Sutherland began chatting about something in the Sunday paper, but Milo was deaf to all except the aroma of melting sweet cream butter, and warm maple syrup flowing down the eggy brioche. Martha's breakfasts were always good, but this was exceptional.

"I said Mary Alice's party made the Trib!"

Having gotten Milo's attention, breaking through the food-induced hypnotic trance, Sutherland continued stifling a smirk. "There's a lovely picture of Mary Alice with some vagabond private detective in a well-cut suit standing behind her."

"You're kidding!" Milo was shocked.

Sutherland held up the picture, and sure enough, there he was in the background talking to Creedence Durant. "Gee they never get my good side."

"You mean from the back?"

Rathkey laughed at the dig and glanced back at the picture of Mary Alice and those blue eyes. The rest of her wasn't bad either, beautiful and sexy. "They certainly got her good side."

"I don't think Mary Alice has a bad side."

Annie rubbed up against Milo, reminding him that breakfast was about feeding the cat. Several tiny pieces of bacon later, she was sated and headed back to the hearth room's roaring fire.

After making a respectable dent in his breakfast, Milo leaned back and looked outside. Snow and wind were predicted, and Mother Nature looked as if she was planning on making that forecast accurate. Gray-white clouds covered the sky. "I hope the weather doesn't interfere with our poker game tonight."

"It shouldn't," Sutherland said, drinking his Sunday morning green smoothie. "Only an inch or two is predicted."

Good, the poker game should be safe. I'm tired from the party. Today is sit-in-front-of-the-fire-and-read day.

As if on cue, to interrupt his Sunday plans, Milo's cell phone rang playing the *da-dunk* sound of *Law and Order*. It was Ernie's ring.

This better not be Gramm cancelling on the poker game because of a few inches of snow!

The annoyance lines in his brow deepened as he pushed the speaker button. "You'd better be coming tonight."

"This isn't about tonight," Gramm said in a serious tone. "This is about now. I need you over at the Bonner house."

Milo felt like joking, been there done that, but the tone in Gramm's voice was too serious. "Why? When?"

"Now!"

"Okay." Milo was not accustomed to being on the receiving end of Gramm's gruffness.

"Is this damn thing on speaker?" Gramm growled.

"Yeah, you know I can't hear squat from these cell phones."

"Who's listening?"

"Me and Sutherland. We're having breakfast. It's spectacular, if you care."

Gramm ignored Milo's breakfast review. He was not in the mood. "Bring Sutherland with you. I don't want him making any phone calls."

"Phone calls about what? What's going on? My coffee is getting cold."

"Not as cold as James Bonner! He is currently at his desk with half his head on the wall."

Milo was stunned, but glancing up, Sutherland's face took stunned to a whole new level. "Accident?" Milo asked.

"Not likely."

Sutherland, who had been listening with disbelief, jumped in on the conversation, " He was threatened last night, on the phone."

"What?"

Rathkey motioned for Sutherland to be quiet and told Gramm they would explain when they got there.

"Fine." And the phone went dead.

Sutherland expected Milo to jump up. He didn't. Instead he continued to indulge in his glorious breakfast much to Sutherland's horror. "You can't sit there and eat! You heard the Lieutenant. We need to go!"

"Yes, I did, and yes, I can. I haven't finished Martha's French toast. You really should try some."

"But James Bonner is dead!"

It had been a long time since Milo woke up to a *not likely* accident, but some things were like muscle memory. He knew a full belly would be important. "Bonner's not going anywhere. Trust me, it's going to be a long day, and unlike last night, this morning will not be catered."

As Martha refreshed Milo's coffee, Sutherland, ignoring the practical advice, continued quite caught up in the drama of the moment. "But we know he was threatened, and they need to know what we know." Seeing the perplexed look on Martha's face, he explained the situation.

In steady, measured tones, Milo instructed through bites of French toast. "We will tell 'em, but right now they are processing the scene, talking to the family, and stabbing Bonner's liver with a thermometer "

"Okay then, that's enough for me this Sunday morning." Martha retreated to the kitchen, "By the way liver and onions will be off the menu for a while."

"Sorry Martha, too much information?" Rathkey apologized. He recognized his own grim, self-protective cop-speak coming out and tried to curb it.

"I gotta say, I didn't see this coming," Milo said. "Guys like Bonner get threatened all the time. They love it. Rarely does anyone have the guts to carry out the threat."

"So, you think he was murdered?"

"From Ernie's tone and the fact that he ruled out an accident, the chances are pretty good. And from what I saw last night, there will be a lot of suspects."

"Gramm wants to see us because we're suspects?" Sutherland asked, as if it were a joke.

Rathkey looked up with a completely straight face. "Well, we were at the party, that might give us opportunity. Motive and means are questionable, at least for me."

Sutherland had only known Milo for a few days and didn't know if he was serious. Not sure, Sutherland ventured, "You're kidding, right?"

Pleased with his little joke, Milo decided to let Sutherland off the hook. "Yeah, I'm kidding about you being a suspect. But a piece of advice, when we go over there, answer only the questions Gramm asks. Do not volunteer anything."

"Why?"

"Police are looking for a motive, a suspect, anything at this point. Like I said, just answer their question. Don't elaborate unless asked. You might screw up and cast suspicion on some of your friends. The cops will find the murderer on their own, and you don't want your friends being hassled, unless of course, they did it."

Sutherland was silent for a minute, looked back at Rathkey to be sure he wasn't joking with him again, and then took a deep breath. "This is for real isn't it? I mean, James Bonner is dead. It's possible someone I know killed him."

Milo cautioned, "Don't get ahead of the game. We don't know anything yet."

Sutherland muttered to himself, "We know he was threatened on the phone."

Milo pretended not to hear that last statement and pushed back his chair. "I'm done here. Great breakfast, Martha. My casual Sunday is over. Let me get dressed and then we'll head over to the Bonner place"

"You're welcome, Mr. Rathkey. What about dinner and the poker game?" Martha wasn't sure if she should begin the poker feast she had planned.

"There's a good chance we'll be back. If they arrest Sutherland, I'll call and let you know there will be one less for poker."

"That's not funny," Sutherland said with exasperation. "How can you joke about this? I mean, I don't know a single person that's ever been murdered."

Milo wished he could say the same.

Sutherland bounded upstairs, wondering what one wears to a possible murder scene.

§

"Goddammit!" Leroy mumbled as a third television truck pulled up in front of the estate, blocking his view of the gates. By now, a crowd was beginning to gather, gawkers wondering what all the police activity was about. Richard and his money could be in all that mess, but Leroy couldn't find him. He elbowed Stan who was getting back into sleep position. It was time to go over there and check it out.

"If I can't sleep, I want to eat," Stan mumbled.

Great Party! Sorry About The Murder

As Leroy closed the door to the car, he knew the clock was ticking on Stan's temper. The man was tired and hungry, and when Stan needed food, he needed it now. Even back in juvie, Leroy controlled Stan by conning inmates for extra food to make Stan happy and Leroy safe.

Despite the shoe lifts and extra jacket under his leather coat, even a casual observer could see that Leroy was much smaller than Stan as the two walked toward the crowd.

§

Sutherland pulled the Porsche up to the gates of the Bonner estate. He was shocked to see his neighborhood, usually empty of humankind on a cold Sunday morning, turned into a circus of gawkers and television trucks.

While waiting at the gate for the policeman to check with Gramm via radio, Milo spotted two unlikely, but familiar, faces in the crowd. "Leroy Thompson and Stan Shultz? What the hell? What are they doing here?"

Sutherland ignored him.

The two men that took Rathkey's attention were trying to blend into the crowd, but to Rathkey they looked like walking mug shots. The hulkish Shultz made eye contact, bent down, and elbowed his shorte puffed up partner to look. Thompson recognized Milo, but, not wanting to be noticed, jerked Shultz's beefy arm and pulled him further into the crowd. Milo knew these two miscreants were always around trouble.

Sutherland was waved in and parked behind the multitude of police cars and one hearse. No valets or pretty girls greeted them . As the two trudged to the front door, a policeman approached Rathkey to tell him the lieutenant wanted to see him in the dead guy's office.

Sutherland whispered to Rathkey as the two entered the house, "The dead guy?"

"What would you call him?"

"Mr. Bonner?"

"He could have called him the stiff. You had better get used to this."

Sutherland's eyes narrowed, and his forehead creased in disapproval of Milo's offhandedness.

The gallery was quiet and empty of the warm, celebratory throng of people from last night. A few sad, solitary yellow balloons drooped from the wall sconces. Milo hadn't noticed balloons at the party, but he was sure they must have been bright and festive a few hours ago. The bandstand was gone, as were the bars at each corner, and the tables once laden with food. This party was indeed over.

Milo noticed the physical changes, but to Sutherland the house itself was under siege. This was no longer a familiar place, the home of his friend, Mary Alice Bonner, where he would come to festive parties and be greeted by her in stylish evening gowns or pert tennis outfits.

Strangers, officials, had taken control. Permission was needed from police to move around the house. Polite conventions were being ignored. In fact, everyone seemed to be going out of their way to be crass, including Milo.

The dead guy? The stiff?

Sutherland tried to bring civility to the situation. "They could call him the deceased. They use that word on crime shows you know."

Great Party! Sorry About The Murder

Milo heard Sutherland but kept walking towards the office in a kind of giant slalom, avoiding the piles of litter strewn leftovers from the Happy New Year's celebration. Sutherland followed several steps behind.

As they approached Bonner's office, Milo stopped and warned Sutherland, "You know, you should stay here. It's going to be pretty gruesome in there."

Hearing Milo's voice, Gramm came stiffly out of the office, arching his back and cricking his neck from side to side. "About time!" he barked.

"I had to get beautiful."

"You wasted your time," Gramm chided, before turning his attention to Rathkey's companion. Holding out his hand, Gramm softened his tone. "You must be Sutherland McKnight. I'm Lt. Ernie Gramm. If you could do me a favor find a seat out here, and I will be with you shortly. I have a few questions to ask."

The smells of rare caviars, roasting meats, and good liquor were replaced with a sickening, sweet stench coming from the office.

"That smell! What is that awful smell?" Sutherland asked.

"Putrid body decomposition combined with a lot of blood. If you sit in the middle of this…party room…you should be fine," Gramm answered.

Sutherland walked away mumbling to himself. "It's a gallery not a party room." He kept moving until he could no longer smell the stench. Glancing back, watching Gramm and Rathkey enter the study, he wondered how they could tolerate that awful odor.

How could any of this become common place?

The crime technicians had left several boxes of gloves on the floor near the door. Gramm pointed at them indicating both he and Milo needed to glove up.

Milo had taken his Excedrin and had extras in his pocket. The bend for the gloves could be felt, but the ribs were definitely better. As they entered the room, Sgt. White acknowledged Rathkey with a nod.

James Bonner was at his desk, head down in a mass of brownish red liquid that had pooled on the slick, see-through, shiny surface. Small bits of brain matter floated in the liquid like islands dotting a lagoon.

On the right side of Bonner's head, the side that was pointing up, the entrance wound—a single black hole—indicated a shot at close range. The bullet went into Bonner's head neatly but was messy on the way out. It took a large chunk of skull and brain matter with it, leaving half of the dead man's skull, complete with blood and brains, streaked on the far wall and the adjacent door to the bathroom.

He didn't seem so boastful now, thought Milo.

The pool of blood that had exploded from the dead man's skull had not yet dried but was no longer flowing.

That damn gun he waved around last night is still on the desk, but it's been moved!

Looking to his left, Milo noticed an open safe on the inside wall.

That was hidden by a painting last night—robbery?

Moving to his right, avoiding White and the crime techs working on the brain debris, he stuck his head into an adjacent office.

Maybe for Agnes Larson?

Turning back to the room, double French doors on the left led outside to what looked like a back driveway. A crime tech was kneeling down out there taking close-ups of tire tracks.

A private entrance…interesting.

Milo closed his eyes and tried to imagine the murder as it happened, something he did when he was a cop. Bonner was seated at his desk. The murderer was at his right, holding a gun, could be Bonner's gun. It had to be somebody known to Bonner because the bullet entered at close range from the side. The dead man had not turned to acknowledge the person or had just turned away.

In Milo's mind he saw the shot, Bonner's head explode, and fall onto the desk top. The murderer then returned the gun to the desk and left. How? There were two ways to get in and two ways to get out.

"So, Ernie, what are you liking? Family member through the office door, or outsider through the French doors?" Milo asked.

"Family member through the office door is always a possibility, but the brief snowfall last night was in our favor. There are three distinct, and one muddled set of tire tracks back there. Using the side street that leads to this back lane, anyone could pull up to the office without alerting people in the house."

Dr. Cyril Smith, the sixty-something medical examiner, interrupted their conversation. He was eager to bag up the body, having finished his cursory examination. Gramm introduced him to Milo, explaining that Milo was consulting with the department on this one. He asked Smith to bring them both up to speed.

Consulting was news to Milo, and the idea of doing police work still bothered him. He thought he was here as a knowledgeable witness, but figured that conversation with Gramm could wait.

Smith checked his notes. "It's pretty straight forward. He died between two and five in the morning…shot in the temple…close range …probably a hollow point round. You know what I know. Are we done here?"

Gramm nodded. "Doc's right. It was a hollow point. We found the remains of the bullet in the doorframe to the bathroom."

Milo pointed to the gun on the desk, "If the shot came from that gun, he was killed with his own weapon. Is it loaded with hollow points?"

With more than polite offhandedness, Gramm asked, "How would you know that's Bonner's gun?"

"He pulled it on me last night. It's been moved."

Gramm's eyes crinkled in puzzlement, not pleased with what he heard. "Last night? Were you at the party?"

"Don't ask me why, but yeah."

"This is getting better by the minute. Why the hell would the dead guy invite you to his party and then pull a gun on you?"

"He was bragging to me how well protected he was and immune to death threats."

Gramm checked with White to see if a picture had been taken of the gun. After she said it had, he picked it up, took out the clip, and examined the bullets. "Hollow points! We indeed may be looking at the murder weapon."

Gramm walked around the desk behind the body. "Come over here, Milo. I have another question for you." Pointing to the farthest computer screen, Gramm asked, somewhat fearful of the answer, "What's this about?"

Milo joined Gramm at the screen and was shocked to see **MILO RATHKEY CONFIDENTIAL** at the top. Underneath was information from a private security firm about Milo's personal and professional life.

"Son of a bitch! What's with this guy? I just met him last night. What a piece of crap!"

Gramm raised his bushy eyebrows. "Jesus Milo, first the guy waves a loaded gun around then he has you investigated. What the hell went on between you two last night?"

"Nothing. I swear. I just met the guy. Maybe he wanted to hire me? I wouldn't have worked for him. He was a total asshole."

"So, you don't currently have a business relationship with this guy, right? You know why I'm asking."

Milo knew where he was coming from. This case was high profile, and Gramm could not afford to have anything screw it up, or have the decision of adding Milo to the case questioned. Milo indicated that his only contact with Bonner had been last night. They had two conversations, and that was it.

In Gramm's long association with Milo, he knew the detective to be a straight shooter, and chose to believe him. Hoping he was right, Gramm moved on to the safe, asking if Milo had seen it open last night. Milo said he didn't know there was a safe, adding it had been covered by a picture on the wall.

"So, what's this about a threat on the phone McKnight was talking about when I called you?"

Milo filled Gramm in on the phone incident with Agnes Larson, and how shocked she seemed to be. He added, her upset was the reason he went to see if Bonner was okay, otherwise he would have never gone to the office.

"What time was it?"

"It was just after midnight, maybe about twelve-twenty, twelve-thirty or so."

Gramm and Rathkey stepped back to allow the medical examiner's team to remove the body. White said she was pretty much done, and Gramm indicated it was time to start interviewing the family. White pulled out her notebook.

Gramm summed up his conversation with Milo, "Three notes from Rathkey. He talked with Bonner shortly after midnight, the safe was not open, and the gun, if it is the murder weapon, belonged to the victim. Let's go talk to Sutherland McKnight."

§

Stan Shultz rubbed his large hands together and stomped his boots in an effort to keep warm in the overcast seventeen-degree temperature. "I want to get out of here Leroy, it's cold, I'm hungry. I don't like all these cops. I don't know what the hell is going on," he snarled.

In his head, Leroy knew time was up on Stan. He needed his food, or there would be an incident. With all these cops around, that would be stupid. Leroy had to admit to himself that the cops also made him nervous, but he needed his payoff from Richard Bonner.

The stupid kid hadn't spotted the set-up over the last few games, and Leroy cleaned him out last night. Checking his phone one more time, he saw a text from Richard. "Holy crap, Stan! The old man has been murdered!"

Stan didn't comment except to say he wanted to go to Louie's. It was his favorite restaurant because Louie had big oval platters, instead of plates, and filled them up.

Leroy's mind was racing. He texted Richard that the delay would cost him a couple of grand in interest, and then moved on to worry about his second problem, a much bigger problem for him, the murder of James Bonner. This was bad, really bad.

§

Sutherland was sitting on a bench in the middle of the gallery. An officer had brought him coffee. *Maybe Milo was wrong, and murders on London Road are catered.* He smiled at his own grisly humor as he saw the trio heading in his direction.

"Mr. McKnight?" Gramm asked.

Sutherland stood. "Call me Sutherland, everyone does."

"Tonight, at the poker game you're Sutherland. Right now, you're Mr. McKnight."

Sutherland raised his eyebrows, a little surprised at Gramm's abruptness. "Okay."

"Tell me about last night. Start when you arrived."

Wanting to get this right, and only answer the questions he was asked, per Milo's instructions, Sutherland began. "Okay, Milo and I arrived about eight. We came into the house and proceeded to the gallery—this room. I introduced Milo to Mary Alice."

"The dead man's wife," Gramm added for clarification.

"Yes. Then I went to find Paul Taylor." Looking at White he added, "He's a financial advisor I wanted Milo to meet."

Refocusing on Gramm, he added, "I brought him back, introduced him to Milo, and then mingled, I guess. I really don't remember everyone I talked with, but I can try."

"Did you talk to the deceased?"

"Oh no, I avoid him." Looking at the surprise on Gramm's face, he knew he had added too much information.

Gramm seized on it immediately, "Why would you avoid him?"

Milo smiled to himself. *Down the rabbit hole we go.*

Sutherland tried to answer the question without adding anything else. "Quite frankly, he was odious, and I didn't like being around him."

Gramm did not give up. "Describe odious?"

The gallery was chilly with all the police coming in and out, but Sutherland was sweating. He now realized the wisdom of Milo's earlier advice, but he was caught and had to answer the question. "Describe odious...okay...he was insulting, aggressive, and mean. Nobody liked him. No one could have a normal conversation with him without a disagreement."

"Define no one." Gramm knew he was pressing Sutherland, but he was fishing for a third-party assessment of the relationship between Bonner and his wife.

"Pardon me?" Sutherland was lost.

"You said no one liked him. Define no one. Who's no one?"

"Well, no one I knew liked him," Sutherland said, getting a little flustered.

"What about his wife? Did she like him?"

Milo felt sorry for Sutherland. That rabbit hole was getting deeper.

Sutherland was slow to answer. He didn't want to get Mary Alice in trouble. The thought of her murdering anyone was absurd.

How am I going to get out of this…I am taking too long to answer…damn…Mary Alice despised her husband. Come on Sutherland get it together, answer the question.

"I only knew him from business; I don't know about his personal life." It wasn't quite the truth, but Sutherland didn't think it was a total lie.

"You were at his party. That's not business," Gramm persisted.

"I never considered it James Bonner's party. I was invited to Mary Alice's party."

"So, this was not his party. It was hers?"

Sutherland nodded. "For me it was."

"Did you see them together at the party—Mary Alice and her husband?"

"No, I didn't"

"Isn't that strange, the host and hostess not getting together?"

"I don't know. I'm not married."

Milo smiled. Sutherland was climbing out on his own.

Gramm figured he gotten as much about the spouse as he was going to get from Sutherland, so he took a left turn. "Tell me about the phone call."

"Oh, right, the one with Agnes?"

"Was there another one?"

"Oh yes…no…never mind, sorry just a little nervous. I've…"

Cutting off the nervous jabber, Gramm refocused Sutherland. "I understand this phone call took place in the library. Why did you go there?"

"It did. I was looking for Milo. A friend—do you need his name?" Answering his own question by the look on Gramm's face, Sutherland continued. "Right. My friend said Milo had gone into the library, so I went in search. I found him eating dinner with Agnes Larson, Bonner's administrative assistant. After the fireworks…"

"Fireworks?" Gramm's bushy eyebrows raised.

"That's why I was looking for him. Mary Alice always has fireworks at her New Year's Eve Parties. I forgot to tell him. I thought he might enjoy the show. Anyway, after the fireworks, Agnes said she wanted to call Lyft and picked up the phone."

"I guess Milo and I were talking or something. I only know, when I looked back at Agnes, she had a…pained… shocked look on her face as if she heard something horrible. I clearly remember that. I rushed over. She said that Bonner was on the phone, and someone had threatened to kill him. She was really worried, I mean, she was really over-the-top worried. Milo agreed to check on Bonner, you know, to see if he needed help or something."

Sutherland noted that the Sergeant had written everything down. His job was done. He had informed the police of what he knew. There was a long pause and Gramm was not filling it.

Sutherland was puzzled. *Am I finished? Where are my thank-yous? Can I get out of here? Is there something else he wants?*

Gramm turned to Rathkey. "Does that match your recollection?"

"Pretty much. He hit the high points."

"Any idea who was making the threats?"

As Sutherland shook his head, Milo answered the question. "Sutherland and I didn't hear it. You would have to ask Agnes."

Sutherland was relieved to be off the hot seat. Milo looked around and asked Sutherland where he got the coffee.

"An officer brought it."

"Coffee's in the kitchen. Sgt. White, we need to start interviewing family members."

"Give me a second, and I'll figure out which room they're in. There are so many."

"I think they may be in the sitting room, that door down there," Sutherland offered.

"Before we go, Mr. McKnight, I would appreciate it if you did not mention the Agnes phone call to anyone, especially family members of the deceased."

"Got it. And for the record, I didn't do it." He glanced at White and said, "Please write that down." She laughed and wrote something in her notebook.

"Look, Sutherland, I'm sorry if my questioning made you uncomfortable, but in these cases, like it or not, I need to figure out relationships quickly from as many sources as I can. You are one of my better sources."

Sutherland was taken aback by how Gramm went from official *Mr. McKnight* to friendly *Sutherland*. He also questioned how he was a *better* source. *Better than what? Or Whom?* Rather than ask, he nodded and decided to go with the flow, heading down the gallery to the sitting room.

Needing coffee too, Gramm suggested they go to the kitchen which was empty except for the large urn of coffee and a huge basket of pastries. White sat down on a nearby stool so she could drink coffee and take notes, while Rathkey and Gramm stood leaning against the marble countertop.

Munching a donut, Gramm asked, "So fill me in on Sutherland McKnight."

"I've only known him since Wednesday! That's what? Four days?"

Gramm gave Rathkey a look that said they were in interrogation mode not chit chat mode, and he wanted Rathkey's best assessment.

"My gut says he's okay, and I think you can trust him to do what he's told. Actually, he may be very useful. He knows the players and much of their history."

"Okay, we'll go with your gut for now."

Gramm was about to ask another question when Rathkey interrupted him. "You told the doc I was a consultant. Do you plan to tell me?"

"You're a consultant. Feel better?"

"You know I don't want to do full blown police work anymore."

Gramm ignored Milo's usual angst and took another bite of his donut. "It's rare to have a trained policeman on scene before and after the murder. This murder will become a public relations nightmare unless we solve it now. I'm hoping you can help in the *now* part. So, relax and tell me what you saw starting with your arrival at the party?"

"Well, we arrived," Milo glanced at White who stifled a smile.

"We can do this downtown," Gramm kidded.

"Okay, okay, I'll get serious. First thing, I met Mary Alice Bonner."

"Tell me about my prime suspect, and don't give me the 'I just met her' crap."

He could have spoken about how he felt when he was with her but followed his own advice and just answered the question. "Beautiful, gracious..."

"Did you only make small talk?"

"For the most part, but she did say that her husband was a nasty man. I saw that for myself when she introduced me to him. At the time, he was yelling at a short guy. I think about some business deal. I didn't like him."

"How long did you talk to him?"

"A minute or two at most. Later, I saw him in yet another argument with a bigger, taller guy...again about business... some sort of land deal."

Milo thought about how to phrase this next bit of info. He decided to simply say it. "I don't have any proof of this, but I think that the widow and that taller guy have a thing going."

Gramm raised his eyebrows. "Interesting. But the argument was about business?"

"That's all I heard."

"Any more?"

"I met the son twice. The first time was early in the evening. He seemed nervous, anxious to see his dad about something. The second time, late in the evening, after the phone call, he was bolting out of Bonner's office when I was going in. He was none too happy."

"Angry?"

"No, more worried. He almost ran me down."

"Okay, so you go in."

"Right. Bonner was at his desk doing something on the computer. Probably reading that report about me," Milo snarked. "Ms. Larson didn't want him to know that she had overheard him on the phone, so I made something up. I said I had heard him being threatened several times at the party, and I wondered if he thought the threats were serious. The asshole had the nerve to pull that 9mm Glock out of the low file drawer behind him and point it at me. I was none too pleased, especially when he said the damn thing was loaded. After waving it around like an idiot, boasting that nobody worried him, he bragged he could take care of himself. Boy was he wrong."

"What did he do with the gun?"

"Before I left, I saw him set it down on the desk by his right hand. However, this morning, I noticed it was on the far end of the desk, still on Bonner's right but closer to the door."

Gramm leaned back, put his hands behind his head, and gazed at the ceiling, stretching out the stiffness in his back.

"It's most probably murder; motive: hatred, or—with the open empty safe—robbery, or a combination of the two?"

"Oh crap!" Milo said. "Speaking of two, I almost forgot about the two bottom feeders lurking outside when I came in."

Gramm perked up. "That's why you're here. Who were they?"

"Leroy Thompson and his good buddy, Stan Shultz."

"Outside this house? This morning?"

"Yeah. When Leroy saw me, he grabbed Stan and moved back into the crowd. He didn't want to be seen. I'm thinking those two could kinda take this murder into a whole new neighborhood. Of course, they could have been walking the dog and noticed the crowd."

"And I'm Miss America."

9

Sutherland had survived his first police interrogation—not his usual Sunday morning, but better than the victim's. He hadn't liked James Bonner, hated his business practices, but wondered how somebody could have shot him in cold-blood. He knew death, but death from illness like his mother or old age like his father. This was different.

He walked to the end of the gallery and turned around to catch Rathkey, Gramm, and White heading down a hallway, to the kitchen. Stopping in front of the closed door to the sitting room to collect his thoughts, he wondered what he should say. This was not a normal condolence call that came with its own set of rules. 'Sorry about the murder' wasn't going to work. In mid thought, the door to the sitting room opened. Agnes Larson exited in a rush, almost bumping into him.

"Mr. McKnight?" she stammered, backing up, shocked to see anyone but police in the house. "Hello? I didn't expect you. Why are you here?"

"Mrs. Bonner called me early this morning," Agnes said, closing the door. "She asked me to come in. But why are you here?" There was an odd edge to her voice that wasn't there last night.

Feeling uncomfortable and awkward, Sutherland struggled to explain. "I understand why you would ask. It is a bit odd. I'm not trying to be intrusive. The short story is, Milo seems to be helping the Lieutenant. I guess…well…the Lieutenant asked us both to come over. He will eventually talk with everybody, I guess."

He wasn't sure Agnes had heard him as she turned and sat down on a nearby bench midway through his rambling explanation. She said nothing.

Undaunted, Sutherland sat down next to her and continued, "This is pretty awful. I don't know what to say."

"I guess you tell the police what you saw and heard."

"I've done that." He was pleased to have her at least respond like this was a normal conversation. "I mean, I don't know what to say to Mary Alice. I know I'm far too early for a condolence call. The family, I'm sure, is nowhere ready to receive visitors, but I'm here. If Mary Alice knew I was here and I didn't say something, it would be rude. It's quite an uncomfortable situation all around."

Agnes looked at Sutherland again as though her thoughts were elsewhere, and his too many words were confusing to her. "You give comfort," she said, almost to herself.

"I told the police about the phone call you overheard and Mr. Bonner being threatened and all."

"Oh…yes…that's okay…I understand."

"Have you told anyone about the phone call?"

Agnes looked at him as if she didn't quite hear him or understand. Sutherland was about to ask again when she stated, "I haven't said anything to anyone."

"Well, the Lieutenant told me to keep quiet about it. I assume this applies to you too, so don't tell anyone until the Lieutenant says it's okay."

Agnes nodded her head in agreement.

Knowing it was going to be awkward, Sutherland asked Agnes who was in the sitting room and what to expect.

"Mary Alice, Richard, and a policewoman named Hughes."

He tried to get a bit more information. "Did they send you out for some reason?"

"No, I needed to get out of that room for a while."

Although she seemed tired and in shock, Sutherland thought Milo would approve of the way Agnes answered his questions, brief and to the point, unlike himself he noted with chagrin.

Placing his hands on his knees, he announced, "Well, I have to go in eventually. It may as well be now." Standing, he added, "Kind of a changing of the guard."

"I'm better now. I'll go back with you. I might be needed."

§

Unlike most of the stark-white angular house, the sitting room was all rounded edges and soft luxurious fabrics: light blues, grays, and soft whites predominating.

Mary Alice, clad in a baby-blue cashmere sweater and ivory slacks seemed to be custom made for the room. She was sitting with her legs tucked under her on a crescent shaped, off-white camelback sofa in one of three sitting areas beautifully-appointed in the massive room. A faux antique, white phone was cradled between her shoulder and ear as she reached down and poured herself another cup of coffee from the antique silver coffee service.

Richard's wavy blond hair brushed the collar of his ivory, turtle-neck sweater as he stared out the window scanning the area outside the gates for Leroy Thompson. He was oblivious to his mother's phone conversation. Neither son nor mother was paying any attention to Officer Hughes who stood by the door allowing Agnes to enter but stopping Sutherland. After asking who he was and why he was there, she seemed satisfied that Lt. Gramm was aware of his presence in the house and let him enter. The easy comings and goings were gone. It was official and permissioned.

Agnes proceeded back to a small writing desk, while Sutherland, not wishing to intrude, waited by the door for Mary Alice to finish her phone conversation.

"So, is the next step the reading of the will? Please tell me that James had a will." After a pause she continued, "I don't know when the funeral will be, I mean the police are still here." The strain was beginning to show in her voice. "I guess I'm in shock." She paused again and listened to the response, taking a few notes on the legal pad on her lap. "As I said, he was killed…maybe murdered…last night, I think shot…I don't know the police haven't told me a thing."

Her voice became less upset and more demanding of the person on the other end of the line. "Look, I need to know if there are some legal things I need to do. I mean, I assume

I am now in charge of his business. How do I proceed?" She smoothed her shimmering blond hair. "No, I don't think you need come over, unless there is something I need to sign."

Again, there was quiet as she listened to the response. "What!" She exclaimed straightening up. "Why?" Again, there was a slight pause. "No! I…I don't know. I will get back to you on that. Yes…okay."

As Mary Alice hung up the phone, she caught Sutherland standing by the door. Her quick smile told him she was pleased he was there.

Gracefully unfolding herself, she stood up and hurried to give him a quick hug. "Sutherland! I didn't expect anyone to come over so soon, but I am so glad you are here. Come, sit down with me. I need some advice." She guided him to sit next to her on the couch.

While pouring himself another cup of coffee, he felt the need to explain himself. "I'm sorry about everything that has happened, and I know I'm here too soon, but...well…I'm here with Milo Rathkey. Do you remember him from last night?"

"Oh certainly." Taken back she asked, "But why is he here?"

Despite Mary Alice's warm welcome, Sutherland still felt ill at ease, but tried to answer her question as though it was the most normal thing in the world. "He's helping the police with their investigation, and I was asked to come along to answer a few questions about the party which was outstanding by the way. Thank you for your gracious invitation."

"The party—now that seems like years ago. Please, don't you worry about polite convention. Nothing about this day is polite or conventional. As a matter-of-fact, maybe you can both help me. I was asked the most incredible thing by our business lawyer. He was wondering if I needed a criminal attorney. I was stunned."

Reaching for his hand, she asked, "Am I a suspect? What do you think?"

"That would be crazy, but at the same time, I think we're all suspects including me, I've been told. As far as getting an attorney, when Milo comes in, I will ask him if any or all of us need attorneys."

She gently let go of his hand to take tighter hold of his arm and said in hushed tones, "Sutherland, I am so glad you are here. Now I don't feel so alone."

Sutherland was surprised at her intimacy, having never been in Mary Alice's inner circle, but he thought with the trauma and all, maybe she needed a familiar arm to lean on.

"Oh Sutherland! It was horrible. I went into the office and found him. Richard heard me scream and came running!"

Upon hearing his name, Richard turned and stared at his mother but said nothing.

"Richard come here and sit. Eat and drink something. You look pale," Mary Alice said with concerned authority. Turning back to Sutherland she whispered, "This has been a shock for all of us."

Richard obeyed and sat on the matching couch opposite the large, eighteenth century coffee table and placed a croissant on a glass plate Mary Alice held out for him.

She also offered Sutherland a pastry from the ornate silver platter. "Agnes, come join us. Please have some coffee and something to eat. I pulled you out of your cozy warm house on a Sunday morning under atrocious circumstances, and Officer Hughes, please have something."

Both Agnes and Officer Hughes declined.

Richard set his untouched croissant on the table in front of him and stared at it.

Gramm entered the room followed by Milo, and White. Tension increased ten-fold.

Richard rose from his couch and once again moved back to his station by the front window. Sutherland felt Mary Alice's arm tighten around his as he too felt a wave of apprehension at their arrival. The police didn't belong here, yet they were here moving about as if the house was theirs.

Gramm introduced White, and Milo, explaining that Milo was consulting on the investigation. Mary Alice nodded but remained seated with her arm still wrapped in Sutherland's.

"Can you tell us anything?" she asked Gramm.

"Not at this point, but we need a room where we can speak with each of you separately. This is a formality. Also we need a list of all who attended and worked the party last night."

Mary Alice was disappointed at the lack of information but, wanting to hasten the police process, she suggested the library. Agnes added that she would send the guest and vendor lists to the library printer.

"Thank you. Mrs. Bonner, we can start with you then."

Worried, Mary Alice watched Richard who was staring at his phone, and urged him once again sit down and have something to eat. When he seemed not to hear, she disentangled herself from Sutherland, walked to Richard, put her arm around his waist, guiding him back to the couch.

Milo thought it was a good look, ever the concerned mother, protecting her son who had violently lost his father.

Sutherland took the opportunity to get up and whisper to Rathkey about Mary Alice's question of getting a criminal lawyer. Milo glanced at the window and then back at Sutherland. He was torn. "I'm really not in a position to advise her on that. Having a lawyer never hurts but lawyering up this early may make her look guilty."

§

In the library, Gramm picked the glass-topped table in the center of the room, away from windows and distractions.

He sighed. This was always the part he hated, beginning long complicated investigations, interviewing numerous people, and checking alibis and backgrounds. What he wanted to do was get home to Amy's New Year's Day ham dinner and the grandchildren before tonight's poker game.

White was looking at the guest and vendor lists from the printer.

"Let's do these interviews and go home. We can come in early tomorrow morning and do the reports. That way we get a little bit of New Year's Day," Gramm suggested.

White agreed. Looking at the long guest list, she knew they faced a busy week.

Milo guided Mary Alice to one of the comfortable chairs that he and Agnes had shared the evening before. He sat down on the other side of the round table opposite her. Gramm and

White pulled up a couple of straight-backed chairs, completing the circle. They could have been having lunch.

This was a first interview. First interviews tended to be friendly. Mary Alice smiled her beguiling smile. "Are you two comfortable in those chairs? We have other chairs that are much comfier. It would only take a moment to get them for you."

Both Gramm and White declined the offer, saying the chairs were fine.

Mary Alice accepted their statements with a sigh. "Of course, this whole room is uncomfortable." Tilting her head to survey the room, she added, "After today, I won't come in here until it is remodeled."

Milo was intrigued by Mary Alice. *Still the charming hostess, warm and gracious, yet cold and calculating. She found her husband brutally murdered this morning, and now, she is ready to pick out fabric swatches. Who is she really? And could she murder?*

White began taking notes as Gramm asked Mary Alice to describe the events that led up to her finding the body.

She folded her hands together and placed them in her lap. "I can do that. I understand you need my account to be as accurate as possible, and I can be quite specific. I woke up at seven AM," she glanced over at Sgt. White, "my usual time." Refocusing her attention on Lt. Gramm, "I dressed, and came down to breakfast." Once again for Sgt. White's benefit, she said, "I arrived at breakfast about eight AM."

Gramm bothered by her ping pong action, asked her to talk to him and ignore Sgt. White. "Consider this a conversation. Did you notice your husband wasn't in bed?"

Great Party! Sorry About The Murder

The long eye lashes batted a couple of times before she replied, "Yes, I knew he wasn't there. He's never there. We've had separate bedrooms for quite some time." As she explained, her azure blue eyes locked in on Gramm.

Milo realized that this eye thing of hers was part of her manner and part of her charm. Last night it made Milo feel like he was the most important person in the room. Gramm was the man this morning. Milo was a bit disappointed.

If her attention had any effect on Gramm, he didn't show it. "So, you went down to breakfast."

"I waited for a brief time, had some coffee, but he still didn't appear." She started to turn to Sgt. White but caught herself and remained focused on Lt. Gramm. "That was unusual. The cook asked me if James was coming to breakfast, and I had to admit, I didn't know. I went to the intercom and called his bedroom. There was no response, so I went down to his office." She closed her eyes.

"Why not call him on the intercom there?"

"James refused to put the intercom in his office. When he was in there, he didn't want to be bothered by family." Mary Alice turned away. She dabbed at the inside corner of each eye. Did she tear up or not? Milo couldn't say.

"If this is difficult for you…"

She reached out and touched Gramm lightly on the hand.

"Take all the time you need," Gramm offered.

"Thank you so much. You are too kind, but I would prefer to get this over with."

White glanced over at the gesture and was aware of the noticeable softening in her boss' manner. *Was this a calculated approach on his part, or was he succumbing to this blatant maneuver?*

She thought maybe she should be taking notes on how Mary Alice manipulated men rather than the widow's testimony. Deciding Mrs. Bonner was not going to run this interrogation, White picked up the questioning. "Tell us about finding your husband."

Surprised, Mary Alice looked at the Sergeant. Her tone had an edge not present with Gramm, "This is not particularly pleasant. I went into his office. He was dead. It was horrible… all that blood. What else do you want me to tell you?"

Mary Alice refolded her hands on the table, her eyes following the movement of her fingers. "I guess I screamed and Richard, who was in the kitchen, came running. We left the office together, ran back to the kitchen, told the cook that James was dead. Then I called the police."

White noted, for someone who was not sure of events, Mary Alice knew where everyone was and in what order everything happened.

Gramm had the same thought. "When you saw the gruesome scene in the office, what went through your mind?"

Mary Alice didn't hesitate to answer. "I was shocked of course and revolted, and then I became frightened. I wondered if the person who did this awful thing was still in the house. We were terrified. Richard, the cook, and I huddled in the kitchen until you arrived." She used the word *terrified*, but her voice was assured and strong.

"Any idea of who might have done this?" Gramm continued.

Closing her eyes and smiling, Mary Alice seemed almost amused by the question. "Anyone who knew him. Your sergeant has the list of guests, half of whom James insisted I invite, yet I'll bet every one of them had some issue with him. He was not a nice man."

Turning to Milo and smiling, she said, "Ask Mr. Rathkey here. When I introduced him to my husband last night, James was in the process of belittling poor Mr Lund. I think that's his name. I'm not sure who he is. He owns a furniture store. I only met him last night when he arrived. He seemed to be a pleasant enough man. James ordered me to add him to that list," she said, pointing to the papers in White's hand.

Gramm changed the subject. "Do you know the combination to the safe in the office?"

Startled, her fingers clenched as she snapped at Gramm, "No, why would you ask that?"

"The safe was open, or didn't you notice?"

For a moment, she looked confused and uneasy. *Oh, good god! Richard didn't close the safe? He told me he closed it!*

The lady has just flashed fear, Milo thought. It was only a flicker. *What about that safe was so frightening?*

She was forced to ask Gramm to repeat his question before saying no, she hadn't noticed the safe. Beyond that, she offered no further explanation.

Gramm wondered, if she's so sure about everything and everybody, why not that safe. "What was in it?"

Mary Alice stroked the back of her hand and straightened her rings. "I don't know. Were we robbed?"

She's back in control, Milo thought. *She's not concerned about a robbery, just about the safe being open.*

"Did you know he had a gun?" Gramm asked.

This was not a question that took her off guard, she answered with assurance. "He has guns," she said, adding, "Most are locked up in a gun safe in the room that adjoins his bedroom."

"What about a Glock semi-automatic handgun that he kept in his office?"

"I don't know about that gun, but he loved guns."

"Do you know how to use a gun?"

Mary Alice smiled remembering her father. "Yes. I'm a marksman."

Gramm, Milo, and White all looked surprised, maybe a little shocked. This lady, with the perfect manicure, beautiful jewelry, and lithe figure, did not add up to a gun totin' mama.

Pleased at their response, she continued, "As a child growing up, my father taught me how to handle guns and how to use them—both handguns and hunting rifles. I am not aware of James' Glock, but if you are asking me if I could use it, the answer is yes. Did I use it? No."

Milo thought of his own sorry record at the pistol range and wondered if Mary Alice gave lessons—if she wasn't going to prison of course.

Not having found any, Gramm asked about the possibility of hidden security cameras, but, much to his disappointment, she said all the cameras along that back lane had been removed by James two years ago. He did not want comings and goings recorded.

"When can I plan a funeral?" Mary Alice asked, again touching Gramm's hand. "People will want to know."

"There will be an autopsy, and after that, we should be able to release the body. I guess Wednesday or Thursday." Gramm stood up signaling the interview was over.

"When will all of this be gone? It's so upsetting," she asked as she got up, putting her perfectly manicured hands into her perfectly tailored trouser pockets.

"It's hard to say. We could be out of here this afternoon; however, your husband's office will be off limits. The investigation will take time, and there's no way to predict it."

Mary Alice turned to Rathkey. "Thank you for being here for me," and, with that, she left the room.

Milo was flummoxed. "I guess I was here for her."

White rolled her eyes. "I guess you both were here for her."

"She can turn on the charm," Gramm said, before turning to White and adding, "We have an experiment to do before we leave here. Remind me later. For now, go get the son."

Rathkey knew what the experiment would be, and he knew it wouldn't go well. The office was too far away from the kitchen. The blue eyes lied.

10

As Mary Alice left the room with White, Sutherland felt it was his place to attempt small talk with Richard to take the boy's mind off the gruesome reality of the situation. However, Richard's reality was far more complicated than Sutherland could imagine. Small talk failed.

Why won't this man shut up! I've got to think! I can't get out of here. Everything is messed up!

Richard stood and began pacing from one end of the sitting room—an uncommonly long room—to the other, Leroy's text made him glad he had taken the coin collection along with the cash. Pawned, it could cover the added interest.

I've got to remember what Mother said about the morning. I was in the kitchen...she was in the office...she screamed...I came running.

Richard looked out the window one more time. Still no sign of Leroy Thompson.

Great Party! Sorry About The Murder

§

At Gramm's direction, White brought Richard into the room. The young man sat on the edge of the chair continuously rubbing his thumb on his palm—eyes darting from one person to another.

Unlike his mother, all confidence and charm, this kid is a scared rabbit, Gramm thought. He began with a trick question. "Tell us about finding your father."

The trick didn't work. "No! I didn't. My mother did! Mother screamed, and I went from the kitchen to see what was wrong."

"So, you didn't go into the office this morning?"

"No!" Richard's heart was racing, and he knew, if connected to a lie detector, he would fail.

"Did you leave the house after the party last night?"

"I left the house during the party. That was not my party. I went to play poker at a friend's house."

"Friend's name?"

"I'd rather not say."

Gramm's smile disappeared. "But I'd rather you did say. You need an alibi. So, let's try this again. Whose house were you at?"

Richard went pale, and his right heel began to tap on the floor. "Why would I need an alibi? He was my father. I didn't kill my father!"

"That doesn't answer my question."

"Leroy Thompson…he has a store…" Richard stopped, not wanting to go any further.

Gramm and Rathkey looked at each other. "Did you win?" Gramm asked.

"No." *Oh, good lord, this keeps getting worse. Now the cops are asking about the poker game!*

"When did you get home and what did you do?"

"I got home around four-thirty and went to bed."

"I heard that you and your father argued last night?"

Richard shifted in his seat. "We did? I don't remember that."

Gramm let it go knowing it would come up again at a later time. The kid's body language spoke volumes, arms across his body. "Do you know the combination to the office safe?"

"What safe?"

Gramm shook his head in disbelief. "The one that's wide open and empty in your father's office."

Richard blinked several times as a thousand thoughts rushed through his head.

Did Mother reopen the safe? Why would she do that and not tell me? What's going on? What am I supposed to say?

"I...I...don't know about the safe."

Gramm let Richard return to the sitting room, and he stretched his back. "This family has a major problem with that safe."

Milo added, "He said *the safe* not *a safe*...a slip of the tongue, I think. He clearly knew about that safe."

Gramm smiled. "There's a lot of lying going on." White added her opinion. "You wouldn't need to cheat to beat that kid at poker. So, who's next?"

"I'm getting tired. It's New Year's Day. Let's wind this up for today with that Agnes woman," Gramm said.

Great Party! Sorry About The Murder

§

David Bonner sat at the end of the bar against the wall nursing a beer. He liked the Anchor bar. People left him alone. But that was not the case this morning.

"Hey Bonner!" yelled the bartender.

Bonner looked up.

Johnny, the bartender, pointed to the TV. "That dead guy they're talking about, any relation?"

David Bonner had been oblivious to the TV and to the bartender. Now he fixed his gaze on the screen. "Turn it up!"

A young reporter was finishing her report. "…Police are still here at the Bonner estate and probably will remain for much the day. They are not releasing any details at this time, but we're hoping they will hold a news conference later today. Back to you, Mort."

"So, Barb, do we know for sure who died?"

"Yes Mort, the police have said that the deceased is real estate mogul James Bonner, but so far that is all they've said."

"Thank you Barb. We will update this story as more details become available."

David Bonner continued to drink his beer and asked for a shot of Old Crow. Johnny pulled up a shot glass as David mumbled, "That was my brother."

Filling the glass beyond the white line, Johnny offered his condolences. "This one's on the house. Sorry man."

Bonner acknowledged the free drink. His mind was racing.

D.B. Elrogg

Well, now the world knows about you James. It won't be long before the cops are here, and they won't be offering free shots. I need money, and that damn safe was empty!

§

Sutherland had been sitting with Mary Alice, hoping he was a source of comfort. However, with the return of Richard, it was clear his presence was intrusive. He politely excused himself, left the room, and seeking fresh air, found a bench in the entryway where he proceeded to check his email, and social media. He had done all he needed to do and now planned to stay out of everybody's way until it was time to leave.

Officer Hughes was reassigned by White to guard the front door, leaving Mary Alice and Richard alone for the first time since early morning. Mary Alice got right to the point. "Richard, what happened with the safe!"

Richard stared at his mother. "I closed it. You reopened it!"

Shocked and frightened, it was Mary Alice's turn to stare. "I didn't. Oh my God! Who else was in this house?"

§

Lieutenant Gramm began the questioning by establishing Agnes as Bonner's personal assistant for the past five years.

She told him that Bonner had a larger office downtown where he handled much of the company business, but he handled personal business from the house. He made her sign a confidentiality agreement and reminded her not to talk about anything she saw or heard. Agnes asked if she was still bound by that agreement. Gramm told her that this was a murder investigation, and she had to tell the police all she knows.

"So, from what I understand, you were calling a cab when you overheard someone threatening Mr. Bonner."

Agnes nodded. "I was calling my Lyft driver. I pushed the first button on the phone because it wasn't lit up. I thought it was an unused line…it wasn't. I heard a man talking with Mr. Bonner about killing…murder…it was awful!"

"Did you recognize the voice?"

"No, I didn't recognize it, but I would know it again if I heard it."

"Was Bonner afraid?"

"Not at all."

"So, he didn't take the threat seriously?"

"You'd have to ask Mr. Rathkey. I didn't talk to him."

"Why were you using Lyft?"

Agnes seemed surprised. "I always do. I don't own a car."

"Tell us about the interaction between Bonner and his family."

"I have a small office next to his when we work here, but his office is soundproof so outside noises won't bother him. If he was having a conversation with his family, I wouldn't hear it."

Gramm and Rathkey exchanged glances. "Thank you, Miss Larson. Sgt. White will show you out."

Rathkey stood up. "I'll show her out. I need to stretch my legs."

Once outside the library, Milo asked Agnes to join him on one of the benches. "I need to run something past you," he said by way of explanation.

Agnes seemed surprised.

"Let me get straight to the point. I hate coincidences, and your boss' death has created a coincidence. Two violent deaths in the same office—James Bonner and your sister."

Agnes turned away and said nothing. Milo believed in the importance of silence and letting it run its course. Without looking at him, she said in a whisper, "I'm very tired Mr. Rathkey, and Barbara's death was an accident."

"My point is, maybe it wasn't. I would like to check it out."

"Why? To what end? Sorry to be impolite, but why does any of this matter to you?"

The wound of her sister's death was still raw, and Milo had picked at it. "I don't want to be unsympathetic, but it's possible that the person who killed your sister also killed your boss. Wouldn't it help you to know?"

"You think the same person who killed Mr. Bonner murdered my sister?" she asked to no one in particular. Her face went from distraught to hopeful. "Okay, Mr. Rathkey, what do you need to know?"

§

The police radio crackled. "Sir, it's officer Hughes. A Brad Nelson has arrived demanding to see the widow."

Gramm and White looked at each other smiling. "Milo has a nose for affairs. Tell her to escort him in here," Gramm directed.

Brad Nelson burst into the library shouting, "Who are you? Where is Mary Alice?"

Great Party! Sorry About The Murder

"I'm Lt. Ernie Gramm. Sit down Mr. Nelson, this won't take long." Gramm gestured to the empty chair.

Nelson's square jaw twitched with anger. "You don't understand. I'm not here to talk to you!"

Gramm smiled, "It is you who doesn't understand. This is a murder investigation, and we will talk to everybody. Right now, it's informal. We could make it formal up at the station."

As Rathkey rejoined them, he thought to himself that there was a lot of James Bonner in Brad Nelson. He wondered about Mary Alice's choice in men. She seemed to have a type—not a friendly type.

"I want you to know," Nelson continued, "I'm very good friends with the Mayor and the Police Chief."

"Great coincidence—so am I. Now sit down!" Gramm's patience was over.

Nelson sat down with defiance and crossed his arms.

"So, I understand that you and the deceased had a violent argument last night at the party," Gramm began.

"Violent argument? Are you kidding me? Do I need a lawyer?" Nelson challenged

"You can certainly have one, but that turns this into a formal interview. Your choice."

Nelson thought for a second. "We had a discussion. It's business. If we get angry, we go to court. We don't shoot each other."

"Shooting? Who said anything about shooting?"

Nelson was flustered. "I guess I assumed."

"So, you and the deceased were in business? What kind of a business?"

"That's none of your business."

Gramm gave him a look that said this was about to become unfriendly. "Answer the questions or call your lawyer. I am getting tired of this."

Nelson paused again, weighed his options, and decided to cooperate. "My partners and I bought some land on the Miller Trunk that Bonner had promised to lease for development. It was to be a quick turnaround. He reneged on the promise then leased land from our competitors."

"How much are you out?"

Nelson's hesitation was again met with Gramm's no-nonsense look developed over years of dealing with privileged putzes.

"All right. All right. Over a million. Needless to say, I was angry." Nelson held up his hands as if to stop an invisible force. "I know where you are going, and let me stop you right now. Bonner's company is still in place and could very well go ahead with his development, so his death doesn't help me a bit."

These people are easy, Nelson thought, pleased with himself, until Gramm asked his next question.

"How long have you and the widow been having an affair?"

Nelson, red faced and angry, bolted to his feet. "That's a damn lie!"

"Calm down, Mr. Nelson!" Gramm shouted.

Nelson eased back down. "How dare you insinuate such a thing. I will sue you and your department for slander."

"Why are you here?"

"I came to console a friend, my tennis partner."

"Funny, other friends have not come over, but yet here you are."

"Sutherland McKnight's here. I don't have to justify anything to you."

"Not yet anyway, but we will talk again. I think you need to call that lawyer and have him stand by."

Nelson got up and left the room, slamming the pocket doors back into the wall.

Gramm turned to Rathkey. "You called it."

"It's a gift," Rathkey said, remembering his jealousy at the linty jacket and the low-riding hand on Mary Alice's back.

"The widow does have a type—tall, angry men," Gramm offered.

Rathkey nodded in agreement, sorry he did not fit her type.

§

Nelson stomped into the sitting room, his face red with anger. Mary Alice calmly went to him and took his arm. "Come over to the couch Brad. What has you so angry?"

In disgust, Richard left the room. Being anywhere in the vicinity of the tryst between Nelson and his mother was the last thing he needed. What he needed was to pay Leroy Thompson.

Nelson followed Mary Alice to the couch. "I came to see you, not them, and they accused us of having an affair, which of course I denied."

She rubbed his shoulder, and he sat back in the couch. "What we are to each other is nobody's business but ours," he said through clenched teeth.

She nodded, but thought, *The police will make it their business, and you're a fool if you think otherwise. This has to end.*

§

Still in the library, Gramm walked to the telephone, picked it up, and pressed the first button. There was no light. "Well, Miss Larson told the truth. Let's see if the widow did," Gramm said, leading the way back to the office. The body had been taken away, but, as yet, there was no cleanup crew. The stench remained.

"Sergeant, I need you to stand here and scream when I tell you to. Milo and I will be in the kitchen to see if we hear you."

"Got it," White said, pulling out her radio. "I have a great scream."

Gramm and Rathkey walked down to the kitchen. Gramm keyed the radio, "Okay, Sergeant let it rip!"

The two men waited for a minute or two. White got back on the radio and asked, "Well?"

Gramm looked at Rathkey. He keyed the radio again. "If you were screaming, we weren't hearing."

11

"Deuces and jacks, king-with-the-axe, a pair of natural sevens down takes the pot," said George Shaffer, current dealer and consummate loser of the group. Two cards lay face down in front of each player, and one snapped face up to begin this bastardized version of seven card stud.

The group of five had been playing poker for years, but Gramm's old partner Jablonski—another easy mark—was now seated on a beach in Florida, his place taken by Sutherland McKnight.

Gramm hated change. One modification this evening, however, pleased him. Instead of enduring Rathkey's tippy card table and non-matching folding chairs in a musty walk up apartment, he was seated in a comfortable leather chair, playing on a solid oak poker table in a real-life billiard room.

Sutherland started the bidding with a red chip which, for his father's game was worth twenty-five dollars but in this scaled down version, signified a quarter. Immediately, there were howls of discontent. Shaffer commented that this was already too rich for his blood.

Sutherland looked at him and said, "Really? A quarter? I could cut it to fifteen cents."

The offer was met with more mumbles of, "What's with this guy?"

To his surprise, Sutherland had a defender in Gramm. "It's a quarter. Gees." The support wasn't completely altruistic however, as Gramm had two Kings down, one with the axe, almost a sure win. Besides, he was wearing his lucky socks and feared no evil.

The others caved with chips colliding in the center of the green felt.

Rathkey stayed silent while matching Sutherland's bet. He figured Gramm's quick defense of the bid meant the Lieutenant had something good and would continue to pour chips into the pot. Mentally, he was rubbing his hands together and chuckling, something he never did.

Who chuckles anyway? What is a chuckle? I've got to keep my mind on the game.

As the game progressed, Sutherland folded and left to collect the food. Shaffer threw in his cards, declaring his hand a mess.

As Rathkey predicted, Gramm stayed in to the bitter end as did Feinberg doubling the pot. After the final call, Gramm flaunted his straight flush, King-with-the-axe as a wild card. Feinberg threw in his cards, mumbling something about taking a servant of the people to the cleaners.

Great Party! Sorry About The Murder

With total positive assurance, Gramm turned to Rathkey. "Well?"

Ignoring the full-house he had in his hand, Rathkey turned over his pair of natural sevens, the absolute winner, and without comment, pulled all the chips to his side of the table.

"No, no, no. God damn it!" Gramm moaned. "I hate these gimmick games!"

Sutherland reappeared with a cart full of hors d'oeuvres, the bulk of which this group had never seen on a Rathkey hosted night or any night. Gramm grabbed a puff pastry, popped it into his mouth, and tried to say something through muffled bites, but it came out as unintelligible garble.

After a timeout for the group to devour most of the food, Feinberg picked up the cards and began dealing the same game, much to the disgust of Gramm. Having his usual losing night, Shaffer lost a two-dollar pot to Sutherland who produced two jacks plus the king-with-the-axe to give himself a straight flush. Shaffer was not above a swear word or two when it came to poker and let loose with some of his favorites.

Sutherland pulled in his chips with a smile. "Well George, you may have to borrow from petty cash for lunch tomorrow."

Shaffer laughed, "Where I work, that's frowned upon."

"Where do you work?"

The entire group laughed. Sutherland, not knowing Shaffer, did not get the joke.

"Despite my recent, regrettable, profane outburst, I am a priest. I do PR for the Catholic Diocese."

Sutherland's mouth dropped open.

"What? I don't have holy written all over me?"

"Time to play poker!" Gramm grumbled. "Milo, deal the damn cards."

Milo called five card low ball which made Gramm moan again, but in the end, the lieutenant won.

When the deal came to Gramm, he proclaimed, "Okay children, we are going to play some big boy poker, five card stud, nothing wild." It didn't last long, Gramm hung in to the end, sure his 'adult' game would throw the odds his way. Rathkey again took the pot.

Sutherland dealt next and called for a traditional five-card draw. "At last there is another purist among us." Gramm thought this newbie might not be so bad as he grabbed one of the few remaining munchies. "You know, Feinberg, this food is gonna be hard to top next week at your place."

"I've never heard any complaints before," Feinberg countered.

Gramm nodded. "Now that you mention it, I don't think Amy is going to change her usual winter-chili and corn bread either."

"Always delicious," Feinberg added. "Let's face it, the only leaker here was Milo. He was the chips-and-dip boy. Now, because of our new player, we get this spread twice in five weeks."

Sutherland was pleased to be considered one of the regular poker guys. They were a different sort of group from the business people he was used to, but he liked them.

The conversation moved on to some mechanical work Saul was having done on his van. Sutherland knew a little about Saul Feinberg and the legendary van. He assumed, with a lot of pro bono cases, Feinberg couldn't afford a proper office.

Great Party! Sorry About The Murder

As Saul threw in a quarter, Gramm grumbled again about rich guys bidding too much. Confusion must have shown on Sutherland's face because Feinberg took pity and explained that he was a trust fund baby. "My grandfather began Feinberg's Fine Meats and my father franchised it as a chain of delicatessens then sold it for a fortune. Pastrami has been good to me."

"I miss Feinberg's Fine Meats," Gramm complained. "It was pastrami to die for. Luckily, Saul still smokes and ages pastrami in his basement and hands it out when we play poker there."

"I think it's the pastrami I will miss the most," Shaffer declared with no explanation.

Gramm picked up on it immediately. "Miss? What does that mean?"

"Oh, I thought I mentioned it. I'm going to the Holy Land for a year's sabbatical. This is my last game for a while."

After the obligatory congratulations were over, the more practical issue to the group was discussed. "First Bill and now you, gees. We will have to find a fifth fast," Gramm said.

"I know a guy," Rathkey offered. "I'll ask him tomorrow."

"We need someone else who always loses," Feinberg said.

"Oh yeah?" Shaffer bellowed. "Well, I'm going out with a win, and to that end, I see your quarter and raise you a dime!"

Feinberg threw in the dime. "I call. What do you have?"

"Two pair, deuces and fives," Shaffer prepared to scoop up his winnings.

Feinberg dove under Shaffer's hands to collect the chips. "Like I said, we need someone who loses to replace the padre, two pair, sevens and Kings."

Caught in an embarrassing position with arms outstretched, Shaffer broke into song. "You guys will miss me when I'm gone."

"Amen to that," Gramm said.

"Heathens," Shaffer grumbled.

Feinberg took the cards, announced five-card draw, deuces wild and began dealing. "So, Ernie, what can you tell us about a murder on London Road?"

Everyone stopped, not knowing if this was something that was out of bounds. Gramm took a deep breath and glanced at Rathkey who pretended to stack his chips. Gramm didn't want to talk about an active case, but Saul might have some helpful information. He feigned a protest. "Give me a break! We're at the table with two possible suspects here."

"That would be us," Rathkey announced as both he and Sutherland raised their hands.

"Wait a minute! I was at the party. Why am I not a suspect?" Saul complained.

"Wow!" Gramm exclaimed, as he looked around the table. "I keep horrible company." Sitting back, volleying several chips from one hand to another, Gramm conceded, "Okay, I can tell you James Bonner was alive, and then he wasn't."

Ignoring Gramm's attempt to deflect his question, Feinberg continued. "I understand he was shot."

Gramm's eyebrows narrowed. "Okay, but information for information, Saul. Right?"

"Sure, if I know anything."

The rest of the poker table fell silent. Murder was far more interesting than the next poker hand.

Great Party! Sorry About The Murder

"Okay, Bonner was in his study or office, someone came in and shot him in the head. Now you tell me if you know of a connection between James Bonner, Leroy Thompson and Stan Shultz. The two low-lives, Leroy and Stan, were in the crowd outside the house early in the morning. I'm curious."

Taking time for extra shuffling of the cards, Feinberg finally said, "If I were to guess, I think they were watching their money. Leroy's running one of his poker cons on Bonner's kid. Last I heard, the kid was down at least twelve grand. You know, those rigged poker games Thompson runs above his Adult Emporium."

Jesus! We're betting dimes and quarters, and that punk drops twelve grand. There's something very unfair in this world, Gramm thought. "Anything else?"

More information came from an unlikely source. "I know something about James Bonner and that Thompson person."

Everyone turned to the priest. "Do tell." Gramm seemed almost shocked.

"So, spill padre," Feinberg urged, grinning and wondering how a priest would know about a thug and a real estate mogul.

"James Bonner started our Decency League, and we have been fighting to put Mr. Thompson's smut stores out of business. The city got involved at our urging. It has taken time, but we closed down that same store at two other locations, and we're working on this one too. We're hoping they can't keep moving forever."

Shaffer looked at Gramm with concern. "I pray Mr. Bonner wasn't murdered because of his civic work in cleaning the city of smut."

Gramm mulled over this new information. *If Bonner was costing Leroy money, Stan, the attack dog, might have been let loose. New motive, new suspects. I do love poker.*

"A dime," Rathkey said, throwing in a chip. His mind was also processing something—something Father Shaffer had said.

Gramm reached for his chips. "I see the dime and raise a dime."

Shaffer, ever the weenie said, "I'm out."

"Twenty cents is too rich for your blood?" Sutherland asked, chiding Shaffer.

"When you don't have 'em, you don't play 'em."

The bidding got down to Gramm and Feinberg and soared to an alarming three dollars and change. Most of the table fell into a stunned silence at such extravagance. Feinberg took the pot with two jacks topping Gramm's two nines, a weak hand, but then, Gramm thought Feinberg was bluffing.

As Feinberg added the chips to his winnings, he brought the conversation back to the murder. "Have you talked to his brother?"

"Whose brother?" Gramm asked.

"Bonner's. He has an older brother, David. The guy's got a nasty temper that goes from zero to atomic in a second. I know you know him. He's been arrested multiple times for assault. I never represented him, but I have several clients who've run afoul of him. He's a nasty piece of work."

"Oh, for Christ Sake!" Gramm slapped himself in the forehead. "David and James Bonner, I would have never put those two together. I'll have to check and see if David is in or out of jail."

Rathkey pulled in the cards, shuffled, and called seven card stud. The betting was fierce, and in the end, Father Shaffer actually won a pot. All declared it divine intervention. The game went on for a couple more hours with talk about everything but the murder.

During a brief interlude, Sutherland produced an Irish whiskey to toast Father Shaffer's sabbatical.

As Gramm was leaving, Milo asked for the file on the hit-and-run of Agnes Larson's sister. Gramm raised one of his large white eyebrows, but the lieutenant was too tired to inquire as to why.

§

After everyone left, Milo and Sutherland cleaned up the poker table, and put the empty food cart in the kitchen. Rathkey retired to the library, and Sutherland unexpectedly joined him where each indulged in another glass of smooth single malt and listened to the crackling fire.

Breaking the silence, Sutherland mentioned a couple of bills were due in the coming week.

Rathkey smiled. In his former life, the mention of bills would have made his stomach churn. His finances were usually a step behind. Not anymore.

"I am meeting Creedence Durant tomorrow, so I should have money in…what…a week or two."

"I think sooner. Creedence? Not a bad choice. Your money won't work as hard, but there's less risk. My father used Creedence, and I have some investments with him too."

"So what bills are due?" Rathkey asked.

"Mr. Anderson, who maintains the cars, and I have a guy and his son who refurbish the boats each year. I don't know if you remember, but being wooden, they require yearly maintenance."

Rathkey remembered the boats well. John had taken him out numerous times on both boats. The sail boat was fine, but it was the yacht with its radar and ship-to-shore radio that appealed to young Milo Rathkey. Older Milo Rathkey took a sip of his whisky.

Do I half own the boats? Sutherland said I was a co-owner of the cars, maybe that applies to the boats too.

Not being comfortable with not knowing, Milo asked.

"Of course," Sutherland said. "The boats are part of the estate, and you own half the estate, and the upkeep. Welcome to Lakesong."

Milo thought again about what Father Shaffer mentioned. "I need some information about real estate."

Sutherland was surprised.

"After this Decency League has its way and the city forces Thompson's bookstore to move, Thompson gets paid for the building, right?"

"Well, yes and no. He gets paid fair market value, but I suspect his bookstore has lowered property values. It's like he shot himself in the foot when he moved in. He most likely lost thousands of dollars in the deal. There must be records of the transactions with the city. I can look into it further with my commercial real estate guy if you like."

Milo agreed as the conversation lulled, and both men enjoyed the mellowing effects of the whisky. Sutherland broke the silence asking what would happen next in the case of James Bonner.

"Well, here's the blueprint. The beginning of this week, Gramm will do preliminary interviews like he did with you today. But once the forensic and autopsy info is in, alibis will be checked, and arrows will start pointing to people with motives. Then the questioning will become much more serious and direct. Meanwhile, I promised Agnes Larson I would look into the death of her sister. Want to come along on that?"

Sutherland heard himself say, "Yes." Then he thought, *Maybe the whiskey answered.*

He realized Milo invited him to investigate yet another death. "Wait a minute. Why would we do that? Her sister's death was an accident, wasn't it?"

"Her sister and James Bonner: both from the same office, both violent deaths within months of each other. Could be something that happened; could be someone made it happen."

"Happy New Year! I'm living in Murder Central. Thanks, Dad," Sutherland offered, toasting the ceiling.

12

Snow began falling at midnight and continued until dawn making street parking almost impossible. Plows have priority in Duluth, and parked cars get towed. On any other day, Milo would have avoided venturing out this early, but he had an appointment with Creedence Durant to sort through his new-found wealth. Milo sucked it up and parked his car in a ramp.

Durant's office, which he inherited from his father, had a modern industrial look with exposed brick and a touch of the original oak woodwork. The carpet and dusty window shams of his father's day were gone. The small three-seat waiting room featured a smiling receptionist who welcomed clients to the office.

Creedence's somewhat rotund body was parked behind his antique wooden desk. The rest of the room was filled with a large credenza and a few upright filing cabinets whose function was questionable as many of the files were piled on top of them.

Rathkey sat down across from Durant in one of two comfortable client chairs. To the right, a large trisection arched window overlooked Superior Street with the lake in the distance.

"Nice view," Rathkey said.

Creedence smiled and glanced out the window. "What I do bores most people, so I like to give my clients something to watch."

"With your desk sideways like this, you get to enjoy the view too."

Looking over both shoulders and leaning forward, in a whispered voice, Creedence confided, "I shouldn't tell you this, being a new client and all, but what I do sometimes bores me too." Leaning back in his chair, Creedence began to chuckle at his own joke. He reassured Milo he liked to kid sometimes because money is treated so seriously. "It's almost like being a mortician."

Milo could not picture the avuncular Creedence as a mortician and smiled at the thought. At the end of the morning, an investment plan had been devised to give the frugal Rathkey a yearly income he would be hard pressed to spend or even to have imagined a week ago.

Creedence told Rathkey he should expect access to a checking account, a checkbook, ATM card, and new credit card by midweek.

Sutherland had yet to mention the monthly cost of maintaining Lakesong, but Creedence assured Rathkey his income would more than cover it.

Before Milo got up to leave, Creedence said, "Maybe I should have asked this to begin with, but is there any chance Sutherland will challenge the will?"

"His dad asked him not to."

"When I think I've heard everything, I'm always proved wrong," Creedence said, shaking his head.

"Now let me ask you a question," Milo said.

"Sure."

"At the New Year's party, Mary Alice Bonner told me if her father had used you, he wouldn't have lost his money. What did she mean?"

"It wasn't me. It was my dad. I'm much younger than I look." Creedence once again took time to enjoy his own joke. "It was twenty years ago. Her father, against my dad's advice, jumped into a high risk, high reward investment and lost."

"Lost what, exactly?"

Creedence pushed his glasses up the bridge of his nose.

Milo wondered about this nervous habit he had seen Creedence perform several times during the morning. A time killer? A thought gatherer? Or a nervous tic? He couldn't say just yet. He wasn't ruling out ill-fitting glasses.

"He lost everything, all of his money. He almost lost the house."

"That must have come as a blow to Mary Alice."

"Oh definitely. She liked to spend money, still does. Her father died shortly afterwards. Some say suicide. Eventually, Mary Alice's mother did sell the house on London Road." Creedence paused. He opened his mouth as if he had more to say but closed it again.

"Is there more?"

"Oh, there's much more, but I'm a little uncomfortable spilling it out. Please ask me the salient question."

Rathkey smiled. "You are like the troll under the bridge. Sutherland tells me it's hard to find a buyer for the big houses. So, who bought that house?"

"You have a bankruptcy, a suicide, a family out on the street, and you want to know about real estate?"

"Yeah, I really do."

"You're a good detective. That's the salient question, and the answer is a young James Bonner." Creedence delivered his bomb with the desired effect.

Milo sat, mouth open, digesting that bit of information. "Let me get this straight. Bonner bought that ultramodern house on London Road? I was told he built it."

"You were told correctly. Bonner tore down Mary Alice's childhood home and replaced it with that modern monstrosity."

"Bonner buys her house, tears it down, and then she marries him? Why?"

"Don't know. Nobody does. Shortly after the new house was finished, she shocked the city by announcing her engagement to Bonner."

"Amazing! Was it all about money…the engagement I mean?"

"I assume so, but who knows when it comes to the affairs of the heart." Creedence pushed his glasses up again.

"Let me tell you one more thing, in strictest confidence because we are such old friends." His eyes twinkled at his exaggeration. "In all seriousness, my father always thought the person behind the risky investment was the same James Bonner." He let this tidbit sink in, then trumped it. "Even though Bonner had been an investor too, when everything settled, he may have ended up making money. My father was not privy to all the numbers but always thought Bonner's involvement was highly questionable."

Milo sat in stunned silence. He wondered how much Gramm knew about this, and why Sutherland never mention it?

Could Mary Alice have known and waited all these years to get her revenge, or did she just discover it and snap?

His thoughts were interrupted by the intercom buzz, the receptionist reminding Creedence of a luncheon appointment at the Nokomis Club.

"So, how do I pay you?"

"Don't worry. When you get paid, I get paid. You will notice my fee is automatically deducted from your account."

"Is it a lot?"

"A veritable fortune. I will immediately flee to Tahiti," Creedence joked, showing Rathkey the payment sheet.

"You're going to starve in Tahiti," Rathkey said, looking at his financial adviser's monthly fee.

"I know." Creedence stood to bid Rathkey goodbye. "I think I need a financial adviser."

Rathkey headed for the door smiling at the joke, then turned and asked one more question. "Do you play poker?"

"Absolutely."

"I'll be in touch."

§

Great Party! Sorry About The Murder

An exhausted, shaken Richard Bonner rested his head on the steering wheel of his green Land Rover parked in the secluded tree-covered corner of the lot near Leif Erikson Park. He waited. Early this morning, he was first through the door of EZ Pawn and got enough for the sale of his father's coin collection to cover the late fee with Leroy. With the extra money, this nightmare would exit his life.

After about five minutes, he scanned the empty parking lot and, as instructed, walked behind a stand of trees. Richard shivered. The wind off the lake was wicked and icy. The trees shielded the view from the street but left him wide open to the frigid lake wind.

Damn! Where are they? What if I'm in the wrong place? I'm so damn tired.

He tightly gripped the backpack holding the money.

Standing with his back against the elements, Richard didn't see the two men come up behind him but whirled around and almost fell as one touched his shoulder.

Stan Shultz grabbed his arm to keep him from falling. "Kinda jumpy aren't you kid?" Stan said, holding his arm a little too long, turning the helping gesture into a threat.

"Let him go, Stan," Leroy ordered.

Stan sneered but complied.

"I..I…have the money, all of it," Richard stammered.

Leroy smiled, but his voice was angry. "Well, it's about goddamn time."

Richard opened the backpack, handing Leroy six neat bundles of one hundred-dollar bills plus an envelope containing the pawn money. Leroy, trusting no one, took time to count it.

While Leroy tended to business, Stan did what Stan did best—bully the mark. He pushed Richard hard in the chest, causing him to fall backward against a tree. "Where the hell were you Sunday morning? It was friggin' cold out there!"

Richard thought this had been settled over the phone when he set up this meeting, but that was Leroy, this was somebody else, someone he had never met.

"I…I…explained over the phone. The cops were there… my dad had been shot…I couldn't get out."

"You shot your old man to get out of payin' us?" Stan laughed, poking him again in the chest.

Richard was speechless as Stan glanced back at Leroy who was counting the money. "Are we good?"

"Yeah, we're good," Leroy said, both men having watched Pulp Fiction too many times. Leroy stuffed the bundles into the left pocket of his long leather coat.

Morrie would take a sizeable cut of that money. The envelope with the late fee, however, fell into the category of 'what Morrie doesn't know won't hurt him.' It went into the right pocket. Leroy smiled as he walked away.

Without warning, Stan slammed Richard against the tree and punched him in the gut because he could. Pleased with himself, he followed Leroy back to the car.

Richard remained doubled up. His breaths were rasping. The sharp pain in his gut made him fear that Stan had done real damage. Trying to stand, he fell down on all fours to the snow-covered ground.

How could I be so stupid?

Great Party! Sorry About The Murder

§

Morning in the Rasa bar smelled of old wood, disinfectant, and stale beer. At night it was a rough, serious drinking bar, but only four people were in the bar this early. An old man with an unsteady hand teetered on a bar stool breakfasting on a Miller Light.

Morrie Wolf, who owned the Rasa, was holding court in the back booth. This was his coffee time, his one and only stimulant. Few people realized Morrie almost never had a drink. The crime organization he controlled included most of the illegal activity in Duluth. Even if a criminal didn't work for him, Morrie got his cut.

His number one guy, Milosh, whom everyone called Mike, sat in the booth opposite him. While Morrie was going over last week's betting sheets, Mike was watching the TV along with the bartender, a big burly man named Bennie, who was behind the bar sudsing and rinsing last night's glasses.

Mike shot up and shouted at Bennie to turn up the volume. Mike's outburst was unusual and disrupted Morrie's concentration.

A bundled-up television reporter was standing in front of an iron gate with a white mansion behind it. At the bottom of the screen a red banner read, *Death of James Bonner*. The reporter was saying, "To recap, police have told us little about the death of real estate developer James Bonner, other than to say he died in his house sometime Saturday night or early Sunday morning here on London Road."

The station rolled in scenes from Sunday morning as the reporter continued. "This was the scene yesterday morning when Bonner's body was first discovered. We were the first here to bring you this developing story, and we will continue to update throughout the day."

The TV cut back to her. "Linda Lucash Channel Nine News. Back to you, Ron".

"Bennie, roll that back," Mike yelled in a demanding voice.

"Sure, where to?"

"To that part where she talks about Sunday morning. Yeah, right there. Now freeze it," Mike said. "Damn! That's Leroy, boss! What the hell is he doing there?"

Morrie got up to take a closer look. Mike followed him. "That idiot, Stan's, with him too. Refresh my memory," Morrie asked, "did we have a beef with Bonner?"

"Naw."

"Get Leroy in here. I'm curious why he was there."

The two sat down again, and Bennie resumed live programming. Mike spoke first. "You know Morrie, this means Bonner's brother is unemployed. Do you want to pick him up?"

"Maybe for a job or two to test him out. I'll tell you one thing, if Leroy had anything to do with Bonner's death, David Bonner is going to tear him apart. Even that goon Stan won't be able to save him."

"Do you want to talk to Leroy, or Leroy and Stan?"

"Leroy. Talking to Stan is like talking to that chair."

"I'll see Leroy later today. I'll tell him you want to see him."

§

Creedence had given Milo a folder detailing where his money was being invested. Milo tossed it on the front passenger seat confident he would never read it.

He thought of himself as a good judge of character, and Creedence came up as trustworthy on the Milo meter.

How will Durant be at poker?

A smile broadened on his face as he imagined Creedence at the poker table. Hopefully that glasses-push-up thing was a tell, and he will lose like Shaffer.

The Honda fired right up courtesy of Mr. Anderson. While letting the engine warm for a few minutes, Milo thought about the last question Creedence asked him. "Now that you have considerable disposable income, what do you want to buy?"

He was stumped. From time to time, Milo had some extra money in his life. When he was married, his wife spent it for things around the house. He didn't mind. It made her happy and gave her something to do while he was working…working too much. He shook his head as if to shake off the memory.

The heat was pouring out of the air vents, and Milo was about to pull out of the parking space when he got a text from Gramm to meet at Gustafson's. Durant's meeting had lasted three hours, and a lunch with Gramm would add another hour. Four hours was the magic number. He'd be stuck paying for all day parking.

Glancing at the folder, he remembered the fifteen million dollars parked all over the world. An extra ten dollars wasn't going to break him. It would not have broken him before, but he knew he couldn't do it too often.

Milo shut off the car. All-day parking it was. For the past ten years Milo had been treading water, emotionally and financially. John McKnight's bequest was a life line, at least for the financial part. Milo sighed. Maybe all he wanted to buy was all-day parking with no worries.

He would have thought longer on this change in his life, but his stomach began to growl, and he knew Gustafson's would take care of that problem. Was it the cold but sunny day, no more financial worries for the rest of his life, or the healing ribs that put an extra spring in his step? No need to answer. Rathkey made good time.

Nick waved and shouted, "Do you want hear the specials?"

"No!" Rathkey shouted back.

"Why do I bother?" Nick shrugged.

"Once I find perfection, I stick with it."

Nick turned to his wife and shouted, "My meatloaf is perfection! I should win the Nobel Prize for meat loaf, Nicola."

"Sweden is cold this time of year," Nicola shouted back. "Decline the award."

"We're living in Minnesota!" Nick pointed out.

"Win something in the Bahamas or Santorini!"

Rathkey shook his head as he walked towards Gramm's favorite booth in the back and saw White sitting opposite him. The sergeant moved over, and Rathkey slipped in the booth next to her.

"So what's up?" Milo asked.

Before Gramm could answer, Pat came up to the table and pulled her pencil from behind her ear. "Here are the specials."

"I don't want to hear the specials," Rathkey protested.

"Nick wants me to tell you the specials. I'm telling you the specials," she said it in such a way that everyone in the booth realized there was not going to be any food until she read those specials.

Not hearing anymore objections, Pat continued, "We have beef-and-barley soup, spare ribs with mash potatoes, or a halibut filet with asparagus and rice."

"I will have a hot meatloaf sandwich, mashed potatoes, extra gravy, green beans, and a Diet Coke."

Pat rolled her eyes and took a deep breath. "I love a man that's consistent."

"Love you too, Pat," Rathkey shouted as she walked away.

"I still don't know about the Bonner will," Gramm said, sipping his soup. "but I gotta think the widow and son take in a bundle. That sounds like a motive to me for either Mrs. Bonner or the kid or the two together."

Pausing as Pat delivered his Diet Coke, Milo thought for a few seconds. He took a sip of the Coke. "We know money is a possible motive, but why kill him that night? Why not the night before, or after, or next week? What changed?"

Pat returned with Milo's food and set it down. The conversation ceased while Milo's fork headed for the mashed potatoes, and Pat asked the perfunctory question, "Would anyone else care for anything else?" Receiving negatives all around, she left.

Gramm scraped the last of his soup out of the bowl and continued. "Those are good questions. They need to be answered."

Milo came up for air. "I also have something I learned this morning. It's quite a topper."

"Should I take notes?" White asked Gramm.

"No, eat your lunch, I have a mind like a steel trap."

White took out her pad and pencil.

Milo laughed.

Gramm gave White a mock side-eyed glance and said, "She's getting too comfortable. I don't scare her anymore." He turned back to Milo. "What do you have?"

"It appears as if Mary Alice's father went bankrupt while investing in a shady deal which may or may not have been created by James Bonner."

Gramm whistled.

"There's more. After her father died, the family needed to sell their home. Bonner bought it, tore it down, and built the current house."

"Where did you get this from?" Gramm asked.

"I never reveal my sources."

"Yes you do! You're not a journalist, you're a detective!"

"Creedence Durant, my new financial guy, told me that in confidence. It was what his father suspected. He has no proof. It would have to be verified."

"Hmmm, sounds like Durant is someone I should meet."

"You will. I'm gonna invite him to take Shaffer's place at the poker table."

"Gees, now there are four friggin' millionaires and me at the poker table."

"Ernie, it's nickel, dime, quarter," Milo protested.

"Let's make sure it stays that way. I can see you guys betting a Ferrari and raising a Porsche."

"The Porsche is Sutherland's, and I think a Ferrari beats a Porsche."

"I wouldn't know. I drive a Toyota."

Robin ignored the banter, looked at her notes, and questioned. "So, let me get this straight. Mrs. Bonner's father invests in what may be a James Bonner deal. He loses the family fortune, dies, and leaves the family deep in debt. James Bonner buys the family home, rips it down and builds another, and she marries him?"

"Looks bad, but looking at it another way, he saved the family. How many buyers are there for estates that large? Sutherland says there are none," Rathkey explained.

"I'll take your word on that," Gramm agreed with a hint of sarcasm. "But, Milo, it's not the estate that's at question here, it's Bonner being the architect of Mary Alice Bonner's family's financial ruin? Do you think the widow knew?"

"I have no idea." Inside, Milo squirmed a little. Revenge for betrayal could be an excellent motive.

Gramm changed direction, and brought his partner up to date on the discussions that occurred during the poker game. Summing it up, he said, "Stan and Leroy may also have a motive to kill Bonner to stop the Decency League from shutting down their store."

"They still work for Morrie, right?" Gramm asked Rathkey.

"As far as I know."

"They could have been outside the house to collect the gambling debt, but if they were there because they killed Bonner, wouldn't that also involve Morrie?" Gramm salivated at the thought of putting Morrie Wolf away.

"If Morrie wanted Bonner dead, he has much better people than those two clowns. If they did it on their own, Morrie would not be pleased."

Knowing contact with Morrie was never good for one's health, Milo still plunged ahead. "Look, I know Morrie Wolf from years ago. I could go talk to him."

"Why you, not me?" Gramm asked.

"Because he won't talk to you. He might talk to me. If he does, I could at least get a reaction to some 'gentle' inquiries."

"You're right. Okay, do that now, and call me. I want whatever you can get before we go talk to Leroy and Stan." Gramm finished the last of his sandwich. His mind began putting together a formal suspect list. The widow and/or son were at the top, followed by Stan and/or Leroy.

Beginning to gather his belonging for his trip back to the office, Gramm noticed the file he brought for Rathkey and slid it across the table. He asked Milo why he was looking into a three-month-old traffic accident. Milo said it caught his interest. Gramm's raised eyebrows indicated he was unconvinced.

Milo shrugged, not wanting to get into it.

White, who was checking her email, threw in new information from forensics. "The tire tracks along the lane leading to the back of the Bonner house have been identified. One belongs to a Jeep or off-road vehicle, the second to a high-end car, and the third and possibly a fourth are basic everyday tires…could belong to a number of cars. They were all created after midnight when the snow started falling."

"Three or four cars? Bonner was a busy man just before he died," Milo said.

Gramm shrugged. "Nothing in this case is easy. By the way, I'm hoping for autopsy and tox screen info by Wednesday and maybe ballistics by the end of today."

Pat handed out checks and said her usual, "Remember me at tip time."

Gramm picked up the three checks. "The city will pay for this one; you had good information. Get back to me after you talk to Morrie."

Milo did not mention the McKnight money was on the way.

§

The cinder rock surface cracked underneath Rathkey's tires as he pulled into the Rasa Bar parking lot just before two. Like many of the bars in the Twin Ports, the Rasa was a two-story wooden structure built in the 1920's. He parked on the side of the bar facing a long-faded advertisement for a now-defunct beer. The lunch crowd had gone back to work, so the lot was empty.

Milo had been a kid when he first met Morrie and had no idea about Morrie's side businesses: gambling, theft, and prostitution. Back then, all he knew was that Morrie owned a pool hall which he was glad to see still up-and-running on the other side of the parking lot.

As an adult, Milo knew the cops suspected Wolf of killing a few people here and there or at least ordering the killings. The cops could never prove anything. Morrie Wolf was not a man one casually invited to dinner.

Rathkey sat down at a stool and ordered a Pabst, reminding himself he volunteered to do this. It was going to be a tricky chess game coming at Morrie from oblique angles. Milo couldn't appear to be interested in any of Morrie's businesses, and the most he could hope for was a mild reaction.

At first, he thought that Wolf was not there, but as his eyes adjusted to the darkness, he saw him in a back booth next to the wall. Morrie was wearing his usual—a striped sport coat and skinny tie from 1955.

Where does he still get those skinny ties?

Milo recognized Mike, the bulky body guard who sat opposite Wolf in the booth. Another heavy weight, someone Milo didn't know, sat at a table nearby. Rathkey figured he was also a bodyguard. The unknown man began to stand as Milo approached the back booth, but Morrie motioned for him to sit down.

"Milo Rathkey! My, my. What brings you back to the Rasa? I hear you've moved up to London Road. Local boy does good."

How would he already know about my move? Milo knew better than to ask. He sat down next to Mike, opposite Morrie. "I need some information."

Morrie looked around. "This appears to be a bar not a public library."

"James Bonner was shot yesterday in his home." Milo looked for some reaction but got none.

Morrie went back to his basketball betting sheets. "And what's that to me?"

"I think Bonner's death may involve Leroy Thompson and Stan Shultz."

Morrie looked up. Milo had his attention. "Why do you care who killed that guy?"

"I'm investigating it for a client," Milo lied.

"Why come to me?"

"My client thinks they may have offed Bonner in a rage because…you know…the dead man's Decency League kept forcing them to move their store."

"Continue."

Okay, the chess match is progressing, and I'm not dead, yet.

Milo wasn't clear as to why he was getting Morrie's interest, so he decided to throw out a question he had been mulling over ever since the poker game.

"My client wonders where Leroy gets the extra money to keep moving around. I'm told he loses thousands every time the city makes him move. Can he be making that much on smut and poker? I know Bonner's kid was into him for thousands, but how many times does that come around?"

Wolf was quiet for about a minute and then smiled. "Good of you to come, Milo."

That was Milo's cue. The conversation had ended abruptly but on friendly terms. Not human friendly, but Morrie friendly.

Good of you to come Milo? Interesting. I think I gave him information he did not have.

Rathkey got up, and his place was immediately taken by the unknown body guard. Once outside, Milo called Gramm.

Inside the bar, Morrie ordered, "Get Leroy in here, now!"

13

Leroy Thompson's brain was squirming as he drove the fifteen minutes from his book store to the Rasa Bar. *What does Morrie want…what does Morrie know? How should I play this? If I tell him what's going on, it won't be good for me. Maybe it's not about that. I paid Mike this morning. Does he know about the late fee? No way! I gotta play it cool until I know what's going on.*

Leroy had another thought that made his gut hurt.

Did Stan do something stupid? Maybe that's it. Maybe this is about Stan. I gotta play this cool. If Stan screwed up, it's on Stan. Why does Morrie want to see only me? Don't go there. Play this cool. I'm fine. I'm friggin' Leroy Thompson goddammit.

He spun his car into the Rasa parking lot, hit the brakes, and skidded, sending cinders flying. Temps were below freezing, but Leroy was sweating.

Mike was waiting for him. "About goddamn time! Get in the back!" Mike growled.

As Leroy edged his way through the tables to the office, he noticed Mike fall in behind him, cutting off his only exit.

Oh crap! The pain in Leroy's stomach intensified.

This is bad! This is real bad…play it cool, play it cool…it's probably about Stan. Smile.

§

The conversation between Milo and Gramm was short and to the point. "I suggested Leroy and Stan might have shot Bonner, and Morrie didn't cut me off. He may have just wanted to know what I knew, or the possibility concerned him."

"How do we know he didn't order it?"

"We don't, but I think our conversation would have been far less friendly if he had. Just a guess. Also, on a whim, I threw in Leroy losing a lot of money every time he had to move."

"He loses money? That's new."

"Sutherland thinks he does."

"So, what was Morrie's reaction?"

"The conversation ended."

"As in…get the hell out of here?"

"No, friendlier. Sort of, thank you for coming, like I did him a favor."

"It's like reading damn tea leaves."

§

The A to Z Adult Emporium, was a garish affair painted yellow and black with red neon X's plastered everywhere.

Other neon signs promised adult toys, and sex, sex, sex. A blind man could see it.

Next door, Lund's Fine Furniture, the only other business open on the block, advertised big savings, free delivery, and quality furniture. An antique store down the block had been limping along, but a new sign in the empty window now read: **UNDER CONTRACT**.

Gramm and White pulled up across the street. Gramm sighed. He remembered when the tawdry Emporium was a family butcher shop. As a beat cop, he used to stop now and then at the end of his shift to buy sausages for supper. There wasn't much money back then. He and Amy were newly married, and the sausages were discounted at the end of the day.

"What's the plan?" White asked, pulling Gramm back to the present.

"I want to rile these two guys. I am going to suggest they killed Bonner to stop the League of Decency and watch what happens."

"Got it."

They got out of the car and crossed the street to the Emporium.

Inside was low tech, ill-lighted with a few rows of books and magazines. In the back, the DVD's, sorted by fetish, were stacked next to internet booths for the private viewing of porn.

Stan Shultz, wearing a black t-shirt and jeans, sat behind a glass counter with his back to the wall. His thick, muscular arms were folded in front of him as his eyes followed several customers making sure they didn't pocket the merchandise. Stan readjusted a knit cap on his balding head.

Gramm flashed his badge even though he was sure Shultz knew him.

"Whaddaya want?"

"To chat, Stan. Where's Leroy?"

"Gone. Whaddaya want?" Stan asked again, even less friendly if that was possible.

Gramm wanted both Stan and Leroy together. "Have a good day, Stan. We'll be back."

§

Several drops of blood were already visible in the hard-packed, dirty snow as Leroy picked himself up. He had been thrown out the back door like a half-filled bag of trash. Leroy lay hunched over, catching his breath, scooping up chunks of snow and pressing them on his bleeding nose and lip. He was dented but not dead.

Jesus!

Morrie informed Leroy he had seen him on TV and didn't like it. Leroy began to speak when Mike's first punch connected with his gut. A second made contact with his jaw, sending him sprawling against the office floor.

Morrie, in his quiet way, stood over him, asking what the hell Leroy was doing at the Bonner house.

I was cool. I kept talkin'.

He remembered telling Morrie about the poker game and how the kid wanted to pay off in the front of the house Sunday morning. "I was collecting," Leroy remembered saying. "But all these people and cops were there."

Leroy's ribs and back hurt like hell as he stumbled to the car. He thought about the other two questions Morrie asked, much more troubling questions, like how did he afford to keep moving the store, and worse, did Stan kill Bonner.

That last question was bouncing around in Leroy's own head already.

If that stupid son of bitch was mad, he could do anything, but why did Morrie ask that question?

So many questions.

At least I'm alive but what do I do now?

§

White was about to cross the street to the car when Gramm stopped her. He was staring at the sandwich board placed in front of the business next to Leroy's store.

It read: **Lund's Fine Furniture! Great furniture at low prices!**

"Isn't a guy named Lund on our list of people to talk to?" Gramm asked.

White checked her notes. "Yeah, a guy named Roger Lund had an argument with Bonner the night of the party. He owns a furniture store." She looked up at the sign. "My, my."

Gramm raised only one of his large white eyebrows, "So Roger Lund owns a store next to Leroy Thompson?"

"Well, that's convenient."

"Too convenient! What do Thompson, Lund and Bonner have in common? I don't get it, but I will. Let's go talk to Roger Lund."

Great Party! Sorry About The Murder

Lund's Fine Furniture had been on the corner since Roger Lund's grandfather started the business after World War Two. The block began going downhill in the late nineties, but Leroy Thompson's X-rated store sent it careening off a cliff.

Four cheery bells rang as Gramm opened the door and surveyed the furniture store which seemed at the moment without customers. Roger Lund, a small man in his late thirties wearing a red bow tie and a blue shirt, jumped up with a broad smile, and addressed what he thought were customers.

"Welcome to Lund's Fine Furniture. How can I help you?"

Gramm produced his badge, introduced himself and Sgt. White, and informed Lund they were not customers but had a few questions.

Lund's face went from customer-pleasing to irate citizen in a flash. "It's about time you came. That damn smut store is putting me out of business! Look at the block; it's empty. Somebody needs to do something! I have no customers. Who wants to buy furniture next to smut?"

Gramm held out his hand to stop the diatribe. "Mr. Lund. Stop. We are not here about the Adult Emporium. It's about James Bonner."

"Really? Why? Oh, who cares. I'm going to sit down." Gramm and White followed him to a comfortable living room display, where Lund sat down on a traditional three-color floral sofa. Gramm and White chose coordinated occasional chairs.

Gramm asked the first question. "I understand you and he had a somewhat heated conversation during the party on Saturday night."

"Heated on his part…it wasn't much of a conversation. He humiliated me and my family and then moved on."

"What was it about?"

"It was about this!" Lund said jumping up and crossing to the windows. "This store…this block! Perhaps you noticed, I am not overflowing with customers. A week ago the antique store sold, and what remains, which is me, is barely hanging on. When I took this business over from my father, I had six employees. Now it's me, and my wife does the books."

Lund started to pace and shout about his grandfather and how people, especially his wife, kept telling him to sell out and do something else. He added that he couldn't do that to his grandfather's memory. "I went to that damn party to talk Bonner into redeveloping the block."

Gramm, not wanting to listen to another diatribe about the man's business, told Lund to calm himself, sit down, and the answer the questions. Lund flung himself in the corner of the flowered couch as Gramm asked, "Why Bonner? Why did you go to Bonner for help?"

"Who else? I'm stunned you don't know. He's the one that started the Decency League. I'm a member. We know each other, or at least I thought we did. Bonner was major in getting the city to condemn an area in Morgan Park and get it redeveloped. He led the charge. They were cursed by a smut store too."

"But he wasn't interested in this block?"

"I thought he was. When I got the invitation to his party, I was excited. I mean, I thought it was a sign he was on board. He could have redeveloped this block like Morgan Park, and we could have both made money. Boy was I wrong!"

Lund leaned back defeated. "As it turns out, that bastard invited me so he could humiliate me. I don't understand why. I never did anything to him."

"When did you leave the party?"

"Shortly after I received the dressing down and was informed that I was a waste of his time."

"Where did you go?"

"Home, of course."

"Can anyone verify that?"

"My wife."

"Did she go to the party?"

"No, I went there for business not to party. We don't have money for a baby sitter. Besides, she wants me to sell."

"Can you sell?"

"Some company offered to buy my building at a rock bottom price. I refused of course. I don't care how many thugs they send over to threaten me."

"You've been threatened?" Gramm seemed surprised.

"Yeah I've been threatened!" The yelling and gesturing began again. "Some huge guy came in and said he worked for that…I don't know…some company, and they were 'very unhappy' I wouldn't sell. He had the nerve to make some not-so-vague threats about breaking my legs. I am not having a good year as it is, and now some goddamn company I never heard of wants to break my legs."

"Did you report this threat?"

Lund tightened, his volume became louder, his words more pronounced. "I am so tired of making police reports that get ignored. What can I say, I don't remember the name of the company. I don't know the guy who threatened me. He walked in, and he walked out."

Lund took a breath and jumped up again, pointing a finger at Gramm. "You people won't do anything about that sex shop, and those two bastards are there every goddamn day!"

Lund was quick to anger, Gramm noticed. "How did they contact you?"

"You mean the first time?"

"Yeah, the first time," Gramm repeated with patience he did not feel.

"They called me. The offer was so insulting. I didn't take it seriously. Then this goon shows up…"

Standing, Gramm cut him off. "Come to the station tomorrow and file a formal complaint. We will want you to look at some pictures and see if you can pick the guy out."

"Why? It won't help, nothing does." Utter defeat had quieted Lund down. He finally sat down on the couch with his head back, staring at the ceiling.

"Mr. Lund…Mr. Lund," Gramm persisted, trying to get his attention. "One thing is different. James Bonner has been murdered."

"What?" Lund shouted, jumping off the sofa.

"How do you not know this? It happened early Sunday morning after the party…the party you attended and had an argument with the victim."

"Is that what this visit is about?" Lund screamed, taking a menacing step toward Gramm. "You care more about the death of that bastard Bonner than my life! So, go ahead arrest me! That would be perfect! I am near bankruptcy, and under arrest for murder! Are you kidding me!"

White met aggression with aggression. "Step back Mr. Lund! You're not under arrest—yet!"

Gramm liked White. She got it. Lund was playing poor me at high volume, and White let him know she wasn't buying it. In Gramm's mind, Lund was suspect number five. "Where do you keep your car?" he demanded.

Lund looked puzzled, and crossed his arms. "In the back."

"Show me?"

"Sure, but why. You think I killed him? What did I do, run him over?"

"I need to check your tires," Gramm said, ignoring Lund's question.

"Don't you need a warrant?"

White answered the question. "Not if it's out in the open."

"Just my luck. It's in the parking lot out back. You'll recognize it; it's the only car."

White went out to take a picture of the tire treads, while Gramm continued the questioning. "Did you go back to James Bonner's house after the party Mr. Lund?"

"No, I already told you that."

White returned and nodded at Gramm who informed Lund a forensics team would be sent to take tire imprints. They would have a warrant.

Lund was told not to leave town. As he and White were leaving, Gramm remembered the threat against Lund. "Don't forget to come to the station and make that formal complaint about the guy that threatened you. We can show you mug shots, and maybe you'll recognize the guy."

"Oh good, we can share a jail cell together."

§

Leroy pulled into the Emporium parking lot while Gramm and White were next door inside the furniture store talking to Lund. The bleeding had stopped, but when Mike threw him out, Leroy landed awkwardly on his left ankle. It was swelling and throbbing.

Stumbling into the office, he downed some pain pills and washed his face, all the time thinking of how to question Stan. He didn't need to get hit again. A cold water bottle from his small refrigerator acted as a compress which he put under his eye hoping some of the swelling would go down.

Stan looked surprised as Leroy limped to the front of the store. "What the hell?"

"Morrie's pissed."

Stan looked upset. "Does he know about…you know…about the deal?"

"If he knew about the deal, this conversation would be happening in the cemetery.   Still…he knows… something."

"Oh crap. That's not good, Leroy. That's not good at all."

Leroy readjusted the water bottle and winced. "None of it's good, Stan." Leroy mustered up his courage and tackled Morrie's second disturbing question. "Morrie asked me if you killed Bonner."

Stan's jaw tightened. He said nothing, but his fist came down hard on the counter causing the only two customers to turn and look.

"What'd ya say?" Stan erupted, pushing Leroy against the back wall, grabbing him by the throat with one of his huge ham-like hands.

"Stan! Stan!" Leroy rasped. "The cops are here!"

Stan let go. Leroy cleared his throat and stepped back up to the counter.

Gramm, who seconds ago entered with White, turned to her and said, "I sense a little tension in the air."

"I sense assault," White added.

"We were just playin'," Stan defended himself while brushing off Leroy's collar.

Leroy smoothed his pencil thin mustache and straightened his tie. He always wore a tie just like Morrie's.

White had to stifle a smile as she looked at Leroy's patchy chin hair, his failed attempt at a Van Dyke. Both noticed Leroy's split lip, and growing black eye.

"You play rough," Gramm said to Stan. "It looks like your partner here took a couple of shots to the face."

"I didn't do that," Stan said, glaring at Gramm.

Leroy recovered enough to be his usual uncooperative self. "What the hell do you want?" The two patrons in the place rushed out the door. "You cops are bad for business."

"Let's cut to the chase here, boys. I like you two for the murder of James Bonner." If Gramm was expecting a reaction, he didn't get it.

"Never heard of him," Leroy said.

"Strange. You and Stan were outside his house yesterday, right after he was murdered."

"I wasn't there!" Stan shouted.

"Shut up!" Leroy moaned.

"We have video evidence of you both outside the house."

Leroy blinked. His heart was racing for the second time today.

What can I admit to?

He could tell Gramm about the illegal poker game, but that could lead to arrest and fine.

Is that better than a murder charge…oh hell yes.

The next time I see that damn kid, I'm gonna have Stan work him over. It was his fault we were there. Jesus. This is all going wrong! Wait a minute, maybe Stan was right and the kid offed his old man and set us up.

Leroy's silence was making Stan jumpy, so he filled the void. "We were walking to Louie's for breakfast. I had friggin' pancakes. Leroy didn't have friggin' pancakes."

"Yeah, we were takin' a walk," Leroy picked up on Stan's impromptu scenario, "We noticed the crowd. We were curious."

"Yeah, curious," Stan chimed in.

"I thought you weren't there," Gramm teased.

"I got confused."

"I can believe that. But I'm not confused, and I know your phony poker game hooked Bonner's kid for a fortune."

Leroy's eyes began to dart around the room.

Crap! He knows about the game! That rich asshole is going to pay for this!

Putting his hand through his greased-back hair, and taking a deep breath, Leroy confessed. "Okay, the kid owed us, but he paid up this morning.

White circled that note.

"How did he pay?" Gramm asked.

"We are a cash only business."

"So, why were you outside the house Sunday morning?"

"The kid was going to pay, but all you guys showed up and he didn't."

Gramm played his second card. "So, you don't have a beef with the kid, but you sure did with his old man. Don't tell me you never heard of the League of Decency."

Stan smiled, and Leroy once again told him to shut up, adding, "I hate those damn Bible beaters, but not enough to kill 'em."

"Really? You want me to believe that? Bonner and his league kept closing you down. It had to cost a lot of money to keep moving."

"We do a good business here."

Gramm looked around at the empty store. "I can see that."

"It's a lot better when cops aren't here. Get the hell out."

"We'll be back." Gramm and White turned to leave. "One more thing, where's your car?"

"Out back, you got a warrant?"

"To look at your tires, we don't need a warrant."

Leroy led them through the store, past a storage area, out to the parking lot. He pointed to a new Hummer.

Gramm examined the huge tires, and determined they were not a match. "What about you Stan?"

"I got no car." Stan seemed particularly angry.

"So, you're taking a bus?"

"Taking the Leroy taxi."

"Shut up Stan," Leroy said almost automatically.

Back in the car Gramm asked White, "What do you think?"

"Well, the biggest thing we got was Richard paying up. Where did he get that kind of cash? And why didn't he mention the amount when we questioned him?"

"It's a lie by omission. Those lies are stacking up."

"Other than that, we didn't get much," White said, still looking at her notes.

"When I mentioned Bonner was the head of the Decency League, Stan smiled."

"That's an odd reaction."

"Especially if they offed Bonner, but Stan is crazy and may have smiled at his own handiwork."

"You think?"

"I don't have a clue."

14

By four o'clock, the winter afternoon sun was almost behind the hill, leaving Duluth gray and gloomy. A light snow was falling, one of those lake effect snows that was impossible to predict. Milo had an aversion to this time of day. It made him antsy and uncomfortable. If he was busy, it passed without his notice, but this afternoon he avoided it by taking refuge in the windowless library.

Sitting in his favorite chair, he heard voices and childish laughter coming from the kitchen. It was an unexpected sound. He listened more closely, but the voices were too far away to be heard distinctly.

Those giggles reminded him of sitting in that same kitchen as a boy, talking and laughing with his mom as she cooked dinner for Mr. and Mrs. McKnight. Milo smiled.

Annie arrived from one of her secret hiding places to say hello. Milo bent down, held out his hand for Annie to rub up against. After a scritch under her chin, she stretched, yawned, curled up with her back to the fire and fell asleep.

The voices and laughter fell silent. Milo turned to the Agatha Christie in his hand but decided instead on a real mystery, the police file on the Barbara Cook accident. He hoped Agatha wouldn't mind.

According to the file, at seven in evening, Barbara Cook parked her car, left the parking ramp, and was crossing First Street heading toward the Civic Center. Even though it was dark, a witness walking his dog saw the accident from a block away. He said a "fairly new, gray, souped-up car" came out of nowhere and seemed to accelerate into Ms. Cook. She was clipped by the bumper of the car, thrown into the air, bounced off the windshield, and landed ten to twenty feet down First Street. The car didn't stop, and, according to the witness, didn't even brake.

Where was she going?

Milo knew all the government offices in the Civic Center close at five.

It's like a ghost town.

"Any ideas Annie?"

She sat up, stretched, silently meowed and went back to sleep. Milo took this as indecision on her part and returned his attention to the file.

After the accident, the cops checked body shops for muscle cars with front end damage. Several suspects with a matching car were questioned and cleared. The investigating officer, who Rathkey thought was lazy and stupid, concluded the hit-and-run was an accident, and the driver panicked.

Great Party! Sorry About The Murder

Rathkey shook his head, and Annie looked up for a second. "Look cat, the car accelerated. We have to at least entertain the idea this was intentional." Annie yawned and went back to sleep. Murders bored her.

The report mentioned the victim was divorced, but there was no indication the police interviewed the ex-husband. Also, body shops were still being checked from time to time. "Yeah right," Milo said sarcastically to Annie. Annie did not respond. She was sleeping.

The huge gaping holes in this investigation were obvious. If he was going to find out who killed Barbara Cook, the holes had to be plugged. Then he could focus on the small details.

Something in the minutia bothered him, but he couldn't decide exactly what it was, yet. Milo thought a short snooze seemed like a good idea and closed his eyes.

§

Since Sutherland was the only one in the office this Monday after the New Year, he finished his work and came home early. On his way upstairs, out of habit, he glanced into the library and saw both Milo and Annie sleeping. Hearing footsteps in the gallery, Milo opened his eyes and tried to pretend he wasn't taking a nap.

"Gee, you're here in the library. What a shock. What are you reading?"

Milo held up the folder. "The police file on Barbara Cook's accident."

"They give you the file?"

"Yeah."

"I've never seen a police file."

"Well, this isn't much of one, but I'll let you look through it."

"Okay, right now I've got an appointment with some friends for a virtual bike tour of the lower foothills of Mt. McKinley. I'll be down about seven. Let's talk over dinner. By the way, if you want to work out, I have a complete gym upstairs you are welcome to use, and if you are a swimmer, don't forget the pool at the back of the house."

"Exercise? You think I need exercise? What are you saying?"

Sutherland shook his head, laughed, and headed to his domain on the second floor.

§

Like most estates, Lakesong had a large, formal dining room that was cleaned and polished but rarely used. Sutherland preferred the more comfortable family room where most nights he enjoyed a pre-dinner martini. A vodka gimlet was Milo's choice, as they sat down at the table and made small talk until Martha presented them with hot, steaming bowls of clam chowder.

"When I was in the library earlier, I heard children's voices," Rathkey said, addressing Martha.

"That would be Darian. He was getting the 411 on surviving third grade from his older, wiser, eighth-grade brother, Jamal. I hope our noise didn't disturb you," Martha added. "I can always close the doors."

"No! I enjoyed it. Let's just say it was reminiscent," Milo confided. Martha exited to continue her main course preparation.

Milo turned his attention back to Sutherland. "I met with Creedence Durant today. I should have money by Wednesday…you know…so I can pay you back."

"Good." Sutherland once again brought up the idea of a house manager.

Still not having a clear idea of a house manager's duties, Rathkey suggested that Martha might be a good choice.

From the kitchen they heard a loud, "No, she wouldn't!" "Okay then," Milo said, impressed with Martha's keen hearing. "We will have to look for someone to do whatever that house person does."

Exasperated, Sutherland explained once again, "He or she keeps the house up and running, pays all the bills, does all the things I don't want to do anymore, and I don't think you can."

Taking no offense, Milo agreed, and they ate their soup, praising Martha's culinary talents. Milo was not a fan of shell fish, yet he found this clam chowder beyond delicious.

He handed Sutherland the police file as Martha cleared the soup bowls. "I have salmon and asparagus for the main course with some roasted fingerling potatoes. Are there any objections?" There were none.

"A few things in that file pop out," Milo said.

Martha served the main course, and both men fell silent as they ate. Sutherland, used to reading and eating, took the time to examine the file.

After about fifteen minutes, he set the file aside. "Well, I don't see much there. The witness does say the car accelerated, and the police think the driver got confused. You know, saw her, panicked, hit the gas instead of the brake."

"Possible, but notice this happened at seven at night."

"So, it was dark? I don't understand why that's important?"

"It's not about dark, it's about destination. Do you know anyone in those government buildings that work until seven at night?"

"No. They close at five."

"Where was she going? There's nothing around there but government buildings."

"I see your point, but it can still be an accident."

"True. Or she had an appointment after hours with someone in one of those buildings. The meeting was discovered and stopped—permanently."

Sutherland put down his fork and stared at Rathkey. "You have an active imagination. She was crossing the street and was hit by a car. That's it."

"Tell me where she was going?" Milo repeated.

"I don't know. Do you?"

"No, so the picture is incomplete. There are unanswered questions which, until they are answered, makes my theory as good as yours."

Still not buying the murder idea, Sutherland, nevertheless, asked what Milo was going to do next.

"I think we talk with Agnes, and inquire about that car. Oh, and since Barbara Cook was divorced, we should find out more about her ex-husband."

"Do you think he did it?"

"I don't even know who he is. There's nothing in the file about him. I am going to call Agnes tomorrow to set up a time to meet."

As they continued to eat, Milo mentioned his meeting with Morrie Wolf expecting a reaction. Instead, Sutherland gave him a blank stare. Milo was surprised. "You don't know Morrie Wolf?"

Sutherland shook his head. "No, should I? Who is he? "

Well…if you find a dead body in the trunk of a car, and the car is in Lake Superior, chances are the person in the trunk in some way made Morrie a bit miffed.

Sutherland's eyes widened. "This in Duluth?"

"Yeah, Duluth."

"So, you asked this Morrie person if he killed her?"

Milo winced. He wasn't sure if Sutherland was kidding or not. It appeared he was deadly serious. "See that's a question that would make Morrie miffed. Not a good idea."

"Then why did you go?"

"Sorry, I switched murders on you. I went to see Morrie for Gramm in connection with the James Bonner murder."

"Oh yeah, let's keep our murders straight," Sutherland chided, knowing he had never said those words in his life. "Especially when we are talking about our good friend Morrie Wolf who apparently puts dead people into cars."

"I don't want you to get the wrong idea. Morrie's main business is gambling, prostitution, and loan sharking. He does murder as a problem solver and only when necessary, at least when *he* thinks it's necessary."

Sutherland laughed. "Oh, I'm glad you cleared that up. It makes it so much better. Should we invite him to brunch?"

At that, even Milo had to laugh.

"Seriously, I don't see those two worlds ever colliding… James Bonner real estate developer and Morrie Wolf, what—crime boss?"

"Oh, but they did. The morning of the murder, while we were waiting to get in, I saw two of Morrie's 'employees' outside the house. They had to be there for a reason," Milo said.

"So, what was the reason?"

"It could be they were collecting Richard's gambling debt. Remember Saul told us about the debt at the poker game."

Sutherland was beginning to understand.

"So, I met Morrie to find out if his guys were there for a different reason, say murder. If I've read Morrie right, he had nothing to do with Bonner senior, but it was a loose end."

"Well, better you than me. I avoided James Bonner. I sure wouldn't go near Morrie Wolf!"

Milo couldn't argue with Sutherland's thinking. He didn't eagerly go into the Wolf's den himself. Still, he felt that his new friend could benefit from seeing parts of the city, and people he didn't know existed.

Of course, if he had bothered to think about it, the same could be said for Milo who had been seeing Sutherland's world ever since the will reading.

"So, you still want to come with me to see Agnes?" Milo asked.

"Absolutely! You know all of this is…oh what's the word?"

"Boring? Tedious? You know, most of this is just plodding along. Talking to Agnes is a first step."

"Oh, I find it exciting, and I like Agnes!" Sutherland said, with a tad too much enthusiasm. "So, do we talk to her? What do we talk to her about?"

"We talk to her about the ex-husband, the accident, and why her sister seemed to be going to city hall so late."

Sutherland walked over to the bar cart, poured two small cognacs, and offered one to Rathkey. Milo laughed but accepted nonetheless. His idea of an after-dinner drink was a lite beer.

Settling himself on the sectional, Milo continued, "Creedence told me about Mary Alice's father. I found it incredible, especially the part Bonner played in it. Why didn't you tell me?"

Sutherland was surprised. "I don't know what you're talking about?"

Milo filled him in on the family's bankruptcy. Sutherland was again stunned. "I know that Bonner bought the old house, ripped it down and built his own, but I never heard that other story. How horrible! He was a real louse."

Standing by the fireplace, Sutherland sipped his cognac thinking about what Milo had said, and slowly realized this story had a point. "Oh my God, you're thinking Mary Alice could have killed James out of revenge!"

Milo shrugged. "It's a motive."

"But why now? All that happened so long ago."

"Maybe she just found out. She has opportunity, means, and now motive. Don't get me wrong, I like her. I hope she didn't do it. That's a problem with cases like this. Sometimes people you like go to jail."

15

Sutherland McKnight marched into the morning meeting. This was a new year; he was back at work, a place he belonged. Following the lead of his father, Sutherland had given his employees two weeks off for the holidays. Now the office was over-flowing with well-rested people, chattering and laughing.

"Welcome back everyone!" he announced.

Between cheery choruses of 'Happy New Year' and 'Good morning,' Sutherland poured himself a cup of coffee while Loraine, his administrative assistant, handed him a goat-cheese-filled, honey-fig muffin, his favorite. Loraine always made sure no one else took this muffin, not that any-one was ever tempted.

Sutherland expected the chatter to continue while he looked over his agenda. Today there was dead silence as everyone stared at him. Sutherland glanced up. "Do I have a piece of muffin on my face?"

Great Party! Sorry About The Murder

Marion Caldwell, the head of residential real estate and not one to sit on ceremony, got to the point. "I talked to Sybil over at the Nelson Agency, and she told me that her boss told her that you were part of the police investigation into the murder of James Bonner."

Sutherland was shocked at how word of his involvement in the investigation had spread. "There's not much to tell."

"Oh, come on!" Marion complained, "You can tell us something!" She paused to find the right hook for her boss to bite on. "You know that our clients are going to want to know what's going on." There was a murmur of assent.

Sutherland looked at Marion and at the nodding heads around the table. When asked to join Rathkey on Sunday morning, he didn't think for a minute his name would be tied to the murder investigation and now wondered what the effect would be on business.

Clearing his throat, he began. "Okay. I don't want to take much time with this. After the death of my father, by mutual agreement, Lakesong was left to me and a family friend named Milo Rathkey, a private detective."

A few eyebrows went up at this piece of information, but Sutherland did not pause. "Milo used to be a policeman and is consulting on the Bonner investigation."

"Both he and I were at the Bonner New Year's Eve party Saturday night. Now, please listen. *He* was asked…let me repeat…*he* was asked to come to the Bonner estate on Sunday to help the police. I was asked to join him to give a statement because I was at the party. That is my only involvement. I spent most of the time sitting by myself." He looked around the table and said, "This should clear up any questions from clients."

Several people were eager to ask more questions, but he stopped them. "Look, if I knew more, I couldn't tell you anyway, but I don't investigate murders. I do real estate which is why we need to discuss what Mr. Bonner's death means for us." Tapping on his paper, Sutherland emphasized, "That was number one on my agenda."

Bill Bingham, the head of commercial real estate, picked up on that immediately. "We could grab some of Bonner's business and agents."

Sutherland acknowledged that could happen over time but cautioned against being too aggressive as that sort of thing could start a war.

Pointing to Piper, the head of Development—a new department of the McKnight Company—Sutherland added, "In the coming months, there may be some opportunities, until the Bonner Company recovers one way or another, so check to see if they are pulling back from current projects. It could be an opening to grow this area of our business."

"Who's going to take over the Bonner company?" Bingham asked. "Say what you will about Bonner, he was the company. Maybe the family will sell."

"I think Mrs. Bonner may take it over, at least to begin with. The son may also have a role there."

Having cleared the Bonner situation to his satisfaction, Sutherland moved on to points two and three on his agenda.

The meeting took its usual hour and adjourned exactly at nine o'clock. It was another area of agreement between

Sutherland and his father: no long meetings, adjourn when you're supposed to, and let people get to work.

As they all stood to leave, he asked Bill to come into his office. Bill was tall, and thin, and despite his sixty years, still had a full head of curly, salt-and-pepper hair. As a young man, Bingham was a bundle of energy, always animated, and on the go. Now, a much older man, he still had pluck and pizzazz even though the energy level had diminished a bit. He followed Sutherland into his office. "What's up, boss?"

Sutherland sat down behind his desk and motioned for Bill to close the door. "This question is from left field, Bill. I need to know about the A to Z Adult Emporium —that X-rated store on Fourth."

Bill laughed at the inquiry. "Are we going into that business? We could open a chain."

Sutherland smiled. "Not unless I want my dad to haunt me. I am told that a guy named Leroy Thompson owns that store. I believe it was first located in West Duluth, then relocated up on the hill, and now he's in the central hillside on Fourth. You've been in this job thirty years more than I have. Does any of this make sense?"

Sutherland, not giving Bill a chance to answer, took a deep breath and began to explain what little he knew of Leroy Thompson and his Adult Emporium. "Something called the Decency League has forced Thompson to close each store and move. Here's the tricky part—Thompson should be losing money each time, but he keeps moving to higher rent areas as if he's making money. It doesn't make sense to me. Does it make sense to you?"

Bill said it didn't, but added, "I know a couple small-time brokers who tried to move property near these places. I'll check with them. What's our interest?"

Leaning back, Sutherland tapped his fingers on the arm of the chair. "I'm wondering if we can we get in on some of the development. This might be something Piper could pursue. I know we are new to this development thing, and maybe it's too big a nut for us to chew at the moment, but I'd like to know more about it."

Bingham nodded. "Okay, I'll do some checking and get back to you. Is this urgent?"

"Not 'today' urgent, but by the end of the week if possible?"

§

Hunched over his beer at the Anchor Bar, David Bonner's mind would not shut down.

My brother's a cold stiff, and I'm flat broke. How long does it take to check a will? It doesn't matter, the widow's gotta give me money…now!

Bonner, like his brother, was nobody's fool, except he came with more socially unacceptable problems. He liked to fight.

Being older, he protected his younger brother by taking most of their father's beatings, at least until he got old enough to empty both barrels of a shotgun into his father's head. The beatings stopped.

James had given him work and money regularly. His rent was paid through the month, but beer money was getting low.

Trying to stop the dialogue in his head, Bonner ordered another beer.

What'll I tell the cops when they find me? How should I play this? I hate cops. Dammit, James!

§

Milo finished his last cup of morning coffee and thanked Martha. He grabbed the police file on Barbara Cook as he crossed through the library and billiard room on the way to the office.

In the daytime, the office was brighter than the library but was still John McKnight comfortable. Dark oak dominated the room, on the walls, the recessed ceiling, and the bookshelves. And, of course, there was crown molding everywhere.

Two floor-to-ceiling windows were responsible for most of the light streaming into the room. Or were they doors? Milo wasn't sure. Crossing the room, he realized that the windows were windows, but there was a large door to his left that led out to a snow-covered terrace meant for non-winter activities.

No room in this house was complete without a fireplace, but this one looked somewhat different from the rest. Milo noticed a small switch on the side of the mantle, flicked it up, and was greeted by the dancing flames of a gas insert. John had apparently flirted with modern. Still, the two overstuffed chairs with ottomans facing the fireplace were vintage John as was the executive desk with recessed dark oak panels which mirrored the ceiling.

Milo sat back and made himself comfortable in the large leather swivel chair. No creak in this one. All of the drawers in the desk were empty. With the exception of the books in the floor to ceiling book cases, all of John's personal items had been removed.

A large, dark-blue painting over the fireplace predominated, but didn't seem to fit John's style. The brown-haired girl in the painting looked young and old at the same time, and a rainbow in the background seemed out of place. Jules would be pleased he noticed.

Removing several small pieces of paper from his pocket, he found the two with phone numbers and began transferring the numbers to his contacts. This was Milo's filing system.

The first number was Agnes Larson's, but he managed to type Karson instead. He could never hit the right keys on his smartphone. Correcting that mistake, he moved on to Sutherland's business number with more success.

Milo called Agnes who answered on the second ring. He had to smile. Agnes had spent years answering business phones, and she answered her home phone with the same crisp efficiency. Her voice was friendly but not gushing.

Milo explained that he had some questions after reading the police file on Barbara's accident, and he and Sutherland would like to come over today if possible. She seemed surprised Milo had started the investigation so soon. They settled on any time after two o'clock.

After putting the appointment in his phone's calendar, Milo called Sutherland's business number. He had his cell phone number but didn't want to bother him if he was in a meeting.

A receptionist, not as friendly as Agnes, put him on hold and made him listen to elevator music. After a short wait,

Sutherland answered, and the two discussed the meeting with Agnes, agreeing Sutherland would pick Milo up in front of the Chinese Dragon restaurant at one forty-five.

Milo had a talent for solving murders, something he realized in his first years in police work. Where that talent came from, he had no idea. All he knew was he could see significance in some unimportant detail that others discounted.

Milo held the police file in his hand and tapped its spine rhythmically on the desk. Something in the report was shouting to him, but he couldn't yet see it. He read the report a second time. Nothing.

§

An hour of Sgt. White's morning was spent tracking down David Bonner. She told Gramm he had a couple of rooms at the Gardner Hotel in the West End.

"Not quite as successful as his brother," Gramm remarked as he began to lecture White about the history of the Gardner Hotel. "You know the Gardner used to be on Lake Avenue, but they tore it down to build condos."

White, who learned to tune out Gramm's lessons, didn't even pretend to care.

Gramm sighed. A new partner, same old indifference to his historical insights. "Let's go and meet yet another Mr. Bonner."

The *new* Gardner Hotel looked a lot like the now-demolished old Gardner Hotel—dark, dirty, and uninviting. It was not likely to attract the tourist crowd that came to Duluth for winter skiing or summer biking.

The hotel had one employee during the day, a one-armed man named Slack. If he had a last name, no one ever cared to ask. Of course, Slack could be his last name. Again, no one ever cared to ask.

Gramm and White entered the establishment and immediately found themselves in the lobby which consisted of four mismatched chairs, a faded-plaid sofa, and a plant that refused to die. An old man was reading the paper. He paid no attention to the recent arrivals. Another man, however, slouching on the sofa, stared as they walked from the front door to the front desk.

Slack looked up from a magazine and eyed the two with suspicion.

"They're cops," the slouching man cautioned.

Slack hardened. "You need a warrant."

With a look Gramm let it be known he wasn't new at this. "I want to know what room David Bonner is in, and I don't need a warrant."

"He's in 203. He's not there," Slack admitted.

"He's over at the Anchor Bar, across the street," the man on the sofa added.

Slack glared at the man.

Knowing he had crossed the unwritten rule of cooperating with the cops, the man on the sofa jumped up and confronted Slack. "What! That psycho is no friend of mine!" The man left the lobby and went upstairs.

§

The Anchor Bar had a nasty reputation as a place to go if you like to fight or watch others fight. It was part biker bar, and part railroad worker bar, but it only attracted the nastiest of the railroad workers. Police were called several times a week to break up fights, and the bar's license was always hanging by a thread.

It was getting towards lunch, and even nasty people have to eat. The bar was filling up.

As Gramm and White walked in, heads turned. It was clear to most that these two did not fit in. Several of the patrons could tell they were cops and moved from the bar to a table. David Bonner stayed put on his bar stool. The three beers were calming him down.

He had dealt with cops all of his life and was now ready to meet them head on.

I've got a big surprise for them!

He took a large swig of his beer, draining his glass. That motion drew Gramm's attention. This guy had to be David Bonner. He was a clean-shaven version of the corpse, older, harder but with the same red hair.

As Gramm walked towards his target, those who had not fled the bar earlier did so now, leaving empty stools on either side of Bonner. Gramm showed him a badge and sat down. White went on the other side and pulled out her note pad. Interviewing a prime suspect in a dangerous bar could be a problem. Both were glad it was early in the day before the patrons got drunk and angry.

Looking at the badge, Bonner sneered. "You're a cop. So?"

Gramm got right to the point. "Do you know that your brother was murdered?"

David Bonner was silent but tapped his empty glass on the bar.

The bartender came over with Bonner's refill and asked the others, "What will you have?"

"Nothing," Gramm said.

Glancing at both of them, assessing they had enough money to buy something, the bartender challenged, "Order, or get the hell out."

Gramm flashed his badge. "Leave us alone."

Grumbling, the bartender turned and left.

"When was the last time you saw him?" Gramm continued his interrogation.

"I don't remember."

"Is that your black Bronco out there?" White asked, already knowing the answer.

Bonner didn't turn in her direction, but kept his eyes straight ahead as he downed half of his new brew. "You tell me."

Having dealt with people like David Bonner all of her professional life, White continued unfazed. "Here's what's going to happen when we leave here. I will take pictures of your tire treads and match them to treads found outside the back of your brother's house the night of the murder. So, let's do this again, when did you last see him?"

"I saw James when he was supposed to pay me. It was around five in the morning on Sunday. That's when James told me to come over."

Gramm wasn't buying this new information but continued to see where it would lead. "Was he alive?"

Bonner didn't flinch. "Naw. He was pretty much dead. I didn't make him that way, and I didn't get paid."

Great Party! Sorry About The Murder

White looked up from her notebook taken aback at the callous way David Bonner talked about his brother's death.

What went on in that family?

Gramm was pleased. This was going to be so easy. But before making the arrest, he asked, "Why should we believe you?"

David Bonner downed the rest of his beer. "Buy me another—I'm a little short on cash—then I'll tell you how to catch my brother's murderer."

Gramm acquiesced. One more beer before the arrest might keep him calm. He put money on the bar and nodded to the bartender who again refilled Bonner's glass.

Bonner took a gulp and began. "Like I said, I didn't get paid. James was dead, so I opened the safe. It was empty."

"Again, why should we believe you? You entered the office. Your brother refused to pay, and you shot him."

Bonner erupted, pounding his fist on the bar. "That would be stupid! I'm not stupid. Neither was my brother. That damn safe has a camera." His anger subsided. He took another swig of his beer. "It takes a picture of everyone who opens it. I'm sure there's a picture of me looking at an empty safe. Check it out. Whoever opened it before me stole my money. I'm not happy."

Gramm was surprised but did not show it. "What did you expect to find in the safe?"

Bonner leaned in, close enough for Gramm to smell the beer on his breath. "Hard, cold cash, lots of it."

"Was that all?"

"All that I cared about! He had a bunch of old coins in there he took off some guy in a land deal. Useless to me. I didn't care." Bonner backed off and took another swig of beer.

"Did you close the safe?"

"Hell no. Why should I? It was empty, and I was pissed."

White could hold back no longer. "So, your brother is in the room dead. You don't call us. You don't tell his wife. You open the safe, and then leave."

"Yeah. Not my problem."

"What were you getting paid for?" Gramm asked.

"I deliver messages. My brother is—was—a busy man and didn't have time to deliver them himself."

Gramm with a condescending attitude egged him on, "So, you were his delivery boy."

Recognizing what Gramm was doing, Bonner avoided an angry reaction, "Well, it's a message with an attitude."

"Your brother needed an enforcer?"

Bonner shrugged and said nothing.

Gramm's upbeat mood over a pending arrest had faded. "We're going to check out those pictures, and you can bet, we'll be back. Don't go anywhere."

Bonner growled, "I'm out of a job and out of money. Where the hell am I going to go?"

16

No recent scars or bruises on the body, no drugs, and some alcohol. The ME's official call was death by suspicious circumstances. No surprise there. Ballistics matched the bullet to the victim's gun. The only fingerprints on the gun were Bonner's, and they were smudged.

White groaned, "I bet the killer wore gloves."

Gramm nodded his head in agreement. "Keep going; it gets worse. We can't catch a break on this one."

She read it out loud. "The trigger has a light pull, and this model Glock does not come with a safety." She sighed. "We have a murder, no prints, a hair-trigger gun, and no end of suspects. Piece of cake."

"Well, you bullied David Bonner into admitting he was there the night of the murder, maybe you can bully someone else into a confession."

"I'll practice my bulliness." White quipped.

"We have to do two things, and by 'we,' I mean you."

White smiled.

"First, get some people to check pawn shops for those missing coins David Bonner mentioned. Sweep it wide. Include Superior, Cloquet, and Two Harbors. Also, check the DMV to see if any of our current suspects owns a luxury car that might belong to those tracks in back of the house. If not, expand it to all the party guests."

Gramm mentioned he was meeting Rathkey for lunch at the Chinese Dragon, and Robin was welcome to join them once she finished the DMV search. She confessed she was glad it wasn't Gustafson's again.

§

The Chinese Dragon, a Duluth landmark since the 1950's, was established by a Chinese immigrant named Joey Hun and was now run by his grandson, Henry Hun, Hank to his friends. Outside, it was a formidable stone building that could have been a court house, but inside, it was awash in red, black, and gold with huge lanterns hanging from the ceiling, and tables surrounded by tall, formidable Buddhas.

The aroma of Asian spices filling the room was welcoming as Rathkey and Gramm snaked their way past fast-filling tables of the Duluth business lunch set. The Chinese Dragon was more upscale than Gustafson's.

Here the talk was muted, and the service staff was not given to yelling across the room. There was less clack and clatter with only the occasional clinking of dishes.

They were seated in the back, always Gramm's preference. Hank waited on them. He and Rathkey were old friends, having gone to high school together where they rode the baseball team bench for four years.

Milo often stopped here in the evening for takeout, not so much for lunch.

"Here kind of early aren't you, Milo?"

Falling into their usual teasing banter, Milo replied, "I was wondering if the food was better during the day."

Hank feigned insult while attacking Milo's food choice. "You always order that crappy Egg Foo Yung anyway, so what difference does it make. As I told you many times before, it's an omelet…not even Chinese."

Milo sat back and shrugged, "Then why do you offer it?"

Hank handed only Gramm a menu and countered, "Because bozos like you order it. It's called business."

Milo grabbed a menu out of Hank's hand, "I might order something else. Moo Goo Gai Pan sounds good."

"Okay we'll do this dance. By the way, the special is Gong Bao Chicken."

"You're making that up. There's no such thing."

Hank sighed. "It's chicken breast with peanuts, garlic and ginger. Take your time before you order your Egg Foo Yung. I'll be back."

Gramm laughed at Milo. "You always irritate the people who prepare your food. That could be dangerous."

"Hank and I are buddies."

"Let's hope so." Gramm set his menu aside and began to fill Rathkey in on the dismal ballistics report, the Medical Examiner's murder verdict, along with yesterday's interviews of monosyllabic Stan, slick Leroy, and the volatile furniture store owner.

The possibility of David Bonner being a viable suspect was about to be discussed when Hank returned to take their orders. Jotting down Crab Rangoon and Mongolian Beef for Gramm, Hank looked at Rathkey. "Well?"

"After careful consideration of the imaginary special, I have decided on Chicken Egg Foo Yung and don't skimp on the gravy."

"That's it!" Hank said, ripping the menu out of Rathkey's hands. "No more menus for you."

Raising his hands in a false defensive gesture, Rathkey feigned, "So touchy."

White emerged from the crowd of tables and heard Hank's last words as she removed her coat and sat down. She pointed to Rathkey. "Can I order if I say that I've never seen this man before in my life?"

Hank bowed. "Robin, you can order any time you like."

"I saw the special on the way in, I'll take the Gong Bao. I love that!"

Rathkey put his hand to his forehead. "Stop encouraging him from making up fake names for Chinese food."

Giving Rathkey one of her disapproving sidelong glances, White defended Hank, "It's not a fake name."

Motioning to one of the waiters to bring more tea, Hank commiserated with White. "Don't try to educate him. It's a lost cause."

Gramm asked White about her DMV search.

With a smile on her face, she announced, "We may have caught a break. Someone has a shiny new red Cadillac."

"Someone we know?" Gramm asked going along with White's "ta da" moment.

"None other than…can I get a drum roll… Belligerent Brad Nelson."

Gramm's eyebrows shot up. "Well, Belligerent Brad's afternoon schedule is going to be interrupted. Let's get a warrant to take impressions of his tire tracks just in case."

While pouring more hot tea into his tiny cup, Milo reviewed the tire situation. "Brad Nelson's Caddy is one set of tracks. Before you ordered, you were talking about David Bonner. Are his car tracks number two?"

"We think so. His 4x4 could match."

"Whose cars are three and four?"

"Don't know. We should get the result of Lund's tire mold this afternoon or tomorrow morning."

"Oh, by the way," White added, "I cleaned up some remaining details. No one jumps out from either the guest list or the worker's list…checked out Agnes Larson…she doesn't own a car, and there were no late-night calls to her home for either a taxi, Uber, or Lyft. However, Mary Alice Bonner is a regular visitor at the Duluth Gun Range where she is known to be an excellent shot. The guy there thinks she should compete."

"She said she knows her way around guns, but the shot was at such close range, the killer didn't need to be a marksman," Gramm added.

"Did you ask Milo about the safe?" White reminded Gramm.

"Oh, yeah. I almost forgot. Have you ever heard of a safe taking a picture as it's opened?"

"What? No! Take a picture of what?"

"The person opening it. We've been told Bonner's safe does that."

"Great! So, who opened the safe?"

"Don't know…can't get the pictures. So far, Forensics can't figure it out. They say it's military grade encryption."

Milo thought of Ed Patupick. "To quote Sutherland, I gotta a guy."

"A guy? Okay, call your guy. I want the pictures."

The food arrived, and Milo was pleased by the large amount of gravy on his Egg Foo Yung. Glancing at Robin's dish, he had to admit the Gong Boa looked tasty.

They finished their meal with scattered discussions about grandchildren, holidays with relatives, and the curious late-night business hours of James Bonner. With a wave to Hank, they walked out into the bright sunshine and bitter cold of the afternoon.

Milo waited on the sidewalk, scanning the street, hoping Sutherland was driving the SUV. A brisk wind had turned a balmy thirty degrees frigid compelling Milo to flip the collar on his new overcoat—the one he bought for the Bonner party. He had to admit that it was a lot warmer than his old one.

He retreated into the restaurant doorway, his ears calling it quits in the bitter wind, as the Porsche's tires crunched on the frozen mix of salt, sand and slush. Being careful not to slip, Milo opened the door and attempted the sports car dip, not smooth, but all arms and legs managed to get inside at about the same time.

"The Porsche? Really? What about the SUV?" Milo demanded.

"Not bad enough yet. Definitely sports car weather."

Milo ignored him.

§

Gramm sat in the car and checked for messages while White went through the process of getting a warrant for an imprint of Brad Nelson's tires.

Given the rancor of the last interview, Gramm called Nelson and advised him to have a lawyer present. It had been his experience that such advice often scared the hell out of suspects. Still full-on belligerent, Nelson decried the interruption into his day, demanding to know what this imposition was all about. Gramm gave him nothing but dial tone.

On a summer's day, they would have walked down to Superior Street where the Nelson Group offices took up most of the fourth floor in one of Duluth's newly renovated buildings. On this blustery, cold, winter's day, they drove the three blocks down the hill, parking in the building's ample parking garage.

A short elevator ride and two glass doors later, they entered the office and told the receptionist they had an appointment with Mr. Nelson. She made a call, and a young lady came up to escort them back.

Nelson introduced them to his lawyer, Harold Walters, and offered to get them coffee. Gramm accepted. While waiting for the coffee, there was no small talk or friendly banter to break the awkward silence.

Gramm pulled out his phone and texted Saul Feinberg, asking who was Harold Walters?

Feinberg responded almost at once, stating he was a real estate lawyer.

As Gramm put his phone back in his pocket, the same woman who had led them to Nelson now rolled in a coffee cart.

Gramm took extra time with his coffee, enjoying the unease he was creating.

With Belligerent Brad, as White had coined him, Gramm decided to start with a lie. "Let's get to the point, Mr. Nelson. We have a witness that puts you back at the Bonner house early Sunday morning.

Robin enjoyed the lie and kept a straight face.

Nelson's eyes darted from Gramm to White almost like a frightened animal trapped by predators.

He grabbed his lawyer and dragged him to the far side of the room where they conversed in hushed tones. Nelson's back was to the conference table, so Gramm and White could not tell what he was saying, only that he was angry and animated.

Gramm took the time to enjoy the fabulous coffee, and asked White, "Why don't we have coffee like this?"

"French press is not in the budget," White responded.

Coming back, Nelson threw himself back into the chair, stretched out his long legs in front of him, and placed his hands palms down on the table. "Okay! Bonner called me about one in the morning and told me to come back after three. He had an offer for me. I wanted to tell him to piss off, but we needed a deal."

Gramm was pleased his lie worked. "Continue."

Nelson, unsure of how to proceed, eyeballed his lawyer who only shrugged. With false bravado, Nelson continued. "Nothing happened, absolutely nothing! He refused to come to the door! I banged and shouted and cursed, but the jerk refused to come to the door!"

"Did you see him?"

"No, the curtains were pulled shut. But he was there. His damn light was on!"

White asked, "Was this normal for Bonner? I mean scheduling people to see him at three in the morning?"

"Of course. He was a total bastard."

Gramm, taking his own good time to allow Nelson more discomfort, finally asked, "Why didn't you tell us this before?"

Nelson again looked to his lawyer who once again shrugged. Left on his own, he looked down and admitted, "It looked bad. I wasn't prepared for questioning. I came to see Mary Alice."

Gramm agreed it looked bad. He admonished Nelson for lying in the original interview, and asked for the location of his car, as they needed to take tire prints. True to form, Nelson blustered at the necessity of such an action, saying he already admitted that he was there.

Gramm explained it was procedure, dotting the i's and crossing the t's. Nelson shook his head, gave them the car's location in the ramp, and the interview ended.

"You know that lawyer didn't do much," White said as they approached their car.

Gramm laughed. "He's a real estate lawyer."

"How do you know that?"

D.B. Elrogg

"I have my sources."

§

A little after two o'clock, Sutherland pulled up in front of Agnes Larson's house, a post-World War II, story-and-a-half, yellow bungalow in a neighborhood of similar houses but different paint colors. At some point, a large inviting front porch had been added to Agnes' house. It wasn't a major architectural feature, but it set Agnes' house apart from most of her neighbors.

Rathkey found himself pinned between the car and a large snow bank. Milo was glad his ribs had calmed down otherwise he could not have done the stupid entrance and exit squeeze a sports car in winter required.

Sutherland found Milo's gyrations amusing and said with false innocence, "Did I park too close to the snow bank?"

Rathkey gave him a dirty look.

The sidewalk was shoveled and sanded, which Sutherland found to be efficient and welcoming.

As they climbed the steps of the front porch, Agnes opened the door. "Come in!" she said smiling. They walked into a cozy living room warmed by a small fireplace. It was framed by a comfortable, modern sofa with clean lines, and two complimentary chairs. Cookies, holiday candles, marshmallows and candy canes covered the coffee table in the middle of the seating area.

Considering the season, Sutherland was expecting to find a mix of Santa-and-Norman Rockwell-cozy, but the room was far more complicated than that. With the exception of a few Christmas decorations, it was clean, almost stark. Modern prints of Rothko and Klee were hung on the far wall along with a third painting Sutherland didn't recognize.

"I have coffee and cocoa." Agnes pointed to the two white carafes on the coffee table.

Rathkey thanked her, sat down in one of the chairs, and poured himself cocoa. Scooping a handful of tiny marshmallows, he dropped them into his cup.

Sutherland walked over to the print he did not recognize. "This one doesn't ring any bells," he said, puzzled.

Agnes joined him and said, "Tutti-Frutti. It's a Frankenthaler print."

"I am not familiar with him."

"Her." Agnes corrected.

Embarrassed, Sutherland nodded. "A bit of sexism on my part, sorry. I do like this. I will have to become more familiar with her work."

"I got this at the MoMA store on my last trip to New York. It's my one extravagance. I try to go once a year."

"Can I use that to explain my ignorance? I haven't been in a several years."

Agnes turned to Rathkey. "Do you like abstract expressionism, Mr. Rathkey?"

"Maybe. I don't know."

Agnes led Sutherland back to the couch, settling herself next to him. "I am hoping on my next trip to get de Kooning's Untitled V print." Sutherland offered as to how that would go well here as he picked up a cookie.

"I usually bake," she said, "but with all that's happened with Barbara—we usually have a tree—maybe next year."

Milo put his cocoa down, put his hands together and leaned forward. "Speaking of your sister, after reading the police report, I think there's a stronger possibility it wasn't an accident."

Agnes leaned back, grasped her cup with both hands, and said nothing for several seconds. Again, Milo, being a trained interrogator, knew to keep quiet and wait for Agnes to speak. Sutherland however, being a novice at this work, jumped in like a puppy. "Are you okay?" he asked.

She turned to him and said, "Yes, yes, I'm okay."

In his mind, Milo was choking Sutherland. He wanted Agnes' raw response to the possibility someone would harm her sister. Waiting on the silence often yielded information that would not come out otherwise. He did give it another try however. "Why would someone want to hurt your sister?"

"I don't know why anyone would hurt her. She was wonderful. Ever since her divorce, she lived here with me."

That was Sutherland's clue to take the conversation in an opposite direction. "How long has she been divorced?"

"Five years."

"Was the divorce amicable?" Sutherland asked.

Milo was chagrined. All the right questions at exactly the wrong time.

"Well…I guess as much as any divorce can be. Her husband was a lawyer and spent most of his time in the office. They…grew apart. Then Barbara discovered he was cheating. She was hurt…angry, but she worked her way through it. I convinced her to move here from the Twin Cities and helped get her the job with Mr. Bonner."

"Exactly what did she do for Mr. Bonner?" Sutherland continued.

"She was his personal bookkeeper."

Milo decided to go with the flow. "Isn't that kind of old fashioned? Don't people like Bonner have a company to do the accounting?"

"He didn't trust outside agencies—too many people he couldn't keep an eye on. When Barbara came to live with me after the divorce, she needed to keep busy. Working for Bonner solved that problem, and the added bonus was he overpaid both of us. We used to joke it was hazard pay."

Silence descended once again. Sutherland, helping himself to more cocoa, didn't interrupt, allowing Milo to bring the conversation back to where he wanted it to go. "Do you know anyone who would want to harm her?"

Agnes stared at him and held her breath. Tears welled up in her eyes which she wiped away. "How can anyone do that? End a person's life…like they don't matter?" she whispered.

Sutherland handed her a napkin from the coffee table. Milo leaned back, "She may have mattered too much to someone, and that person wanted her silenced. It was either something she saw, or something she knew."

Agnes eyes were riveted on his. Milo continued. "Do you know where she was going at that time of night? She was walking in the direction of the city-county offices across the street, but they were closed."

"I have no idea. Was she meeting someone?"

Milo softened his tone. "We don't know. It was something we hoped you could tell us."

Agnes shook her head as Milo continued. "Did Barbara leave any papers, date book, calendar that we could look at?"

Agnes stirred her cocoa absently. "I went through all of her papers to settle her estate. I didn't notice anything."

Sutherland jumped in, "Do you still have her work computer?"

"Yes, it's in her bedroom."

"Maybe there's something on that. Milo thinks there could be a connection between Bonner's death and your sister's."

Despite having heard this before from Milo, Agnes stared at Sutherland as tears overcame her and became sobs which she could not stop.

"We've upset her!" Sutherland shouted at Rathkey.

Ignoring the shouting, Milo directed him to take her hot cocoa and hand her another napkin from the coffee table.

After several minutes, the sobbing lessened. Through the tears, she apologized for crying. Sutherland told her there was no reason to apologize. They understood. Agnes excused herself to freshen up.

Milo said nothing while they waited. Sutherland didn't know how to fill the void, so he too sat there in silence until Agnes returned.

As she walked into the room, again apologizing, Agnes stumbled a bit catching herself on the back of the couch. Sutherland jumped to her aid, guiding her to the couch. "I am okay...a little dizzy...I'll be fine."

Sutherland sat down and offered her a cookie. "You may need the sugar."

Agnes accepted the cookie and smiled at Sutherland. "You know, you may be right, it's been a while…I haven't eaten."

As she bit into the cookie, Sutherland gave Agnes a concerned look. "That's not good. I have a solution. Come with me this afternoon to the restaurant of your choice. I will feed you, and you can educate me about Ms. Frankenthaler."

Agnes smiled. "Her first name is Helen."

With eagerness, Sutherland responded, "My first lesson, Helen Frankenthaler. So what will it be, Bellisio's, JJ Astor?"

"The Pickwick! I'm in the mood for onion rings. No one makes them better."

"The Pickwick it is," Sutherland echoed. He looked at Rathkey. "Are you in?"

"No, no thanks. I've got some calls to make."

"We can drop you at Lakesong."

"Not unless Agnes or I ride on the roof. You've got a Porsche."

"You're right, I forgot."

"I'll get a taxi," Rathkey offered.

Agnes pulled out her phone and said, "I can call my Lyft driver to pick you up."

Sutherland, who was Lyft savvy, negotiated the app so the ride was charged to his credit card.

§

Milo got back to Lakesong around midafternoon and informed Martha that he would be the only one for supper. What he wanted to do on this cold winter's day was sit in the library by the fire, but he forced himself to continue to the office. Crossing to the gas fire place, he flicked it on, sat down, and tapped the Barbara Cook file end over end, thinking. Frustrated at the lack of information, Milo decided to see if Feinberg, the Knower-of-all-things-street, could shed more light on the accident or possible murder.

Feinberg answered on the second ring, and Milo filled him in on what he was doing and what little information the police file gave. Feinberg said it sounded familiar.

The lawyer took a minute to check his calendar and informed Milo he was at the police annex in city hall that night dealing with the Wilson kid, the one who didn't rob the liquor store.

"Police annex? What the hell is that?" Milo questioned.

"It's a couple of rooms in the basement of City Hall. They created it when the rest of the cop shop moved up over the hill."

Feinberg told Milo he remembered a lot of activity that night not connected to his client. "One of the cops was talking about a hit-and-run. I didn't pay attention. Along with trying to see the kid, I kept tripping over Fred McGrath from bunco."

"Oh yeah. I know him—Fading Fred. No one can ever find him at one-minute past five," Milo interrupted. "What the hell was he doing there?"

"He was waiting for someone, and he was pissed. The person was a no show."

Milo thought Barbara Cook being run down, and Detective McGrath being stood up was another uncomfortable coincidence. "Tell me more about that night and what McGrath was doing."

"McGrath kept interrupting, asking if anyone had come in looking for him. Finally, he put on his coat, said he was tired of waiting, and went home. I remember how glad I was to have him out of the way."

Milo wrote McGrath's name on the cover of the file. "Saul, this is good. I have one more question for you. Do you have time?"

"Yeah, court got postponed."

"The hit-and-run car was a dark gray, newer model muscle car. Have you heard anything about that car?"

"Hmm, doesn't ring any bells."

"What about right after the accident, any word about anything?"

"Nothing I've heard, but I wasn't looking. I really never knew who had been in the accident. I only knew there was an accident."

"So, no talk on the street?"

"About a hit-and-run? Why would there be talk?"

"I don't know. I have a couple of things rolling in my head. What you gave me now may help fill in some of the pieces."

Feinberg began to ask his own questions. "Okay, back up. Who is this person? What was her name?"

"Barbara Cook."

Feinberg repeated the name. "What is Barbara Cook to you?"

Milo took a second to reply. "Good question, Saul. Barbara Cook worked for James Bonner."

"Whoa, the recently shot-in-the-head James Bonner?"

"One and the same, and I gotta tell you, I can't get rid of the feeling her death and Bonner's death might be connected."

"Well, I'm not hearing anything about Bonner's death or this Barbara Cook woman. But I'll keep my ears open."

§

Since the Pickwick Restaurant was Agnes' choice, Sutherland let her take the lead. The early happy-hour crowd at the Bavarian-themed bar was growing, but the restaurant itself was almost empty.

Sutherland preferred the booths beyond the bar next to the large fireplace. A back room consisted of more formal tables and afforded a wide view of the lake. Agnes asked for a booth, much to Sutherland's delight.

Glancing at the holiday fir boughs on the dark paneled walls, Agnes was glad they hadn't been taken down yet, saying January can be so bleak. Sutherland helped her with her coat, but rather than hang it on one of the booth hooks, she kept it around her shoulders and sat down. Sutherland took off his coat, hung it up, and slid into the booth, opposite her.

An older waiter came over and inquired as to their drink preferences. Sutherland asked for a wine list. Agnes giggled and wondered what wine was best with onion rings. While the question stumped Sutherland, the waiter who had served millions of onion rings was quick to answer. "An Alsace Pinot Blanc."

During the chit-chat, Sutherland realized that he had not been out in a social setting with a woman for many months.

He had known Agnes in passing for several years, but this is the first time he noticed how attractive she was.

He urged her to get some protein along with the carbs the onion rings would provide. She smiled and looked at the menu.

The waiter returned with two glasses of wine, a half basket of large, thick-coated, onion rings and two plates. Sutherland held up his glass and toasted to a happy New Year. Agnes drew a deep breath and echoed his toast. Their glasses clinked.

"You know, I am going to help you with a few of those onion rings. They look delicious."

Agnes sipped on the wine watching Sutherland bounce a too-hot bite of onion ring around his mouth. His attempt to remain graceful made the scene even funnier. Agnes laughed and started to relax. She thought to herself how nice Sutherland was to go out of his way for her. He didn't have to; no one had to anymore. Not wanting to go down that dark hole again, she took another sip of the Pinot Blanc and began to feel its effects.

Agreeing with Sutherland that protein was also needed, Agnes decided on the lake trout with small red potatoes in garlic-butter sauce, and green beans. Sutherland laughed because he was thinking of the same thing. They put in their order and went back to the onion rings.

As they were picking through the final crumbs of their appetizer, Agnes began to fill him in on the strengths and weaknesses of Helen Frankenthaler and her contribution to abstract expressionism.

Agnes allowed as to how she hadn't thought about painting and painters in a long time and how much fun it was to talk with someone who shared a love of art.

She asked him about the works in Lakesong. Sutherland named several pieces he had in his area of the house, but he said the art work on the first floor featured regional artists going back to the 1900's. He added his father had purchased several Heywood Hardy works because he liked them. They were not to Sutherland's tastes however.

"My mother conducted a subversive campaign to lighten and modernize the house. She actually bought an Oskar Kokoschka print and hung it in my father's office. He refused to admit it, but I think it grew on him. It's still there."

Agnes laughed. "She hung it in his office? At least she wasn't trying to hide it."

The trout arrived, and Sutherland ordered a bottle of light Chardonnay to go with the fish. "So what will make the new year happy for you?"

"Wow, that's quite a question." Agnes sipped the wine and took a taste of the trout. "I have been reacting to events in my life for so long, I have not thought about what I wanted for some time."

"What do you mean?"

Agnes debated whether to share exactly what she meant but decided to take a chance. "Barbara and I were foster kids, lurching from family to family. We kept moving. Luckily, we always had each other, that's why all of this has been so hard."

Agnes began twisting the wine glass between her fingers. "I thought that as an adult, I had overcome that feeling of being insignificant. Then someone ran Barbara down and didn't even bother to stop."

Sutherland always felt he mattered and couldn't imagine Agnes' pain. He struggled with a response. "Sometimes you can lose yourself trying to deal with the unexpected coming at you." He wasn't sure it spoke to her experience, but it was how he was feeling with the recent loss of his father.

Agnes looked up and stopped twisting the stem of her wine glass. "You know, I think you're right. I have been dealing with the unexpected all my life."

Sutherland offered a toast. "It's a new year, let's toast to finding what matters for both of us."

Agnes smiled, their glasses clinked, and they continued their meal.

The food and company had improved her mood. "The first thing I need to do is find a new job."

Sutherland was surprised. "Really? Won't you continue on as Mary Alice's assistant?"

"I don't think so. I assume Mrs. Bonner will offer me a position, but with all that's happened…I want a change."

Sutherland thought for a minute. "I can't promise anything. I don't know if we have any positions open, but I can check."

Agnes was surprised and not in a good way. "Oh no, no, no! I wasn't asking you for a job! Let's not even talk about this! This meal is a lovely respite…an island away from dealing with the muddled mess."

She closed her eyes and shook her head as if to reset the conversation. "Let's talk about art."

Sutherland raised his glass, "To art."

Agnes countered, "To art indeed."

D.B. Elrogg

§

Milo was looking at the books in the study. Some of these titles he had never seen before, but some were quite familiar and duplicates of books in the library. He remembered that John had mentioned many valuable first editions he had collected over the years and kept in his office.

Milo didn't know what to do with a valuable book. "John, you left no instructions for this," Milo said to the empty room. "Does one actually read a first edition? Can I Google what I should do with these books?"

His questions to the spirit of John McKnight were interrupted by a phone ringing. It was a first for Milo in this office. "You're off the hook for the moment John, but we will continue this discussion unless that's you on the phone."

Laughing at the absurdity of his imaginary conversation, he walked back to the desk to answer the phone. It was no spirit on the other line. It was Ernie informing him the police had found the missing coin collection at a pawn shop in Superior, the city across the bay from Duluth. Surveillance video showed Richard bringing it into the shop.

Ernie reminded him to call his guy about the safe. As Milo dialed Ed Patupick, he knew tomorrow was not going to be a good day for Richard Bonner.

17

Annie jumped down from her Guiana tree, a clear sign that there was food in her future. Noticing the cat strolling into the kitchen, Martha announced that Mr. Rathkey was on his way to breakfast; within seconds, Milo arrived.

"How do you do that?" Sutherland queried from the morning room.

"I could say it's my professional training, but to be fair, it's the furry, four-legged advanced scout."

As if understanding what was being said, Annie serpentined to Rathkey's chair, forcing him to slow down behind her. It created a comical parade. Rathkey turned to Sutherland and said, "My bodyguard goes first at all times."

"Your bodyguard and Martha's scout. This cat plays many roles." Sutherland smiled.

Rathkey sat down, poured his coffee and, slipped Annie a small slice of bacon. "For all her hard work. The kitchen could have been mined. She saved us all."

Milo put down his coffee, looked at the delicious calorie-filled breakfast before him and sighed. "Today, I am going to exercise. There, I said it!" Spearing a sausage with his fork he joked, "It's all Martha's fault."

Martha turned and looked at him with great surprise. "I can change the eggs, toast, bacon and sausage to fruit and yogurt, or how about some cardboard tasting healthy cereal?"

Milo put out his hand to stop Martha's healthy substitutions. "You don't understand. I love this. So in order to be able to eat it every morning, I will have to…have to…"

"Exercise. The word is exercise. Like what I do every evening."

"What you said."

"So, what kind of exercise?" Sutherland asked. "You can use the upstairs gym. There's a treadmill, an elliptical, and several different stationary bikes. Name your poison."

"I like to swim. Is the pool still a dungeon in the basement?"

Surprised, Sutherland was quick to assure Milo the pool was not in the basement.

"Good," Milo said, between bites of toast. "As a kid, it scared the hell out of me. It was dark, damp—like something out of a horror movie."

"Well, as it turns out, my mother must have thought the same thing because shortly after my arrival, she had the old pool filled in and a new one attached to the house. The old pool was before my time, but the one I know is light, airy, and during the winter months, heated."

"Okay, I am more than in. Where is it?"

"It's off the back of the house. In the summer, you can walk there from your office or the gallery, but in the winter, you get to it from the basement."

"The basement door off the kitchen? Right?"

"Oh no. My mother added another set of stairs from her dressing room closet in the master suite. You'll see a door that leads down to the basement. So, you're a swimmer?"

"After my hitch in the Navy, I had better be a swimmer, and if I don't start soon, at the rate I'm going, I'll be a small battleship by spring. But I don't have any swim trunks."

"We have a closet full of trunks for guests in all sizes down in the pool area. I am sure you can find a pair that fit." Sutherland smirked, knowing he had taken away all roadblocks between Milo and the dreaded exercise.

"By the way, I discovered the cops have a small office in city hall, something created when the cop shop moved over the hill. I'm thinking Barbara Cook could have been going there," Milo explained, while using his toast to help the scrambled eggs onto his fork.

Sutherland thought for a moment on this new information and then expounded on a theory of his own. "Could it be that Bonner was in trouble—being threatened? Maybe Barbara went to the police because James Bonner wouldn't go there himself. Loraine, my administrative assistant, would, I think, do that for me."

Rathkey looked up from his food. "It's a possibility. Something worth exploring."

Sutherland seemed quite pleased. "Maybe we should mention it to Gramm."

"For the moment, let's not bother Gramm with anything about Barbara Cook. He's busy enough. So how was your dinner last night? Did you get Agnes fed?"

"Yes, she has been nourished. You know she is quite remarkable. We talked about art all night. It was so enjoyable. She is also quite attractive."

Rathkey stopped eating. "Remarkable? Enjoyable? Attractive?"

Martha jumped in, "Am I catering a wedding?"

Smiling and blushing, Sutherland remarked, "Ha! That may be rushing it."

"They grow up so quickly," Milo said, going back to the toast and eggs.

Not appreciating the attention on his social life, Sutherland changed the focus of the conversation. "Are you sleuthing today?"

"Sleuthing? I'm not sure I've ever been sleuthing, but I do have to tail Heidi Reinakie for an hour or two."

"Again? Can't you tell her husband he's crazy?"

"Harry won't believe me, and it pays well."

"Speaking of getting paid, is today the day?" Rathkey brightened up. "According to Creedence Durant, today is the day!"

Sutherland smiled. "Good, I will total up what I think you owe me so far this month."

"It comes and goes so fast," Rathkey complained.

"That's the nice thing about that household manager idea. We both make an automatic deposit into a household account each month. Everything is handled. We don't have to think about it."

Annie, sensing that bacon time was over, meandered to snooze before the fire. Sutherland took off for work. Rathkey had another cup of coffee.

§

A pre-blizzard grayness had set in at sunrise. The much-predicted snow storm was due in the late evening and was forecast to last the better part of twenty-four hours.

Gramm had called Mary Alice the night before and told her to expect them in the late morning. He added that she and Richard may want a lawyer present. If he expected Mary Alice to react to that statement, he had been disappointed.

In a calm voice she asked, "What would be the reason for the visit?" Gramm said they had new information that needed clarification.

Usually people attempt to question the police further or become belligerent like Nelson. Not Mary Alice. In her accommodating style, she said she understood, and she, Richard, and their lawyer would be ready. She wished him a good evening.

§

Roger Lund combed over digital images of police mug shots in the hopes of recognizing the man who had threatened him. He had been given a desk, a computer, and large cup of coffee. Hundreds of mug shots later, the coffee was gone, and there he was—the threatening thug. Excited that finally something might get done, Lund glanced around to see the Lieutenant heading in his direction.

Smiling, Roger said, "I found him! This is the guy! This worked!"

Gramm didn't smile or seem friendly at all. "Okay, Mr. Lund, let's see what you have?"

Lund pointed to the picture on the computer screen. Gramm looked and wondered if this case could get any more complicated. But for the moment, he had a bigger question for Roger Lund. "There's a problem Mr. Lund. Our forensics people tell me your tire tracks match the set left outside of Bonner's office the night of the murder. You lied."

Gramm sat down and was joined by White who pulled out her notebook. Lund's joy at finding the mug shot was replaced with the gloom he had been feeling the last several months.

"I was there…he called me…said he wanted to buy my building…wanted me to come around at two in the morning to talk about it."

"Did you? Talk about it?"

"Yeah, sort of. His offer was an insult."

"Why didn't you tell us to begin with. You could have saved us valuable time."

Lund looked down at his hands. "I don't know. I want this nightmare to end."

"The nightmare of murdering James Bonner?" White added.

Lund didn't look up. "No, of course not. The nightmare of my furniture store, my legacy, dying in front my eyes."

"Did you see anyone else coming or going?"

Lund looked up and seemed surprised. "It was two in the morning. Why would anyone else be there?"

Gramm leaned into the nervous man, "Let me give you a scenario, Mr. Lund. You and Bonner argue, you see the gun on his desk, you pick it up, it has a hair trigger, it goes off—an accident."

Lund kept shaking his head and saying over and over again, "No, no, no, no I didn't do that!"

"Why should I believe you? You lied about going back to the house."

"I know. I shouldn't have done that. I'm not thinking clearly these days, but I did not kill him."

Gramm stood. "You know, if you did, we will be able to prove it. You can go for now, but don't leave town."

"Leave town? I can't afford the gas to get home." As he stood up, he pointed to the screen. "What about him?"

"We'll deal with him."

As Lund headed for the door, mumbling about how he heard all that before, Gramm bent down and turned the computer screen toward White.

White read the name under the picture. "David Frederick Bonner. What? He's Lund's thug?"

"Was he freelancing for that company?" Gramm asked.

"Could be his brother found out. They argued, and David shot him."

"Who the hell knows? This time you buy the live Bonner a beer."

Looking over her notes, White said she wanted to get all the stories straight before adding one more name to the list of strong suspects.

"Lund admitted he talked to Bonner at two. He could be lying. He could have shot Bonner at two. Then Nelson comes along at three and says Bonner doesn't open the door. Could be Lund has already shot him."

Gramm countered. "Nelson could be lying, and he shot him at three. Let's not forget the calm collected widow who finds the body at six. She could be lying and shot him any time after Lund's visit."

White added, "The same goes for Richard, and those are the fine upstanding possible murderers."

"In the less-than-upstanding category, first out of the gate, Stan Shultz. He could have entered the office, shot Bonner, and then returned with Leroy to collect that poker money."

"Why let Thompson off the hook?" White argued.

"Not his style."

White pointed to the screen. "We've got David Bonner. He claims to have gone to the house at five, and his brother was already dead. He could be lying too."

"With that gun, anyone could have accidently fired, except Mary Alice who claims to be a marksman. What's the first thing you learned in gun safety?"

"Keep my finger off the trigger until I'm ready to shoot," White parroted.

"Exactly! If she shot him, it was no accident."

§

Milo checked his email while Martha collected the rest of the breakfast dishes. He was surprised to find an email this early from Creedence. The message was short and to the point. It included a web page with a password where Milo could check all of his, as Creedence called them, 'holdings.'

Milo laughed. To check his 'holdings' in the past all he had to do was empty his pockets.

As if on cue, the gate alarm went off. Dashing into the kitchen, where he knew he could find an intercom, Milo pushed the talk button. The woman at the front gate said she had a package for Milo Rathkey. He pushed the talk button again and told her to hang on a moment while he figured out how to open the front gate.

It was simpler than he thought. There was a button labeled, **GATE OPEN** Pushing that button, he heard the courier say 'thank you,' and Milo headed to the front door.

The exchange was simple. She gave him a package. He gave her his signature. Going to the kitchen, he opened the manila envelope and dumped the contents onto the island.

There was a note from Creedence. *"Milo, please find a checkbook, an ATM card, and two credit cards which have been activated. Cheers, Creedence."*

Milo put the cards in his wallet, glanced at the balance in the checkbook, and laughed again.

"It's the new reality, I guess," he said to no one in particular, seeing as how Martha had already left.

Logging off the web page, he checked his calendar and was reminded of the old reality. The old reality had him earning three hundred dollars today following Heidi Reinakie.

Several weeks ago, that three hundred dollars paid much of the rent. Now he wondered why he should bother.

"It's eight-thirty, I have time to swim in a pool in my house, when a couple of weeks ago I couldn't afford a gym membership," he said to himself.

Milo wandered back to his bedroom, looking for the basement door. Entering the large unused closet, he found the door, pulled it open, and discovered a modern well-lit staircase leading down to what he assumed was the pool. This was so much nicer than the single hanging light bulb leading to the dungeon of doom he remembered as a child.

Arriving at the bottom of the stairs was even more inviting. He could see the pool through the glass door to his right, but what had they done to the dungeon of doom?

Curiosity got the better of him. Turning away from the pool, he walked down the now-finished hallway toward the old pool area. Two heavy oak doors barred the way where once a creepy old metal door stood guarding the monster of the deep.

Pushing down the fear of eight-year-old Milo, he opened the doors to a well-lit, climate-controlled wine cellar. Hardly the thing of nightmares. No pool; no sign a pool had ever existed. Instead there were rows of wine racks.

He guessed there were thousands of dollars, if not tens or hundreds of thousands, tied up in these beautiful little bottles of red and white. Remembering every evening meal came with a bottle of wine, he now knew where it came from.

Last fall, when he met with John in the library, Milo remarked at how little the house had changed, but now realized there had been changes, modernizations, that were not apparent then. He had to say that he agreed with this one, and looked forward to more exploring, but not today. Today was for dreaded exercise. Leaving the wine cellar, he headed back down the hall to the new pool.

Opening the glass door, he expected a rush of heated chlorine. Instead, the room was warm and toasty with no humidity and no chlorine smell.

I bet it's a salt water pool.

His attention was taken by the glass dome overhead. Even though this was a cloudy, dreary, winter day, the glass seemed to amplify what little light there was, making the pool area bright enough to swim without artificial light.

Along the inside wall, he noticed a bar and a series of doors. The first one was filled with towels, suits, robes, flip flops, kid's toys and floats. Milo looked through the trunks, found an extra-large, grabbed a towel, and moved on to his next challenge, getting into the pool without doing himself injury. Luckily there were steps leading down into the water, meant for a young child and for Milo with healing ribs.

His big toe told him the water was warm and Milo eased in with confidence. In the Navy, Milo could do ten laps in twelve minutes, the requirement. He still did ten laps, but the time was longer, thirty-five minutes.

Milo could have admitted to being out of shape, but he chose to blame the slow time on his injured ribs.

After floating on his back for fifteen minutes, catching his breath, he marveled at the fact that he could swim in his own house in the middle of January.

He climbed out of the pool and looked to the bar. He was thirsty. Grabbing a bottle of water, he drank it, made some coffee, and sat down in one of the plush lounge chairs.

D.B. Elrogg

Looking at the unobstructed view of the gray skies, snow-covered woods, and the lake, he could only imagine how this view would look tomorrow, if indeed, the predicted blizzard arrived.

Milo's moment of reflection was interrupted by a phone call from Ernie Gramm asking him about the safe guy.

"We are going over to the Bonner house in about a half hour to talk coin collections, and I want to know if I can get those pictures from the safe while I'm there."

"You're in luck," Milo said. "Ed Patupick, not only knows about the picture-taking safe, he made it."

"What the hell does that mean?"

"He invented it, patented it, and installed the first one for none other than James Bonner."

"Okay then, I'm impressed. Your guy is the guy, but can that guy get those pictures to me while I'm there?"

"He doesn't want to leave his shop, but he says he can walk me through the process by phone."

"Works for me. See you in a half hour."

18

Mary Alice stood clad not in black, but in an appropriate dark, navy-blue ensemble. She offered her hand to Lt. Gramm, and nodding to Sgt. White, she introduced her lawyer, Pat Wautkin.

The elf-like Wautkin, whose full salt-and-pepper beard was a dramatic contrast to his shiny bald head, often crossed paths with Gramm when well-healed clients ran afoul of the law. He always liked to begin on a friendly note, and today proved no different. "Well Ernie, you have yet to take me up on a day of fly fishing."

Gramm knew fly fishing was Wautkin's passion. Lawyering was a hobby, lucrative, but a hobby. "It's a little too cold at present," Gramm kidded. Wautkin nodded and sat down.

Richard was absent, causing White to bring the friendly conversation to an end. "Where's young Mr. Bonner?"

Mary Alice smiled. "Sgt. White, I am so sorry. He went for a walk on the grounds a little while ago, but he knows to be here at nine. I expect he will be back at any moment. In the meantime, can I offer you both coffee and pastries?"

Gramm accepted the coffee. White did not. Thinking this excuse was curious at best, White asked if Mary Alice had tried calling him.

Mary Alice said of course she tried calling him, but Richard was not picking up. "It's a reception problem. Our cellular service is spotty here."

White and Gramm exchanged disbelieving glances. Reaching for her phone, White asked for Richard's number, noticing that her phone had full service.

Mary Alice repeated, "I don't think he's getting the call."

White smiled while putting Richard's number into a special app. "I'm not calling him, I'm locating him."

Gramm leaned over to look at her phone as it pinpointed Richard's location about a hundred yards behind the house. He appeared to be stationary.

White excused herself and headed to the back of the house.

Gramm sat down on the couch opposite Mary Alice and her lawyer, accepted coffee, and made small talk about Wautkin's latest fly fishing trip.

Pushing open the back door, feeling the blast of lake wind on her face, White lowered her head and lifted her collar to cover her nose and mouth as she followed the tracking app. It led her to a solitary figure sitting on a bench overlooking the lake.

"Richard Bonner. Are you going to join us?"

Startled, Richard whipped around and jumped to his feet. "I..ah…um…oh is it nine o'clock already?"

"Past nine, you're late. What are you doing out here?"

Richard said in all seriousness, "Do you really need me?"

"You were told to be there. Go back to the house. I'll be right behind you."

Richard shoved his hands in his pockets and, with head down, trudged his way up to the house.

§

Milo managed to avoid Mary Alice on his way through the house to the crime scene. Accompanied by a uniform cop, he entered the now-cleaned office, sat down in the dead man's chair, opened the laptop provided by Gramm, and gave Ed Patupick a call.

Ed directed Milo through command prompts, pings, and IP configs, giving Patupick control of Milo's computer. Rathkey sat back watching windows fly open and close until, finally, he was staring at a folder labeled **January**.

Ed, ever wary of conspiracies, especially those involving the police, instructed Milo to click on the January folder before announcing his retreat. "I don't want to know what you're doing or who you're doing it to."

"Thanks, Ed."

Ed's access window disappeared, and the phone went dead. Milo clicked on the folder, sat back, and let out his breath. There were two pictures. The first was a surprise, the second, a man eerily familiar, but unknown.

§

Richard entered the room apologizing for being late. He noticed there was no signature welcoming smile from his mother. That, and her uncharacteristic silence, let him know how upset she was at his avoidance. He opted for a side chair rather than joining his mother and Wautkin on the couch. White sat down next to Gramm.

Wautkin spoke first. "Okay, Lieutenant, why are we here?"

Reaching into his file, Gramm pulled out a printed photo. Wautkin intervened, grabbing it away before anyone else could look at it. "What do we have here?" he asked Gramm, while inspecting the photo.

Mary Alice leaned toward Wautkin, eyed the photo, glanced at her son, but remained silent.

"What we have here is a still from a surveillance video that shows Richard pawning a coin collection this past Monday morning. Note the time stamp."

Wautkin shrugged. "All I see is Richard holding a box, and who's to say the pawn shop time stamp is accurate."

Gramm ignored the time stamp statement and handed Wautkin a second photo showing the coin collection on the counter with the cover open. "As I said, it's all part of a video I can send you."

"Okay. He's pawning a coin collection. So what?" Wautkin asked.

"According to our information, there should have been a large amount of cash and old coins in the safe the night Mr. Bonner was murdered. They were not there when we arrived at the scene on Sunday morning."

Richard, who was leaning forward with his elbows on his knees, put his head down in his hands.

"Come on Ernie, this isn't much," Wautkin protested.

Gramm held up his hand. "Oh, there is more. There is so much more. We have a witness who says he received a large amount of cash from Richard early Monday morning as payment in full on a gambling debt."

Richard groaned.

The interrogation was interrupted by the policeman who had been with Rathkey. Handing White the open computer, she looked, handed it to Gramm, who passed the computer to Wautkin.

Mary Alice's heart pounded, and her face grew warm as she tried to remember how to breathe. On the computer, she saw a picture of herself opening the safe at four-ten Sunday morning.

"Now what are we looking at?" Wautkin asked.

"You're looking at your client, who told us she knew nothing about the contents or combination to the safe, opening that safe. Notice the camera also caught stacks of bills which she removed. I have to tell you, I'm getting tired of being lied to."

"Where the hell does this come from?" Wautkin demanded.

"The deceased had a camera installed in the safe, that is triggered when the safe is opened."

"Wait. You said she removed the contents? I don't see her doing anything of the sort. Gramm, you know better than that."

The Lieutenant smiled. "There is a second picture, and I assume it will show you an empty safe."

Wautkin moved the curser over and clicked to enlarge the second picture in the January file. "Wait a minute, who the hell is this guy? There's your murderer!"

"That's David Bonner, James' brother. The time stamp says five minutes after five. He already admits to being in the office, opening the safe, but finding it empty. That seems to be the case, seeing as how Mrs. Bonner got there first."

Gramm was on a roll. "Also, Mrs. Bonner claims to have found the body, screamed, which brought her son running from the kitchen. However, we tested that scenario, and a scream from the office cannot be heard in the kitchen. Pat, if that's the story you've gotten, your clients lie to you as much as they lie to us."

Wautkin opened his mouth to speak but Gramm turned to Richard and continued, "You, young man, had a strong motive to kill your father. You were desperate for cash that your father refused to give you. You also had means to kill your father with the gun sitting on the desk. In addition, you had opportunity…you were in the house."

Gramm shifted to Mary Alice. "So, all I need to know is which one of you shot James Bonner, and which one of you is an accessory after the fact?"

Tears were welling up in those beautiful blue eyes.

Pat Wautkin finally grabbed the floor. "I need a moment to confer with my clients. For the record, I think you're way out of line here, Lieutenant."

"Convince me otherwise."

Wautkin got up and took his clients out of the room. Mary Alice put her arm around Richard who looked desolate. He did the same for her.

When the door closed, White turned to Gramm, "Confession time?"

"I see trauma and tears…maybe." Gramm was hopeful.

After fifteen minutes, the three reappeared. This time Mary Alice and Richard sat on the couch and Wautkin took the chair.

Leaning forward, he went on the attack. "My clients now realize they were confused about the events of Sunday morning, which is completely understandable given the horrendous gruesomeness of the scene and their devastating loss. But neither—neither—killed James Bonner. And let me say, had I been allowed to be here when you first questioned them, all of this could have avoided."

Gramm was having none of it. "Come on Pat, we read them their rights before questioning them, and neither asked for a lawyer. Let's dispense with that nonsense and give us the correct version of events."

As White took notes, leaving out the inflated adjectives, Gramm allowed the farce to continue.

Wautkin sat back and began. "As to Sunday morning, my clients admit to a bit of a…charade. Richard came home from his card game at four to plead once again for enough money to pay off his debts. Instead, he found his father dead."

Gesturing to Richard, Wautkin continued in his over-the-top style. "Traumatized—as any normal person would be—he rushed upstairs to rouse his sleeping mother. Shocked at hearing this…unbelievable happening, she tore down to the office where she also was assaulted by what could only be called the horror of a gruesome murder scene. Of course, neither of them killed James Bonner, but the love of a mother compelled Mary Alice to concoct a slight fabrication to protect her beloved son. She knew Richard didn't kill his father but realized finding the body would put him under immediate suspicion. Wanting to take that burden from him, she patiently waited for the cook to come to the house to witness their little charade…which obviously didn't fool anyone."

As if on cue, Mary Alice took Richard's hand and intertwined her fingers in his.

White rolled her eyes.

Wautkin continued. "So, as I said, neither Richard nor Mary Alice committed this heinous act. They may have been imprudent in their description of events, but come on, it was all so traumatic. People panic."

Gramm held up his hand. "Pat, stop summing up for the jury. Were they so 'traumatized' they stopped to raid the safe while James Bonner bled out on the desk? This time, without lying, could your clients tell us step-by-step what happened."

Wautkin gave Mary Alice his best lawyerly nod. With eyes cast down, Mary Alice admitted to opening the safe and giving Richard the money and the coin collection. Looking up at both Gramm and White, she added, "Violent men were threatening my son. Richard didn't kill James and neither did I. And for the record, it was quite clear James was already dead."

Gramm took the time to notice his shoes needed to be shined. The pause made Mary Alice and Richard sweat. Gramm wanted these two to sweat.

He knew he could arrest them for something, but at this point, there were still too many unanswered questions. He had no concrete proof either of them actually did the killing.

Breaking his silence, he said, "I can't get past this point: Richard has a great motive. He had a debt and his father would not bail him out. In fact, the two were seen arguing about it the night of the party. If you argue in public, what do you do in private?"

Richard looked up for the first time. "There was no difference in my father's actions between public and private. He didn't care what people thought."

His tone went from aggressive to defensive. "Besides, he gave me a way out. He told me to skip town, work off the debt, and he would stall those men, the ones I owed the money to. He said he would buy me some time."

Mary Alice looked at Richard with concern. This was news to her. "Go where and do what?"

"I don't know. It was a job with one of his companies… Whitehorse or something."

"Whitehorse in Canada?" White questioned.

"No Colorado. Denver, I think."

Mary Alice stiffened, caught herself, sat back into the couch, closed her eyes, and took a deep breath.

Wautkin, not comfortable with information being leaked unfiltered to Gramm, chimed in, once again stressing the trauma of the situation as an excuse for his clients' poor choices.

Gramm shook his head. "Obstruction of justice and interference in a murder investigation are still on the table.

Your clients need to know their lies have moved them to the top of the suspect's list."

Wautkin sat back. "Ernie, if you had any physical evidence putting either of my clients in the room during the murder, you would be making an arrest. I assume you have the murder weapon?"

"We do."

"Are either of my clients' fingerprints on the weapon?"

"They could have used gloves."

"So, the answer is no. I think we're done here," Wautkin said, standing up.

Gramm and White also stood and Gramm said, "For now, we're done. Don't leave town, and this latest version of events had better be the truth, or our next meeting will end in an arrest."

Richard said nothing. Mary Alice, whose mind had been somewhere else, came to life. She smiled at Gramm, got up, and ever the good hostess, escorted her 'guests' to the door.

§

After handing off the computer to the officer, Milo had slipped out of the Bonner house, not wanting to be around for the interrogation. He expected the picture from the safe to be Richard, not Mary Alice. The blue eyes lied again.

Besides, he had to follow Heidi Reinakie as she led her ordered life of Pilates, dry cleaners, grocery stores, and the constant mani-pedis. No dead bodies, no safes that take pictures, and most of all, no lying eyes.

Heidi was pulling the Cadillac out of the driveway as Milo arrived. He followed, but not too close behind. He knew where she was going. It was her Pilates day.

In the past, as he waited the hour or so for Heidi to emerge, Milo hustled for other work, calling various lawyers and larger detective agencies, checking his email, and voice mail. Today, he sat and did nothing.

This gig, which he tolerated for so many years, needed to end. He didn't like the work, and he no longer needed the money.

Breaking off from his stakeout, Milo headed down the hill to Ilene's. He had made a decision, and now had to act on it.

Ilene waved to him as he sat down at what was known as the employees table, the one near the kitchen. "Coffee and a cream puff," Milo called, "and I need to talk to you when you get a chance."

The place was busy, so it took a while for Ilene to deliver Milo's order. It gave him time to think about his decision. It was bittersweet. Since he arrived back in town, that apartment was where he bunked, and Ilene was his friend and sometimes therapist. But it was always meant to be temporary. Yet Milo could never muster the energy to leave, until now.

After about ten minutes, Ilene returned. Smiling, she said, "You're leaving, aren't you?"

He sighed, poured cream in his coffee and stirred it much more than it needed to be. "Yeah. I didn't think so…but now I think so. I will pay you for everything until you can rent it out."

Ilene laughed. "No worries here. I have an accountant who's wanted that space for a year. He likes the smell of baked goods…thinks it's good for business, and he is going to renovate."

"I'm surprised you didn't kick me out on my ass."

"I thought about it," she said laughing. "So, this mansion thing…it's good for you?"

"Let's just say, I'm getting used to it. Speaking of that, I have a nice, new, shiny check book and credit card. I can pay the back rent, the current rent, and any future rent. Just figure out how much I owe you while I get my files."

"Well this all so sudden," Ilene feigned surprise. "Hmm, let's say six hundred and fifty-eight dollars and thirteen cents. That includes the coffee, cream puff, and tax."

Milo laughed and handed her the credit card. He was glad she had a tenant in the wings who appreciated the smell of the bakery as much as he did.

Ilene returned with his card—marveling at how it had cleared—and invited him to come in anytime with his magic card to buy all the cream puffs he could eat. They hugged, and Milo headed upstairs for the last time.

After boxing up his files and filling the trunk of the Honda, Milo was about to head home when Gramm called him, filling him in on the events of the morning. Milo was somewhat surprised there were no arrests.

He asked Gramm to set up an appointment for him with McGrath concerning the Barbara Cook accident.

"Should I pay attention to this?" Gramm asked.

"Not yet."

"Good. I'll get back to you."

§

Great Party! Sorry About The Murder

Pat Wautkin admonished both Mary Alice and Richard for talking to the police without him present, and especially for concocting the lie about what happened Sunday morning.

"The cops are not idiots. Gramm has been at this for a long time. Don't talk with the police anymore. I will deal with Gramm."

After Wautkin left, Richard excused himself and went upstairs. Alone, Mary Alice poured herself a fresh cup of coffee, sat back, and enjoyed the silence.

She felt peace in knowing this house and the grounds were now hers again. Her father would be pleased. James was dead, no loss, and Mary Alice had confidence that Wautkin could keep the police away from both her and her son.

The ringing of the phone broke the calm. She glanced over and saw it was Brad Nelson. At one time, he was an amusing escape, but now he was a loud liability. The idea of a dalliance with her husband's competitor was no longer pleasing.

After six rings, the phone stopped making noise. It rang again. With a sigh, she picked it up.

"Where the hell were you? I just called!"

Mary Alice closed her eyes. If there was any doubt this was going to end, the doubt was gone. "What can I do for you Brad?"

"The police were here...at my office!"

"Why?"

He hesitated before speaking. "I went back to the house after the party to have it out with James...you know, about the Miller Trunk project."

"That was unwise."

Brad erupted. "Well, I didn't know he was going to be murdered, did I?"

Mary Alice said nothing.

"Hello? Are you there?" Brad shouted.

"Brad, I care about you, you know I do, but things have changed, and under the circumstances, we need to end this relationship for both our sakes."

It was Brad's turn to be silent.

"I take your silence as agreement. Goodbye Brad." Mary Alice hung up the phone.

It immediately rang again. She ignored it, refreshed her coffee, and walked the length of the room to the far window. Her tennis courts were encased in snow.

I will have to find a new tennis partner.

Richard returned and asked who was on the phone.

"No one of any consequence." She patted the cushion of the settee near the window. "Come sit by me."

With reluctance he moved to his mother and sat down looking at the floor. "I'm sorry about the gambling. I got in over my head, way over my head."

"You know you can tell me anything Richard. I realize you wanted to take care of this on your own, and spare me the concern."

Richard blurted out. "You never asked me if I killed Father."

Mary Alice gently locked her arm around his and leaned against him. "I didn't have to."

They sat for a moment in silence finally broken by Mary Alice. "All of these people…all of this mess will go away, and when it does, we will continue on. Now, tell me about this job James offered you."

"I don't know what it was."

"And you're sure it was called Whitehorse, the company I mean?"

"Oh yeah, I remember that. It didn't sound like a real company name. Why?"

"No reason. I agree, it's an unusual name for a company. I want you to know, I will need you to help me run my company here, not off in Colorado somewhere."

Richard laughed. "I was never going to go."

Mary Alice disentangled herself saying, "Good, and don't worry about the police. Wautkin says we are fine."

For Richard, a dark cloud had been lifted. His mother wasn't mad, or worse, disappointed in him. He now had the guaranteed future that should have always been his. The gambling debt was paid, and the police were at bay, at least for today. Richard felt at ease for the first time in weeks.

Standing up, he pronounced he was hungry, not having had any breakfast, and was going to the kitchen to make a sandwich. Life without Father was going to be grand.

Mary Alice sat alone on the settee in the sitting room. Her smile faded as she watched her only son, her joy, leave the room. Her eyes narrowed, and her jaw clenched in an uncharacteristic fashion.

"Whitehorse!" she said out loud. "Bastard!"

19

The blizzard hit around three in the morning, and by the time Milo arose at seven, ten inches of snow had piled up on the ground with more still coming. A stiff wind in excess of forty miles per hour added to the misery, keeping all but the brave indoors. It was Thursday, but schools were closed, and businesses were shuttered as Duluth hunkered down to ride out the storm.

As Rathkey walked through the gallery, he could hear the wind-driven wet snow smack against the windows. The rotunda glass was completely white.

"Good morning!" he said to Martha as he made his way past the kitchen. "How was the walk from your house to ours?"

"High and dry, Mr. Rathkey. Remember, I can take the tunnel," Martha said. Gesturing to the morning room windows which were also encased in white, she added, "Too nasty out there today."

"As a kid, I would ride my bike in those tunnels. I'm glad they're still safe."

"We have a guy who keeps them safe," Sutherland said, not looking up from yesterday's paper. "That reminds me, we need to pay some of our guys, and since nothing is moving, let's do it today."

Milo looked pained.

"By next month, we could have a house manager to do it all."

Milo sat down and agreed to the financial powwow, but first, he wanted to experience swimming during the blizzard. Sutherland having 'been there, done that' in his youth, agreed to meet after lunch and talk finances.

Martha served Milo and announced she was leaving to check on her sister and brothers who were home without adult supervision.

Enjoying his breakfast, Milo talked murder investigation between bites. "So, it looks as though the story Mary Alice and Richard told police was not exactly true."

"They lied to the police? What part of their story was false?"

"Let's go with all of it," Milo said, biting into some toast, explaining all of the lies Mary Alice and Richard had perpetrated on Gramm.

"Why would they lie? That makes things worse."

"It sure does."

"But the Lieutenant knows neither of them did it, right?"

Milo looked at him with disbelief, "No, he doesn't know that, not at all. Both had the big three: motive, means, and opportunity. They're in trouble. Oh, and don't share this with anyone."

"I won't, of course, but I can't believe either of them had anything to do with Bonner's death."

"Look, I like Mary Alice, but she and her son have admitted to raiding the safe while James Bonner's still-warm, bloody body was a few feet away. Not exactly Rebecca of Sunny Brook Farm."

"I have played tennis with her!"

Confused as to what difference that made, Milo suggested, "If you were to collapse on the court, I'm afraid it's possible she'd hit a winner before coming to your aid. She sees the big picture."

"She must have despised him."

"I think it went beyond hate. She didn't care about him one way or another. Hate would require her to care. Oh, by the way, I found the wine cellar."

"Where the old pool used to be—good use of that space, and it doesn't scare small children."

"I was wondering who orders the wine. Do we have a guy?"

"Yeah, me. I order the wine."

"Good, no complaints here. By the way, are those old furnaces still in the basement? They also used to scare the bejesus out of me. I thought they were monsters guarding the dungeon with thick disjointed arms waiting to grab me and red-hot fire exploding in their mouths."

"You must have spent most of your childhood frightened to death." Sutherland grabbed one of Milo's bacon strips.

Without warning, the wind picked up and threw more snow against the windows. Annie jumped up, and glared at the storm outside, deciding if a retreat to her safe place was needed. Opting to remain, she went back to a tight curl in front of the fire. Even the smell of bacon could not draw her away from the warmth.

Finishing his omelet, Milo inquired, "Assuming this storm eventually ends, how do we dig ourselves out of that long driveway these days?"

"We got another guy. He will be here as soon as the storm ends. We also have an old converted army-surplus WWII half-track with a plow." Sutherland had gotten Milo's attention. "When I was a boy…"

"Oh my God!" Are you talking about Goliath?"

"You know Goliath?" Sutherland seemed surprised.

"Sure do. You don't forget Goliath! The sound of that engine. So loud! What a rush! The engine made so much noise, it required hand gestures to communicate, and once the grinding gears took hold, I was sure the damn thing was going to explode. John laughed at me. I would always jump when he dropped the plow and when those tracks began to roll…oh man! The snow flew back on either side of the cab! It was a carnival ride!"

"Yeah, it was fun when I was a kid. Years later, he found another playmate in Martha's brother, Jamal. In fact, I think they went out in it last winter." Sutherland saw the glee on Milo's face. "You're going to drive that thing today aren't you?"

"Certainly not! I mean, I'm a grown man. Why would I want to play with a really cool half-track?"

Martha arrived back in the kitchen in time to overhear the two talk about Goliath. "Let me know when you're going, and I will get Jamal out there. He will love it."

Sutherland shook his head at the thought of getting jostled about in a blizzard in a vehicle meant for war. "Play on the lane behind the house. My guy will do the front. He's used to Dad playing in the back."

Rathkey finished his breakfast and announced, "First, I'm going to take a swim."

Then I'm going to play in the back too. Goliath will ride again!

§

Floating on his back, Milo looked up at the snow-covered glass above the pool area. The wind outside was making a wild whistling sound as it skidded around the curved corners of the pool house. Snow was still coming down, and Milo watched it pile up on the glass dome as he began a moderate back stroke. After several laps, the snow slid off the dome, and Rathkey realized that the glass itself must be heated, causing the snow to melt and thud to the ground.

If this blizzard had occurred two weeks ago, he would be trapped in his apartment. He was still trapped but trapped with so many toys. As he flipped over and transitioned into a breast stroke, he had to agree with what he told Ilene yesterday—this mansion thing was indeed working out.

After adding five more laps to yesterday's total, he emerged from the pool and headed to the bar to make coffee. At this rate, he figured he would lose at least twenty pounds in a month. He always lied to himself when it came to weight. At least he wouldn't be a battleship.

Milo relaxed on a lounge chair, drank his coffee, and watched the storm.

§

Upstairs, Sutherland pedaled up the Andes via his virtual biking app while the techno rhythms of *Chasing the Sun* by the Wanted pounded in his earphones. As his legs circled to the beat, he started to sing the lyrics. When he got to the line about being forever with you, the face of Agnes Larson—smiling, pretty, and animated—somehow worked into his mind's music video. He was surprised but undaunted as he continued his quest up the Andes. *Agnes Larson? Hmm interesting.* The trail steepened, forcing Sutherland to stand and pedal harder.

§

Milo finished his coffee, and went up to the master bedroom to get ready to take on Goliath. Pressing the intercom button labeled Martha's House, he waited for a response.

Seconds later, he heard Martha's voice. "Yes, Mr. Rathkey?"

Hurrying back to the intercom, he asked, "How did you know it was me?"

"If you look at the top of the intercom console, you will see a caller ID."

"It has my name?"

Martha laughed. "No, Mr. Rathkey, only location. You pressed the button from the master bedroom."

More mansion stuff to learn.

"Tell Jamal I'm heading to Goliath in about thirty minutes. Also, so much has changed around here, are the tunnels in the same place?"

"In my experience, tunnels are tough to move, Mr. Rathkey. The entrances are still in the basement past the furnaces. They're marked."

Rathkey thanked her, enjoying her sarcasm. After showering and dressing, he headed for the basement with some trepidation, still remembering those furnaces.

He passed the old pool room, now the wine cellar, and opened a new door that led to the unfinished basement. To his relief the old coal furnaces with attacking arms were indeed gone. Three modern gas furnaces had taken their place. They were silent.

It's amazing how old fears from childhood hang on.

Rathkey put on his old overcoat, leather earmuff hat, and his old galoshes. He noticed a door labeled, *Tunnels* and opened it. The blast of cold air hit him square in the face reminding him the tunnels were not heated, but they were underground, and protected from the worst of the weather.

There were four tunnels, all clearly marked. Rathkey wished he had taken a flashlight with him as he entered the darkening tunnel to the maintenance shed. Thirty years ago, John had always brought the flashlight.

Having come unprepared, he had planned to follow the wall, but two steps into the tunnel, the lights came on. "Okay, this is new," Rathkey said to himself. "Jamal, did you do that?" he yelled. No response told him these must be motion-activated lights.

Cool.

Making his way to the maintenance shed, Milo opened the door, and once again overhead lights came on automatically. It was hardly a shed in the true sense of the word. Large and open, it held many different devices, but in the center, in drab army green, lived the wonderful monster known as Goliath. To Rathkey, it was like meeting a long-lost friend.

He walked around it, touching its metal sides and treads. He expected it to be smaller than he remembered, but Goliath was still Goliath. It had stood the test of time and did not disappoint.

The door from the tunnels opened, and a handsome young man entered the shed. "Hi, Mr. Rathkey. I'm Jamal."

Milo walked over to shake his hand and noticed he was looking up. "How old are you?"

"Twelve. Thirteen in February."

Taking what he knew from Martha, he figured Jamal had a sense of humor. "Too bad you're so short," he chided.

Jamal shot back. "Yeah, it's a curse in the family."

Milo noticed that his young companion had an Air Force Parka. It was green, overstuffed with a large fur-lined hood.

"I have to get one of those," he said, pointing at Jamal's coat.

"Oh yeah! I hated it when my sister bought it, but I don't go outside without it these days. I have been spoiled."

Not seeing the keys, Milo asked Jamal if he knew where they were kept.

"Sure, there is a panel on the wall. Here let me show you."

They walked over to the far wall and a closed metal box. Rathkey opened it revealing numerous keys, all labeled. "I gotta admit, this place is well marked."

"I know." Jamal laughed. "That's Mr. Anderson, the guy who keeps Goliath running. I'm surprised I'm not wearing a label that says *Jamal*."

Milo laughed. He liked this kid. "I keep hearing about this Mr. Anderson. I've got to meet him. When does he come to the estate?"

"Tuesdays and Thursdays usually, and he spends the whole day here." As Rathkey took the key for the half-track, Jamal asked if he could ask him a question.

Wondering what a twelve-year-old would want to know from him, Rathkey invited Jamal to ask away.

"Martha told me you are now a co-owner of Lakesong. How does that happen? I mean, I've never seen you before." The question was asked with genuine curiosity and spot-on to the situation.

"You should be a detective. That's a good question. I'm a private investigator who, as a boy, lived on this estate. My mother was the cook for John McKnight, just like your sister is our chef. John, for reasons known only to him, decided to leave me half the estate when he died. So, Sutherland and I now co-own this place."

"Your mom was like Martha?"

"Yeah. We share that. Now, can I ask you a question?"

Jamal gave Milo a guarded look as only a soon-to-be teenager can.

Opening the door to the half-track, Milo asked, "Are you ready to ride Goliath?"

The teenage guardedness disappeared, and Jamal, the child, reappeared. "Let's rumble!"

They climbed into Goliath, and Rathkey remembered where the garage door opener had been stashed. It was still there!

"I wonder if this still works."

"It's Mr. Anderson. Of course, it works."

Gears began to spin, chains moved, and the large wooden door shuddered its way up. "Oh wow!" Rathkey said, more to himself than to Jamal.

The fierce winds had calmed some, and the wet icy mix had given way to a softer snowfall. Yet massive drifts formed a wall at the door blocking any vehicle that was not Goliath.

Milo sat in the cold, all-metal, unpadded seat refamiliarizing himself with the WWII controls. Goliath had standard transmission, no synchromesh, and Milo remembered it needed to be doubled clutched between first and second gear. It all came back to him as he turned the key and brought the monster to life. The engine's howl vibrated the entire cab, including the occupants.

"I love this thing!" Jamal yelled over the roar of the engine. Rathkey nodded his head, forced the shift lever into first gear with a grind, and popped the clutch. Goliath lurched forward, it's plow destroying the snow wall.

Rumbling along, Milo had to make a quick choice. Left to the estate service roads, or right to the side street.

The last time I drove this thing, I was seventeen. I need a little practice before I take on the narrow estate roads.

Milo pointed to the side street. Jamal gave the thumbs up.

Rathkey made a wide left turn out the side gate and then another left turn onto the side street. Staying in second gear but getting some speed on the straight away, the snow hurled past the side windows the way he remembered.

"Whoo hoo!" Rathkey yelled.

"We're killin' it!" Jamal shouted.

When Rathkey got to London Road, he turned around and shut down the half-track.

"What's wrong? Why are we stopping?"

"You want to try it?" Rathkey gestured to the wheel.

Jamal's eyes opened wide. "Really? You bet!"

They got out into the light wind and snow and traded places. Jamal sat down, pushed the seat back, and wiped the snow from his face.

"Let me explain the gears to you."

Jamal's eyes glinted as he turned toward Milo. "Oh, I know all about the gears. This is not my first snow storm. Don't tell my sister, but Mr. McKnight started me driving this when I was eight. I'm tall for my age."

Rathkey laughed as Jamal fired up Goliath, shoved it into first, eased off the clutch, and sent the rumbling half-track down the street back toward the estate. Like an expert, he double clutched it in second, and the snow began flying once again. It was wet and heavy, but the tracks held firm to the ground, no slipping and no sliding, just slicing through the snow.

Jamal made the turn past the gate, drove beyond the maintenance shed and then turned onto the service drive that led to the gardens and the tennis court. If he had kept going, he would have gone past the house where he lived with his sisters and brother.

"Don't want to go that way," he called out to Rathkey. "Martha will see me driving, and that won't be good for either of us."

"It's a blizzard," Rathkey hollered back, "How would she see us?"

"She has x-ray eyes. Trust me, she sees everything. It's kind of spooky." He powered Goliath down.

Milo and Jamal changed places once again. After another fifteen minutes of clearing back estate roads at max speed, Rathkey backed Goliath into the shed. As instructed, Milo and Jamal left the front of the estate for Sutherland's guy to plow.

"Now that was fun!" Rathkey said.

Jamal was smiling. "I hope we have a couple more storms before spring."

"Me too!" Rathkey agreed. He pushed the garage door opener and the old wooden door creaked and groaned back into place. It was as old and noisy as the half-track.

As they exited the vehicle and headed down the tunnel together, Milo knew the Goliath torch had been passed to a new generation.

His next thought, not nearly so metaphysical, concerned the Air Force parka . He needed to get one before the next blizzard.

20

A massive barrage of snowplows, road graders, and front loaders began working at midnight. Clearing Duluth's streets would take the entire day.

As Milo got his morning coffee, Sutherland explained, "With the bad roads, I've closed the office. Since I'm home all day we…"

"Since no one is leaving," Martha interrupted from the kitchen, "would you like me to do lunch today?"

Sutherland agreed and told her to bring the 'sibs,' using Martha's affectionate term for her sister, Brianna, and brothers, Darian and Jamal.

"That works. I'll have them here about one," Martha said, taking off her apron, preparing to head back home through the tunnel.

Sutherland continued where he left off. "Today is a good day for us to talk finances since somebody was successful in avoiding it yesterday."

There was no evading the conversation this time, but Milo tried, spending an inordinate amount of time feeding Annie her bacon.

Sutherland, having none of it, began to detail all the various expenses that they now owed.

Milo interrupted. "I get it. We owe these people. I'm not trying to be a dead beat, but it's boring. Just tell me my share."

"Oh no, no, no!" Sutherland exclaimed, waving his index finger. "That makes me your accountant. Either we do this together or get that third person to do it for us."

"Let's do that house manager thing," Milo said between bites, not caring nor wanting to hear any more about it.

"Excellent! I will play accountant this month; next month we will be set up with a house manager!"

"Good plan."

Annie meowed.

"Feed the cat. She's still hungry."

Rathkey complied.

§

Gramm rose early Friday morning, hoping to follow a plow into work. He was in luck, latching on to both a plow and a sanding truck almost all the way up the hill to the cop shop.

Doc Smith called at eight sharp to say they had finished with Bonner's body and were releasing it. Nothing had changed from the preliminary report. Gramm thanked him and looked up Pat Wautkin's home number.

Wautkin was sleeping and not happy to get a call this early in the morning.

"Pat, it's Gramm. Your clients can take possession of the body anytime. Let me know when they schedule the funeral."

Wautkin yawned. "Don't tell me you're at work."

"Unlike private attorneys, we servants of the public must be at our desks come flood, famine, or snow storms."

Wautkin laughed, "Shouldn't there be violins in the background when you say that?"

"The violinists were let go in the last budget cut," Gramm joked, "So let me move on to the will. What's in it?"

"Good grief Ernie! You want to talk wills before coffee?" Hearing no 'sorry, I'll get back to you,' Wautkin pleaded, "At least let me go grab some coffee as we talk."

Gramm waited through clanking cups, and a whooshing, foam-making coffee machine while sipping his own coffee, no cream, one sugar.

Finally, Wautkin was ready to approach lawyer mode. "As you know, I don't handle estate law, but since our firm drew up the will, I have read it."

White entered the office. Seeing Gramm on the phone, she began to turn around when the lieutenant motioned for her to sit down and start taking notes. She darted out, grabbed her note pad, and returned as Gramm put the call on speaker.

Wautkin paused, "Okay, I have some coffee now, so I might be able to make some sense. The will is basic. Mary Alice gets the bulk of the estate. There are trusts for Richard, and for James Bonner's brother, David."

"Trusts? Why trusts?"

"Because he didn't trust them," Wautkin laughed. "Okay, that's a lawyer's joke, but this time it's probably true. They each get a set amount each month with no ability to get advances."

"What about other bequests?"

"Are you kidding? You think James Bonner left money to charity? Did you ever meet him? That reminds me, I was going to call you later this morning, after coffee to clue you in on another line of inquiry."

Gramm leaned into the speaker, his interest piqued. "Do tell."

"Our firm is having difficulty determining all of the deceased's assets."

"What the hell does that mean?"

"It means we have discovered Bonner was paying huge sums to companies that don't seem to exist. We've tried contacting these companies in the usual manner. No one answers their phones. There are no web page, and their addresses are post office boxes. What services they provided are completely unknown, and I need to figure it out. It's now Mary Alice's company and her money."

"My first thought is money laundering or embezzlement." Gramm was a little suspicious. "Why are you telling me this?"

"Under normal circumstances I wouldn't, but the murder complicates things. I'm thinking the same way you are. If Bonner was doing something illegal, that activity could have gotten him killed. You should be looking for his shady business associates rather than hassling the widow and her son."

"Should our forensic accountants be looking at this?"

"Look Ernie, I'm walking a fine line here. If James Bonner was doing something illegal, and I turn everything over to you, the bulk of the estate, the money, the house, and the business, all legitimate, could get tied up in court. That would be against my clients' best interest. So, no, I don't want your forensic accountants anywhere near my client's money. I don't know yet who was involved with Bonner, but whoever they are, they could have murdered him. You know…a deal gone bad."

Gramm was not sure if what Wautkin had to offer was a solid line of inquiry or a convenient diversion away from his clients. "I can't do anything unless I have information."

"I understand that. I will send you what I have now and update you as we uncover more." Wautkin hung up.

Gramm looked at White. "What do you make of that?"

"I think a smart lawyer is trying to send us down a path other than the one that leads to his clients," White said.

Gramm nodded, "I think you're right, but we can't ignore it. More suspects to add to the list. Exactly what we need."

§

In Sutherland's mind, an avid cyclist pedaling the steep and rocky terrain of Hau' Ula Loop in Oahu should not be interrupted. Wanting to ignore the ring, he glanced to see it was Bill Bingham. Changing the bike's program to the easier level, Ka' Ena Point ride, he reluctantly answered Bill's call.

"Bill? The office is closed today. Did you miss the text?"

"No, but you asked me to get back to you about that X-rated store by the end of the week."

Sutherland nodded his head as if Bill were in the room. "Oh right."

"I've talked to a number of people. No one had the whole story, however, putting it all together, I've come up with my own theory. It's a wild one, but it fits."

Sutherland was intrigued. A theory from Bingham? He was a just-the-facts kind of guy. "Great! What do you have?"

"I think it's a scam."

Not waiting to be interrupted by his let's-see-the-best-in-all-people boss, Bingham plunged ahead. "As you mentioned earlier, the owners of the X-rated store bought the building at a normal price. Their property values, along with the whole block, begin a downward spiral. It's understandable. No family business wants to be on the same block as one of these smut stores. A moral outcry from a group of residents forces the city to act and create a development district. They use eminent domain to buy up the block and redevelop it."

Sutherland stopped pedaling. "How is this a scam? I get the property values falling. Doesn't everyone lose?"

"No, everyone does not lose. I didn't get it either, so I thought, what if we were buying these properties instead of the city. That gave me an insight, and, if I'm right, this scheme is as devious as it is brilliant."

"Go on."

"Think about the entire block not only the smut store. Each property goes down in value. Legitimate store owners are desperate to sell and get out. They sell at panic prices... pennies on the dollar. I actually made inquiries as if we wanted to buy the buildings. I discovered out-of-state companies have already bought every single building on the entire block, except one—the smut store. That's odd, right?"

Sutherland nodded.

Bingham, hearing only silence, continued. "The guy who owns it, Leroy Thompson, has not sold, and has no interest in talking to me."

Curious, Sutherland thought, but he had to pay attention to Bingham who was continuing his theory.

"Let's say each building costs a hundred dollars. This Thompson fellow, like everyone else, buys one store for a hundred. Because it's a smut store, all property values, including his, drop. Each store is now worth fifty. Everybody wants to get out with some money, so they sell to what they think are the only buyers, the out-of-town companies. They low ball. Most of the stores go for twenty-five dollars or less."

Sutherland was pedaling harder. "Everybody is still losing, Bill."

"Stay with me here. That was the set up. Later, the city comes in and buys each building for fifty dollars or more. Remember eminent domain has to pay a fair market price, and surrounding blocks are taken into account. The companies, who now own the buildings, sell back to the city for fifty dollars per building. They make at least a hundred percent on their investment."

"I hate it! If not illegal, it's at least immoral. These companies make a windfall on the backs of the store owners. The only saving grace is the guy who causes it all, Thompson, still loses."

"He doesn't lose. What if the companies own the smut store and are using it to manipulate the market. This Thompson guy is the front man. He's paid for pretending to lose."

"That's fraud!"

"I'm no lawyer, but I think you're right."

"It sure explains how Leroy Thompson can open new stores. Hasn't this been done several times?"

"Twice here in Duluth and it seems to be happening a third time. This guy Thompson is always the smut store owner."

Sutherland stopped pedaling, clicked his calendar app, and typed the names of the three companies mentioned by Bingham.

Bingham warned that this last part was all his conjecture, pieced together, and some of it could be wrong.

He added that in some cases, the owners sold because they had been threatened. Fraud and extortion in Duluth—not something Sutherland thought possible. He thanked Bingham, switched back to Hau' Ula Loop, and kept on pedaling, not as happy as before.

§

Milo spent the early morning swimming before calling Harry Reinakie to end their relationship.

At first, Harry was not pleased, but Milo sold him on fellow detective, Joe Ripkowski, who he said would do a great job, be much more enthusiastic, and look at this serious situation—Heidi's possible infidelity—with new eyes. In the end, Harry was excited, and Milo was off the hook.

The next call was to Joe, a so-so detective, but a good guy, who made even less money than Milo. On top of that, Joe had a couple of kids. This was going to be a profitable year for him and the family.

"PI Inc!" Joe answered.

Inc took Milo by surprise. "What the hell is PI Inc?"

"Milo?"

"Yeah. What's PI Inc?"

"I was looking for a new name for the agency, and my daughter came up with PI Inc. I thought it sounded classy."

"Are you incorporated?"

"No, what's that?"

"Never mind. I have some work to throw your way."

"Great."

Milo explained he didn't have time for Harry and a few other clients.

"Jesus, Milo, you're giving up Harry? He's a cash cow! Are you dying? I don't want to take advantage of a pal who's dying."

"I'm not dying Joe, just busy. I know you'll do a great job for Harry."

"Well thanks, Milo, I will. If you ever need Harry back, just ask."

"I don't think that will happen, Joe. Have a happy New Year."

"Happy New Year to you too, Milo!"

Milo hit call end.

21

Breanna checked her phone. She and her sibs were already late for lunch. The snowball fight, as fun as it was, had to end. She pelted both of her brothers with her saved arsenal, declared herself the winner, and began hiking back to the house. She knew she'd take a couple of retaliatory snowballs in the back, but better that than disappoint Martha.

Rushing into the garage, the trio flew out of their jackets, snow pants, and boots. With comic composure, they walked into the hallway trying to be as grown up as possible.

Martha called from the kitchen. "You three are only ten minutes late, congratulations."

Breanna countered. "I'm sorry. We would have been on time, but Darian was slow as usual."

"I'm eight! I have short legs, and that snow is high! I'm not giants like you two. Besides, Jamal kept knocking me down."

Martha gave Jamal a disapproving look to which he said, "You're not going to believe that runt are you? He kept tripping over his own feet."

"Sit! We are going to eat."

"Great! I'm starving!" Darian exclaimed as they all walked into the family room.

Both Milo and Sutherland stood up to greet the menagerie. Jamal shook hands with both, Breanna introduced herself to Milo, and Darian waved.

Martha had set lunch up family style, with large platters of sandwiches, a tureen of hot soup, pitchers of milk and water, and a large pot of coffee.

"I won the snowball fight!" Darian proclaimed as the platters went around and Martha ladled out the soup.

"You did not!" Jamal shot back.

"Did so."

Breanna jumped in. "You both were so pathetic. I pummeled you."

The debate, banter, and camaraderie over the morning's snow activities continued unabated between chews of sandwiches and sips of soup. Milo asked if anyone made a fort out of the stone wall near the lake.

"Martha doesn't want us that far down the hill," Breanna said, "but it would be great—as we have pointed out to her numerous times."

Martha sighed. "Well, as you are all getting older, perhaps I will reconsider. But you'll have to promise to stay away from the lake. The ice is still thin."

Darian looked at Rathkey. "How do you know about that wall?"

"When I was your age, I would try to grab it first."

Darian looked puzzled. "You lived here? Are you two brothers?"

Both Milo and Sutherland laughed.

"Not brothers," Milo explained. "My mother was the…" He thought about saying cook but looked at Martha and changed it. "The chef here when I was a kid." He hoped his mom enjoyed her new title.

"Did you two play together?" Darian asked of Sutherland and Milo.

Jamal laughed. "You're an idiot."

"I am not! I'm inquisitive."

"That's shorthand for idiot," Jamal shot back.

It was Sutherland's turn to explain. "When Milo lived here, I wasn't born yet. It was years, and years, and years before I would be born."

"Years and years and years? I don't think so!" Milo protested.

"Let's say Milo is much, much older"

"Much, much?"

Martha and the kids were staring at the two, until Darian said, "You sound like brothers." Everybody laughed.

"Can we go back outside after cookies?" Darian asked.

"Everything is wet!" Breanna protested. "I'm not going out with a wet jacket and gloves."

Darian looked disappointed.

"I have an idea," Sutherland said, "I have to go down to the vault to get some papers. You could all join me."

"What else is in the vault?" Jamal asked, thinking papers could be dull.

"What's a vault?" Darian quizzed.

"It's a large room in the basement with a huge door and a secret combination. It holds all sorts of old stuff, including old games and toys," Sutherland explained.

"Can we play with them?" Darian asked.

"Sure, the toys would love it." Looking around the table, not seeing any dissenting votes, Sutherland said. "Then it's set. This afternoon is for vault exploration."

After lunch, Sutherland led the troupe of intrepid explorers down the back stairs into the basement past the furnaces to a locked door. He opened it, to Darian's delight, with an old-style skeleton key.

A casual mishmash of chairs, sofas and a large table filled the ante room. It had not been disturbed for a long time. Serious dust had settled. The far wall was taken with a massive vault door that looked like it came from a bank about to be robbed by Jesse James.

"I've never seen this before," Milo divulged.

Although the door had a dial and a wheel, both had been replaced by a modern keypad. After Sutherland punched in the code, which Rathkey noticed was 2-6-6-4-3 or A-N-N-I-E, there was a click, and the heavy door swung open.

A sweet, pungent aroma of cedar came rushing out of the vault as the group stepped inside.

"It's like something out of Harry Potter!" Breanna exclaimed as her eyes scanned the myriad of wooden drawers, doors, and shelves that lined the walls, floor to ceiling.

Each door and drawer had its own unique, antique wood carving. It was as if each one was telling a story. Breanna turned to Sutherland. "Is it okay to explore? I won't open anything. I just want to look."

Sutherland laughed, "Go ahead, enjoy, open and touch everything. If you find anything fabulous, let me know. There are places way in the back even I haven't explored."

Breanna walked along the wall. Her fingers traced the intricate carvings of plants, animals, and other strange designs. "Who did all this?"

"I don't know who did it, or why," Sutherland admitted. "I do know it's a form of Scandinavian wood carving, but I always thought it was a lot of work for a room that is rarely seen—kind of odd."

Breanna was mesmerized. "It's so intricate, so detailed. Look guys, over here there are tiny dragon heads on these doors!"

Jamal and Darian rushed toward their sister. On the way, Jamal's eye caught two large dragon heads exploding out of the arm rests on an ornate, oversized chair. "I have dragon heads too, but mine are bigger!" he yelled as he hopped up, regally placing his hands on the heads of the dragons.

Bending over to examine them more, he exclaimed, "Mine have huge teeth and a long tongue!"

"And roundy eyes that bug out!" Darian yelled, being almost eye level with the carved throne Jamal had claimed.

"I am the lord of this domain!" Jamal announced, sitting back, relishing his role as a Viking king. "Obey me, or my dragons will devour you."

Martha turned to make sure the enthusiasm didn't break objects or bones. "Breanna, Darian, Jamal, be careful, some of the things in here may be quite delicate—could be broken."

Sutherland intervened. "Oh, don't worry about it. They aren't the first kids in here. I enjoyed my time in that chair too. I was king...."

"Look at the snake!" Darian yelled, having discovered a stand-alone carving of a yellow, green, blue, and orange snake lying on the floor under Jamal's throne. Darian picked it up to get a closer look and began pulling at the tail of the creature being devoured in the snake's mouth.

Martha rushed over to do a Darian-extraction. "Stop it Darian!" she admonished.

He ignored the order. "I'm trying to figure out what it's eating!"

Breanna came up behind him, gently removing the snake from his hand. "It's not a Lego, Darian. It doesn't come apart." Examining it she declared, "It's a rat! The snake is having a breakfast rat. Let's put it back."

After she stepped away from her brothers—the king and the snake whisperer—her eye was caught by three plain cardboard boxes. They seemed so out of place. Inside were faded, soft-covered, tattered books. After inspecting them, she called to her sister. "Martha, these are diaries!"

Sutherland joined Martha and Brianna. "That's where those ended up!" he said. "Thanks for finding them. This is my dad's collection of diaries from the eighteen-hundreds. He wanted them to go to either the Historical Society or the University. I'll have to get on that, but go ahead and read them if you want."

Milo was taking stock of a room he didn't know existed. "Some of this stuff looks really old."

"It is, and not all of this is ours. In fact, items in the back belong to the people who lived in this house long before we bought it," Sutherland explained. "My dad bought this house as is, furniture and storage. Story is, it had been abandoned. It's a mystery—maybe one you can solve Milo."

Milo, not even feigning interest in a real estate mystery, continued to poke around in the vault. Wedged between the cardboard boxes of diaries, he found a picture in a black and gold, art deco, metal frame which showed four young children sitting on the stone wall by the lake.

Sutherland walked over to Rathkey to look at the find. The picture was too old to be of him.

Jamal had been doing serpentine moves through the bookshelves until he came to a large plywood table top with train tracks and a miniature town. "Is this yours?" he called out to Sutherland.

Leaning around the book shelves and spotting Jamal's find, Sutherland exclaimed, "My old train! Milo, we need to carry it out into the ante room."

Milo placed the picture back on the shelf and joined Sutherland and the boys. The train set was heavy, but the two men and Jamal managed to get it around the bookcases, through the vault door, and onto the oversized table in the ante room.

"Where are the engine and the cars?" Milo asked.

"Follow me." Sutherland took Jamal's circuitous route around the bookshelves back to where the train board had rested. They came to a stop in front of an elaborate cabinet. "This was my favorite. On the outside are all these dragons, snakes, birds, and fierce dogs coiled and wrapped around each other in fierce battle. I would make up stories about who was fighting whom and why."

With a grand gesture, he flung open the cabinet doors. "On the inside is the answer to your question, Milo."

Long orange and white cardboard cartons were stacked each with the name *Lionel* written in black on the side. Sutherland began handing them out to Milo, Jamal, and Darian.

With all hands contributing, it took no time at all before the little town on plywood once again had its regular train service with two ten-car trains whizzing around the board. A steam locomotive that blew real white smoke was pulling one train. The other sported a more modern diesel engine.

Eight-year-old Darian was excited operating the trains. His hands were hesitant at first as they worked the black and orange handles of the dual transformer. But soon he got the hang of it. Crashes were avoided by Sutherland who took command of the electric switches.

They made a great team, and Milo wonder out loud which one was in third grade.

About midafternoon, Martha announced that if anyone wanted dinner, her crew would have to round up their found treasures and head upstairs.

Noticing the kids' arms overflowing with old toys, games, and books, Milo suggested they use the elevator.

Sutherland turned and looked at him as if he had two heads. "What elevator?"

Milo stared in disbelief. "The one that goes up and down—over there just past the furnaces."

"There's no elevator past the furnaces or anywhere in this house!"

"Well, there always was one. Who would take out an elevator?"

Not deterred at the obstinate look on Sutherland's face, Milo forged ahead past the furnaces to a pile of boxes against the far wall. "Help me move these dishes, my ribs have had it. They're complaining."

"Dishes?" Sutherland ripped one box open. "They are dishes! How did you know these were dishes?"

Milo shrugged. "They were always stored here—overflow from the basement kitchen."

Martha tapped Milo on the shoulder. "What basement kitchen?"

Finding all this rather amusing, Milo said, "Let's do one thing at a time. First, the elevator."

Sutherland and Jamal managed to move the heavy boxes of dishes revealing an oversized door. Sutherland tried the door, but it was locked. "I don't have a key for this one."

Milo shooed him back out of the way and ran his hand over the top of the door frame.

"Really? Is there a secret button up there?" Sutherland asked.

"No, a key," Rathkey said, wiping the dust off the key onto his pants.

"Okay," Sutherland said, now more curious than doubtful.

Rathkey opened the door to reveal a cobweb laden old iron gate blocking the way to an elevator car.

"I'm stunned!" Sutherland exclaimed. "I have never seen this before!"

"Does it work?" Martha asked, peaking into the room.

A light came on inside the elevator, as Milo brushed away the cobwebs and pulled back the metal gate. "It still has power, let's see if it moves."

Sutherland started expressing concern about the cables being worn, but Milo interrupted, explaining the elevator was hydraulic and didn't have cables.

"I'm game, but I don't want to test it with the kids on board," Sutherland said. After Jamal deposited the toys, games, and books into the elevator, Martha ushered the sibs up the stairs as Darian complained.

Closing the gate behind them and pushing the dusty number-one button, Rathkey braced for the elevator's jerky but brief starting vibration. Sutherland, who had never been in this elevator before, had to grab the gate to keep from stumbling as the elevator lifted them up to the first floor.

"I can't believe this! I've never seen this elevator in my entire life! It was never even mentioned," Sutherland insisted as the elevator bumped to a stop.

Milo, having fun at Sutherland's befuddlement, opened the gate and knocked on the door, yelling, "Martha we're here behind the locked door in the hallway outside the kitchen. Check for a key above the door!"

"I've got it." After a little fumbling with the lock, she swung the door open. "I always wondered what was behind this door."

The sibs grabbed the treasures and only Sutherland stayed in the elevator, pointing to the buttons, *B, 1, 2*. With disbelief leading to outrage, he began at an un-Sutherland-like volume. "Are you telling me this goes up to the second floor?

Furniture and gym equipment, and who knows what else, was lugged up those stairs, and this elevator goes to the second floor? Are you kidding me!"

Rathkey shrugged. "Up there, it used to open to a large closet in the old servants' quarters. I'm surprised you didn't see it when you remodeled."

"I didn't touch that side of the house. All these years, no one told me there was an elevator. Why didn't my parents use it?"

"I don't know. It was being used when I left," Milo responded. "However, the one addition to the house after I left was you. I bet they were worried about your safety."

"I didn't stay a toddler! You think they could have…"

Martha interrupted the elevator talk with a request to see the basement kitchen.

"Let's go down in the elevator," Jamal suggested

"Us too?" Darian asked.

"I think it's safe," Milo said, checking with Martha who would have the ultimate say. Martha's half shrug and smile gave permission to load up the new toy, and they descended to the basement.

Sutherland said to no one in particular. "We'll have to get a guy to maintain this thing."

Milo walked to where the kitchen should be and was puzzled at a bifold door where swinging doors used to stand. "I bet they put this up to keep you out, Sutherland."

"I was such a curious child."

Milo unlatched the bifold door and behind it he saw the familiar swinging doors marked *in* and *out*.

"Oh my god!" Martha exclaimed as she pushed open the IN door and rushed to the large commercial Thermador stoves which stood along one wall in front of two massive islands. "Why is any of this here?"

"I don't know. When I lived here it was used by people who prepared the food for John's bigger parties. I remember waiters rushing out the *out* door and in the *in* door and one idiot kid who got it wrong once, but I never did that again."

"I bet it taught you how to spell in and out." Brianna quipped.

Rathkey laughed.

Sutherland was the last to leave the kitchen.

What else don't I know about my own house and my own parents!

Martha and Breanna went upstairs. Milo, Sutherland, and the boys returned to playing with the train. After everyone had gone up, Sutherland stayed behind to collect his papers, send both trains around the board one last time, and closed the vault. When he came upstairs, Milo noticed he was carrying the picture of the kids sitting on the wall.

§

Perkins arrived late Friday afternoon. He plowed out the long, tree-lined driveway, took a snow blower to the sidewalks, salted and sanded everywhere so the ice would melt.

From the window, Darian watched Mr. Perkins rip through the snow. "That looks like fun!" He exclaimed.

Rathkey leaned over and whispered to Jamal, "Looks like we have a junior cadet for our next ride on Goliath."

Jamal smiled in collusion.

Martha rounded up her sibs, so she could get them fed before going back to work. As they made their way through the tunnel, the boys were chattering about trains, snakes, and dragons. Breanna was trying to read a diary and walk at the same time. It had been a wild day of discovery.

Martha recalled a couple of years ago, John McKnight had told her in confidence about his plan to include a man named Milo Rathkey in his will. Filling her in on his history with Milo, he thought it would be stimulating for both Milo and Sutherland. Martha smiled as she reflected on that day, especially watching Sutherland McKnight interact with the boys while they played with the train. She had never seen that side of him.

I think you were right, John. I don't know why, but this Milo Rathkey seems to be a game changer…for all of us.

Since it was a day for nostalgia, Sutherland settled in a gallery sitting area overlooking the lake to have a drink and relax before dinner. It was one of his mom's favorites.

The winter sun was setting, casting long shadows across the lawn in the back of the house. Sutherland loved the beauty of Lake Superior any time of year, but enjoyed its calming effect tonight. As darkness encroached, the view was enhanced by the soft yellow lights flickering on in Martha's cottage.

Swiveling away from the view, back toward the gallery, Sutherland pulled a remote control from the side table drawer. The up-lighting in the gallery came on, casting a soft glow about the room. Milo, who was heading through the gallery to the family room for a beer, was surprised. Spotting

Sutherland by the far window, he said, "Well that's fun. Does it do more?"

"There's music and more lights."

"Of course. Do we have a guy who maintains the remote?" Milo called as he made his way to the bar fridge in the family room.

"That would be us. It takes double A's."

Returning to the gallery with a beer, Milo added, "Well if we have a problem, I have a guy named Ed Patupick who can fix it."

"Patupick? Patupick? I think that's the guy who installed it."

"Oh rats," Milo huffed as he leaned against a chair. "My guy is your guy."

Sutherland took a sip of his drink. "Speaking of guys… pull up a chair…my guy, Bill Bingham got back to me earlier today about that smut store. Remember I asked him to look into how the owners could afford to lose money, yet reinvest in a new store."

Milo was all ears as Sutherland explained Bingham's theory. Rathkey leaned back and closed his eyes. Finally, waiting no longer, Sutherland asked what he thought.

Milo didn't open his eyes but said, "I think this is important, but we need to know more, and we need to tell Gramm."

Sutherland was surprised and pleased that Milo wanted to pass on his information to Gramm. This was unusual. He felt bolstered by new self-confidence. "Oh, by the way, I'm calling Agnes tonight and offering Mr. Perkins' snow removal service. We paid him for the day, but, thanks to you and Jamal, he only needed half a day."

"You're wasting your time. Without a car, why would she use her garage? Besides the snow storm was a day ago. Aren't you a little late?"

"It's not about snow removal, Milo. Remind me not to take you along as my wingman," Sutherland complained. Milo laughed.

"Okay, call her. See if her roof needs sweeping."

22

In anticipation of the Sunday night poker game, Milo texted Feinberg who assured him the roads on Hawk Ridge were clear, info he passed on to Creedence and Gramm. Creedence responded with three smiley faces. Gramm texted that because of the storm, his wife was caught at her sister's. He wondered if Milo wanted to join him somewhere for lunch. Milo invited him to Lakesong for a late breakfast. He refused to use the word 'brunch.' Milo Rathkey does not do brunch!

Sutherland was parked in the family room enjoying a cup of coffee and reading the paper. Milo plopped down on the sectional, grabbed the remote control, and turned on the TV.

"Just checking to see the time on the Packer-Viking game today."

"Primo rivalry, but it's on Monday Night."

Rathkey tossed the remote, disappointed his team was not playing today. "By the way, Viking fan, the primo rivalry is Packers-Bears."

"Wait a minute! Are you a Packer fan?"

"Of course."

"Get out of this house. Get out now!" Sutherland joshed.

"Too late," Milo said, looking around. "Where did I put my cheese head?"

Sutherland groaned. "What trauma occurred in your childhood that would have made you a Packer fan? You live in Minnesota, not Wisconsin!"

"My dad was a Packer fan, so I'm a Packer fan. By the way, I invited Gramm over for whatever this meal is called."

"It's called brunch. Tell Martha."

Milo shot up from the couch shouting as he headed for the kitchen. "Lt. Gramm is coming over for food if that's okay."

Martha turned off the mixer, so she could be heard. "It's okay with me, there's plenty of food."

Staring at Darian, she added, "and I'll make sure another place is set at the table." Darian dallied but eventually stopped constructing his Lego Starship and dealt with the task.

Milo was heading back to the family room when the intercom buzzed. "I know how to deal with that!" He walked over to the kitchen console and pushed the talk button. "Yeah?"

"Milo?"

"Yeah."

"There seems to be a large iron gate between me and your house."

Milo pushed the *Gate Open* button, and a few minutes later Gramm was at the front door. The aromas from the kitchen filled much of the house, and Gramm took a healthy breath as soon as he entered.

He walked through to the family room and shook hands with Sutherland while Milo found two beers in the bar refrigerator and handed one to Gramm. Sitting down on the sectional, the three made small talk about the upcoming poker game, Rathkey's dubious football affiliation, and the delicious aroma coming from the kitchen.

Martha and Darian began filling the table with serving dishes of ham, eggs, waffles, and hot-from-the-oven au gratin potatoes. After setting down the carafe of hot coffee, Darian introduced himself to Lt. Gramm.

Upon learning that Gramm was a policeman, Darian complained he was being held against his will as a sous-chef when his desire was to be a star-fleet commander. Gramm countered, because the food looked so delicious, he wasn't going to pursue the matter any further, at least until after he ate.

Martha, liking that solution, told Gramm he could stay.

The three sat down at the table and began filling their plates. Milo asked Gramm if there was anything new in the Bonner investigation. "Oh, the usual reports, but this is new, and kinda odd. Roger Lund—you know the furniture guy—told us a guy threatened him if he didn't accept a low bid offer on his furniture store. He came up to see if he could ID the guy. It turns out to be David Bonner, James Bonner's brother. I don't know what to make of that."

Milo furrowed his brow and leaned back in his chair. "That is odd. We have odd too. Sutherland you're up. Tell him about your guy's theory with the real estate and everything."

All eyes turned to Sutherland. "Well, I don't want to over sell it. It's my guy's theory." Sutherland told Gramm about the way the scam may work and how it might be orchestrated by several out-of-state companies.

"Funny you should mention that threat by Bonner's brother," Sutherland said. "Some of the other building owners said they had been threatened too. That's extortion, isn't it?"

Gramm nodded and asked for the names of the companies. Sutherland pulled out his phone to find the list. "Rampart, Larimer, and Whitehorse."

A puzzled expression spread over Gramm's face. "That's the second time I've heard Whitehorse in the last couple of days. Bonner offered his kid a job with Whitehorse which the kid claims his father owned!"

"Bonner?" Rathkey questioned, turning to Sutherland. "Would Bonner have enough money to pull off a scam like this? According to your guy, somebody has to buy all these buildings. I bet that costs a fortune."

Sutherland thought for a minute. "I don't think Bonner could put his hands on that kind of money. I mean his company has millions, but that's company money not personal money."

Gramm remembered his discussion with Pat Wautkin and the difficulty of finding all of Bonner's assets. "Could money from Bonner's legitimate real estate business be siphoned off into dummy companies with the idea that it could fund a scam like this?"

"Well...no. There are tax laws against raiding the corporate bank account."

Gramm smiled at Sutherland's guilelessness. "But what if you're a crook? Could you actually do it so no one else in your company knew you were doing it?"

Sutherland shook his head, "Not the way we are set up."

"What if you only had one person doing your corporate books?" Milo challenged.

"Oh yeah, I suppose you could hide it from one person because there would be no checks or balances, but nobody has one person doing it all anymore. I mean we have a multi person department…"

"What about Bonner?" Gramm interrupted, not interested in Sutherland's operation.

Before Sutherland could answer, Milo said to himself, "Barbara Cook."

Sutherland stared at him. "Oh my God!"

Confused, Gramm looked to Milo. "What about Barbara Cook?"

"Barbara Cook did Bonner's books. She was the only one who did Bonner's books."

"One lone bookkeeper, now dead." Gramm put his hand on Milo's shoulder. "Your investigation, and my investigation have merged. Tell me everything you know about Barbara Cook."

§

Following church, Roger Lund sat in his living room, shoulders sagging, brain filled with dark blues and black grays. Moving was painful. Normally his children's giggles as they played brought joy to him, but not now, not today. If this was depression, he was in it and sinking fast.

Donna, his wife of eight years, perched on the arm of his chair, gently put her arm around his shoulders, and gave him a hug.

He tensed and didn't look up.

"I know all of this has been hard, but we love you, not your business, you."

He relaxed a bit, reaching up, laying his head on Donna's hand. "Thank you. You and the kids mean everything to me…it's…I don't know." He took a deep breath. "I made a mess. I have to tell you, I lied to the police about the night of the party. They figured it out, and I think they are going to arrest me."

"That's silly. For what?"

"Murder!" he shuddered. "I told the police that I left the party and didn't return, but I did. I went back because Bonner called me. He told me he wanted to buy our building. They know I was there. They checked my tires."

He looked up with tears in his eyes. "They are going to accuse me of murder." He leaned forward, putting his head in his hands. "I will bring shame to you and the kids. I don't know what to do."

The short, pixie-like Donna drew back her hand from around her husband's shoulder as he leaned forward. Roger had always been quick to anger, but lately, with his business failing, he ricocheted between volatility and depression several times a day. There was no middle ground.

As Donna placed her hand on his back, she knew what the answer to her question from the old Roger would have been, but in his current state, she felt she had to ask. "Roger… did you kill that man?"

The kid's playing spilled over to the living room.

§

After brunch the trio wandered into the billiard room where Milo and Gramm played eight ball on the pool table. Sutherland practiced on the billiard table waiting to play the winner. Watching him out of the corner of his eye, Milo vowed to never play Sutherland for money.

Milo filled Gramm in on what little he knew about Barbara Cook's demise. "I'm pretty sure she was going to meet McGrath. We thought for a while it was to protect her boss. Knowing what we know now, she was probably turning him in."

Gramm, going on a three-ball run, added, "You can find out tomorrow at eleven in the downtown annex. I made the appointment for you. I will want a full report. I also want to get ahold of Barbara Cook's computer."

"Agnes still has her sister's computer at the house." Sutherland spoke up from the billiard table.

Gramm was pleased. "Good to know. I'll call her in a few minutes to get that computer, but I'm still wondering where all this leads. I mean, look at what we have. Let's say James Bonner was running a real estate scam which involved his brother, and I suppose Leroy Thompson and Stan Shultz. Let's also say Barbara Cook was taking evidence of this scam to the police when she was killed. I gotta tell you, as dramatic as all this intrigue sounds, it's still based on theory, and I have a number of old-fashion, lying suspects with basic motives that are leading the pack in the rush to murder James Bonner."

Milo called the eight ball in the side pocket but missed. "Basic motives are good, and now that we've tied Stan and Leroy to James Bonner, Stan has one of those basic motives.

I wouldn't put it past Bonner to try to cheat him. That would not be advisable with Stan."

Gramm agreed. "Count 'em up, a lot of angry people and a bunch of liars, all with motives, opportunity, and means. I can only hope this connection to that Cook woman leads us to some solid evidence."

"Don't forget Sutherland," Milo kidded.

"Always been number one on my suspect list."

Sutherland didn't even look up from his three-cushion shot. "I'm not confessing—no matter what you do to me."

"See! No one in this case is cooperating."

"Sutherland aside," Milo said. "If Bonner was using Stan and Leroy to make a lot of money without giving Morrie Wolf his cut, that would be another dangerous thing to do."

"Oh great, add another name," Gramm said sinking the eight ball. "But chances are, Morrie would kill Stan and Leroy not Bonner."

"You people say that like it's a normal response," Sutherland complained.

Gramm re-racked the balls. "For these characters it is. Milo, I killed you in eight ball."

§

Mary Alice Bonner set up shop in the sitting room, topping her white, Louis XV, French provincial writing table with notebooks, financial statements, and her laptop computer. All of this modern finance played against the decorative gold leaf and the beautifully carved cabriole legs in a perfect combination that aptly described Mary Alice Bonner, a beautiful, decorative woman who could handle herself in the modern world, a perfect melding of form and function.

Meetings all week with lawyers, financial people and employees of her husband's business had completed her understanding of her current financial situation. The only missing piece was the exact nature of her husband's unexplained money transfers as described by Wautkin.

As she removed her not-for-public-consumption glasses, the phone rang. It was James's private line. Out of habit she hesitated. He always insisted his line was never to be answered by anyone else. She defiantly picked up the phone and pushed the button.

"Who is this?" The guff voice on the other end demanded. She recognized the voice; it was almost that of her husband's.

"David?"

"Yeah."

"It's Mary Alice."

"Do I get any money?"

"Yes, David," she said with a sigh. "James would not forget you. You get a trust that will pay you a healthy amount monthly. You need to call Patrick Wautkin, the lawyer, to get the exact amount and finalize the details."

"How much?"

"I don't know. Patrick knows. Call him." Mary Alice was more than ready for all things Bonner gone from her life. "James' funeral is on Wednesday at ten at the First Protestant Church in Lakeside."

The phone went dead.

Mary Alice put her glasses on and got back to work.

§

Sutherland versus Gramm in eight ball lasted only ten minutes with Sutherland running the table. After the trouncing, Gramm called Agnes from Milo's office.

When he finally returned to the billiard room, Milo complained, "It took you long enough, what do you know?"

Smiling, Gramm grabbed one of the comfortable poker chairs and sat down. "I think we are making progress. Agnes went through the computer, after you two mentioned it to her, and found a folder labeled *Not Important* which Agnes said was a joke between her and her sister. I guess they always put important things in folders labeled that way. Inside the folder were three spreadsheets labeled none other than—are you ready—drum roll please—Rampart, Larimer, and Whitehorse."

Sutherland dropped his pool cue.

"Boy, do I have to talk to McGrath!" Milo exclaimed.

Picking up the pool cue, Sutherland muttered, "I don't think it's a theory anymore. James Bonner was a crook!"

"That may be true, but don't get ahead of yourself," Gramm admonished Sutherland. "We don't know if any of this got him shot. I told Agnes to shut the computer off and bring it in tomorrow so we can look at it. I'll send a patrol car."

"I can take her!" Sutherland volunteered. "What time?"

In reaction, Rathkey stifled a laugh, and Gramm raised his white bushy eyebrows. "Okay, you pick her up about twelve-thirty. I'll be dealing with Thompson and Shultz in the morning now that we think they were working for Bonner."

"What about their cars. Could either one be the fourth tire track?" Milo asked.

"We know Leroy has a Hummer that doesn't match, but we weren't able to find a car for Stan. Now that you mention it, we may have dropped the ball on that one. We need to dig deeper."

"What does that mean?" Sutherland asked.

"We never checked Leroy's car situation further because he was open about the Hummer. Now that I think about it, he could have another car. I'll text Robin. Monday morning is going to be busy."

§

Saul Feinberg's house on Hawk Ridge was deceptive. Modest from the front, it looked like a simple modern one-story ranch house. From the back, its impressive, glass-encased, three stories were engineered into the hillside. While the physics that held it in place were sound, standing on one of the three large decks always made Milo nervous. It was a long way down from those balconies.

Sutherland and Rathkey were the last to arrive at the Sunday poker game. Once inside, Feinberg offered to take Sutherland on the grand tour but neglected to include Creedence. Surprised that Feinberg didn't include him, Milo asked Durant if he would also like to see the place.

"I've been here before."

"Did you forget, Creedence is my financial guru," Feinberg said, as he and Sutherland disappeared down the staircase.

When did Duluth get to be such a small town? Milo wondered.

Spying the tray of pastrami, basket of rye bread, and the assortment of condiments on the side island in the well-appointed kitchen, Milo wasted no time leaving Gramm and Durant alone in the living room. Gramm seized the opportunity to learn more about Mary Alice's father.

Creedence, who was mixing himself a vodka and tonic, obliged. After all, it was public knowledge and didn't fall into client confidentiality, so he repeated what little he knew for Gramm.

It was the same information Milo had related to him, but Gramm followed up with an obscure-detail-question cops have to ask. "Do you remember the name of the company —the one involved in that deal?"

"I do. My father talked about it from time to time as a lesson for me to avoid deals that looked too good to be true. He also enjoyed the irony in the name…Whitehorse Company… you know, hero on a white horse, riding into town to save the day. After the deal fell through and bankrupted everybody, the company evaporated."

Gramm wasn't surprised. It was the answer he expected. This was yet another time that name had surfaced, and each time it was associated with James Bonner. "Tell me, did James Bonner lose money in that deal?"

"Well, he appeared to lose, but my father was always suspicious," Creedence said.

Sutherland and Feinberg returned from the tour. "This place is spectacular!" Sutherland proclaimed.

"I thought you'd like it," Milo said, returning with his pastrami masterpiece. "Modern, sleek, not a piece of extra woodwork to be found."

Gramm was coveting the sandwich. "Make me one of those, Milo, while I make a quick phone call."

"Sure. Yellow mustard or that French stuff?"

"Yellow, like you have on your shirt," Gramm joked, while asking Feinberg where he could make a phone call. Feinberg took him to his office.

Once alone, Gramm looked around the room. It was a professional lawyer's office complete with an extensive law library. Gramm mumbled, "So much for the van," as he called White.

"What's up?"

"The company—Whitehorse—remember it?"

"Yeah, the one connected with Richard Bonner. His father offered him a job there I think. I don't have my notes."

"That's it. It keeps coming up. There is a file on Barbara Cook's computer."

"Sorry, tell me again. Who's Barbara Cook?"

"Was. She was Bonner's bookkeeper who was run down last November."

"Oh, yeah, got it. What are the other references?"

"It's part of a real estate scam which I'll explain tomorrow, and it was the company that bankrupted Mrs. Bonner's father thirty years ago."

"You think all these Whitehorses are the same company?"

"I don't know. That's why I'm calling. When you get in tomorrow, in addition to those DMV records, have someone start checking it out. I want to know if they are all the same company and, if so, who owns it."

"Richard said his father owned it."

"Yeah, but I want to know if he also owned the first Whitehorse company which I'm told evaporated with all the investors' money."

"Including Mary Alice Bonner's father's."

"You got it, Robin."

"So, thirty years ago a company called Whitehorse destroyed Mrs. Bonner's life, and now the same named company, owned by her husband, reappears. Do we think she just found out about it?"

"If she did, it's another motive for murder." Gramm added, "answers the question, why now?"

23

On this Monday, Sutherland was not reading his Wall Street Journal, nor sipping his green smoothie, but instead stared out the window, waiting for Rathkey to join him. He was nervous. His chatty self may have gotten the better of him last night, divulging too much information to Agnes.

Walking into this scene, Milo thought it odd. "What's up?" Sutherland turned and blurted, "Agnes wants to join you when you meet McGrath."

Milo nodded, poured himself a cup of coffee, and then enjoyed quizzing Sutherland, fully knowing the answer. "And exactly how does the remarkable, enjoyable, attractive Agnes know about my meeting with McGrath?"

"Well, I might have told her by accident. We talked about many, many things last night. I visited her after our poker game broke up."

"Did you now? And you talked about many things, including my meeting. What did you do? Run out of artists? No, don't tell me what you did! Okay, let's see if McGrath is up for a crowd. He wanted to meet downtown at the annex rather than up over the hill. If she wants to be included, you have to get her there by eleven."

"I can, and I'm sorry. It slipped out."

"It's done. Besides, this could be interesting."

§

Gramm was tired. Grabbing a much needed second cup of coffee from the break room, he began to plot out the interrogation of Leroy Thompson and Stan Shultz. Gramm was hoping to get one to turn on the other, so he could put this wretched case to bed. Gramm and White headed for interview room A.

Leroy's rodent face was pinched and hard. His hands were folded, the skin stretched taut across his knuckles, giving away his anxiety.

Manic bluster began the minute Gramm opened the door. "I'm a legitimate businessman, and I'm not going to put up with this crap. I closed the shop to come down here! I am losing money right now! I…"

"And this is your high-volume time, right?" Gramm cut him off as he and White sat down opposite him. "Leroy, I'm not in a playing mood, so save the harassment BS for your lawyer. We know a lot more than we did the last time we talked. We know you and Stan were working for James

Bonner. We know your 'legitimate' business was a front for his real estate scam. You two are his stooges."

"I'm nobody's stooge!"

Getting the outburst he wanted, Gramm shifted into a fast-forward attack. "Shut up Leroy, your time to talk is coming. Bonner started cheating you and Stan, and you guys didn't like it."

He lifted his hand to stop the whine he knew was coming. "Now I'm not saying you went to his house to kill him, but that's what happened. Maybe you shot him…"

Leroy began to rise from his chair in protest. Again, Gramm's hand went up in a sit-stay gesture. Leroy obeyed, and Gramm, never losing eye contact, continued. "But I'll entertain the idea Stan shot him. Either way, both of you are in this up to your necks."

Leroy stared at him. Gramm could almost see and hear the wheels spinning in his head.

"It's your turn, Leroy, talk, and make it good."

Leroy swallowed, "I want my lawyer."

Gramm sighed. "Okay, we'll make a day of it." He stood up and told the officer guarding Leroy to get him a phone.

"Don't need it," Leroy said pulling out his cell phone. "I got my lawyer on speed dial."

"As well you should," Gramm said as he and White got up to leave the room. Turning back to Leroy he asked, "Would that be the same lawyer provided by the now-deceased James Bonner. Who's going to pay him?"

Leroy jerked away, turning his back to Gramm, but the comment had made contact

Once in the hallway Gramm said to White, "Well, we rattled the rat's cage. Let's go talk to Our Man Stan."

Looking through the one-way glass in the observation room both Gramm and White noticed that Stan was not as anxious as Leroy, but he was angrier and far more menacing. He raised his bull-like body from the chair several times and began to pace, only to be ordered to sit down by one of the two officers in the room, Tasers and nightsticks at the ready.

"Relax, Stan," Gramm said, upon entering the room. "Want some coffee?"

"Screw you!" Stan snarled, pushing his chair back from the table. "I'll get my own damn coffee. I want out of here."

Gramm and White remained standing. "Get your ass back to the table, Stan! Do we need to cuff you?"

Seeing the beefier guard pull out his cuffs, Stan inched his chair closer and spread his hands on the table. His eyes downcast he mumbled, "I'm good." Stan didn't like restraints.

"Good," Gramm said as he and White drew up chairs and joined him at the table. "Your partner is in a much more cooperative mood."

Stan looked up and almost smiled. "Screw you! I know what you're doing."

"And we know what you've been doing for your boss, James Bonner."

No sound came from Stan, but his eyes began to dart as if looking for help from Leroy.

Gramm continued. "You're in big trouble and you know it."

Stan said nothing.

Reaching forward with palms open, Gramm continued. "Stan, thanks to Leroy's chat this morning, we know Bonner ran the real estate scam," Gramm lied, "and you guys were on the front line."

Leaning back in his chair, Gramm delivered the kill shot. "You know, Bonner made millions, Stan, and you guys got cheated."

Stan slammed his hands on the table, causing White to flinch, and the two officers to respond, making sure he did not rise. Leaning into Gramm with the officer's hands on his shoulders, he screamed, "Nobody cheats me, cop!" The veins in his neck stood out and his face reddened.

"Exactly. So, when Bonner cheated you…you killed him!"

Stan settled down once he figured where this was going. "We opened a store. That ain't illegal. We made some money. That ain't illegal either."

"But let's get back to this cheating thing. Bonner cheated you, and, like you said, no one cheats you. You went to confront Bonner. It ended badly. So, who shot him, you or Leroy?"

"You ain't gonna pin that on me. If Bonner was cheating us, I didn't know about it."

The door to the interview room flew open and a shady character named Frank Ugger entered. "This interview is over gentlemen. I represent both Mr. Thompson and Mr. Shultz, and I am advising them not to answer any more questions."

Gramm smiled. Ugger, a low rent, ambulance-chasing attorney, would not have been the one provided by Bonner. Gramm had called that one. The high price lawyer was no longer theirs.

"Bottom feeding again, Ugger? Well, you're a bit late on this one because Mr. Shultz just admitted to working with the deceased in a real estate scam."

"No I didn't!" Stan yelled.

"It's on tape, Stan."

"Screw your tape!"

"Stan, you have to work on expanding your vocabulary."

Ugger thought for a second. "My clients will admit to running an adult enterprise for the late Mr. Bonner. This is a legitimate business, and I am at a loss as to why Mr. Thompson and Mr. Shultz are here. So, either charge them with something, or let them go back to their business."

Agnes was struggling. Her friend Sutherland, whose company she enjoyed last night, seemed to be his usual affable self, but his words were coming to her from far away. She tried her best to respond, her sister's computer clutched to her chest, but the only thought going through her head was the question, *Why? Why did Barbara have to die?*

Sutherland had asked a question. Her mind tried to roll back to hear what it was. It didn't work. She turned to him, "I'm sorry, what did you say?"

Sutherland smiled. "Did you have breakfast today?"

She had to think. "Coffee. I think I had coffee."

Concerned, Sutherland asked, "Anything with the coffee?"

"I'm fine." She managed an insincere smile, hoping her response answered his question. Sutherland pulled into the parking garage across from the city-county complex.

Her thoughts slid back to her childhood with her sister. Their parents died within a year of each other, leaving her and Barbara orphaned. From there on, a series of relatives—and one or two foster homes—scarred both with the idea that they were not important to anyone but each other.

Now Barbara was gone, and Agnes was important to no one. Squeezing her eyes shut, she lowered her head in an attempt to endure the crush of physical and mental pain these thoughts brought. The waves of empty desolation were back.

Agnes found herself on the street outside the parking ramp, but she couldn't remember how she got there. This was that place. That awful place where her beautiful sister died, left on the road like garbage, of no importance. Milo said she may have been killed because she was too important. Not important. Too important. The two phrases flashed in her mind as she stared at the cold, salt-stained, concrete in front of her.

She stepped into the street not hearing the horns until she felt Sutherland's strong arm around her waist leading her to the far sidewalk. "I'm…I'm sorry, I…"

"I understand. That's where it happened. Let's get you inside where you can sit down."

Agnes allowed herself to be guided to the police annex where they found Milo already waiting. Sutherland sat her down on a chair. She heard Milo tell Sutherland he had checked in, and Lt. McGrath was ready for them.

Agnes was fighting to join the present. "Lt. McGrath? What will he tell us?"

"Not much," Milo explained. "This is the way these investigations go. You talk to everyone and learn small bits and pieces which start to fill in the puzzle. We think your sister was on her way to talk to McGrath about some sort of fraud, and today we'll either verify it or dismiss it. Meanwhile, give me the computer, and I will hold onto it until we see Lt. Gramm."

Agnes looked at him as if not fully comprehending.

"Agnes, you're holding the computer. Agnes? The computer," Milo said, gently.

She looked down. "Oh, yes, here, I'm sorry. I forgot…"

Milo gave Sutherland a knowing glance that said take care of her, and disappeared to put the computer into the trunk of his car. He didn't want to show it to McGrath. That was Gramm's call.

Sutherland spotted a vending machine in the far corner of the lobby but was torn. Should he leave Agnes to get her something, or would it be better to sit by her side. He opted for sitting.

"I am so sorry. I'm not…"

"That's perfectly okay."

"This is so unlike me. I was fine last night. I don't know…"

"It's okay. We'll sit here until Milo comes back."

Five minutes later Milo returned saying that McGrath was waiting for them. Sutherland helped Agnes up, and with Milo leading, they followed him down the hall to McGrath's office.

The younger Lt. Freddy McGrath was the smiling All-American boy, but the All-American boy had gotten older with a sprinkle of gray in his fortyish, thick, black hair. Rathkey introduced everyone and thanked McGrath for seeing them, explaining why they were there. Expecting a brush off, Rathkey was surprised. McGrath seemed interested.

Consulting his computer, McGrath asked "What day was this again?"

"November twenty-third."

"Ahh yes, I did have an appointment to meet Mrs. Cook at seven that night."

Agnes looked up. *Barbara was going to the police!*

As he leaned back in his chair, McGrath continued. "I remember it now. I usually don't make appointments that late, but it was the only time she could come in. She seemed anxious to see me. I was upset when she didn't show. My wife has MS and was having a bad day. I usually get home a little after five, so I can cook for her and the kids."

Rathkey thought how perceptions change with information. From what he had heard of Fading Fred, he thought of him as a guy who didn't care about his job. Now he had a much different picture of him.

Agnes continued to hear everything as if it were filtered through an echo chamber with questions interrupting the flow of information.

Why was Barbara coming here? Why didn't she tell me? Could I have helped her?

"I'm very sorry about your sister. I didn't realize what had happened," McGrath offered.

Oddly enough, it was Sutherland who asked the obvious question. Maybe it came from years of getting to the point at endless meetings. "Why was Barbara Cook coming to see you?"

McGrath went back to his computer. "My only note is she had evidence of fraud she wanted to show me. I gathered from our brief phone conversation it was complicated."

Sutherland continued the questioning. "Did you follow up after she missed her appointment? Is that something you do?"

"Of course," McGrath said. "I called her back several times, left several voice mails, but she never responded. Now I know why."

Milo looked at Agnes who nodded. "The police gave me her phone. It must have been turned off."

"I'm curious. Do you know what she was coming to tell me?"

Milo picked up the conversation, "It may be tied to the murder of James Bonner."

McGrath looked surprised. "Really?"

Milo went on to explain the situation, not divulging too much information. He didn't want to step on Gramm's investigation. He thanked McGrath, saying they had another appointment up over the hill.

§

As Sutherland started up Mesabi Avenue, Agnes stared straight ahead. Her mind reeling from what she had learned.

This is all my fault! Barbara's death is all my fault! I failed her!

Sutherland was at a loss, not knowing what to say to fill in the quiet. He blurted, "Well, that meeting was interesting."

Agnes remained quiet and stared straight ahead.

§

"You sons-a-bitches are not going to keep getting away with this crap!" Stan shouted as he burst out of the interview room, slamming the door against the wall. Having been released, Stan was striding toward the front door with his lawyer and Leroy double-stepping to keep up.

In a room where outbursts are common place, Stan's menacing acrimony caused everyone to look up. Several officers put their hands on their guns. Stan's volume was increasing and could be heard throughout the building.

"For Christ sake, Stan, shut the hell up!" Leroy shouted at him, running to grab his arm.

He turned on Leroy, eyes wide with anger, and shook him off. "Don't tell me to shut up! I'll kill you! Nobody does this to me, NO BODY, you sons-a-bitches will pay for it! You'll all be sorry!"

With that threat, several guns came out of their holsters, cooling Stan enough to allow Leroy to grab one massive arm and Ugger to grab the other pulling Stan into the lobby past Rathkey, Sutherland, and Agnes. Stan could still be heard shouting outside.

Agnes opened her mouth, but nothing came out. She struggled. "I…I..I can't breathe," she said gasping and grabbing at her chest. "I need to leave! I can't breathe!"

Feeling his own panic rising, Sutherland led her to a nearby bench while Rathkey yelled, "Can we get some help here!"

The desk sergeant whirled around and saw Agnes in distress.

"She can't breathe!" Sutherland shouted.

The desk sergeant hit the button on his intercom, "We have a medical emergency near the front desk, we need EMT help ASAP."

Several officers, including Sgt. White, rushed out of the bullpen area. Agnes was on the bench and Sutherland, frantic, was scanning the hallway.

White took over, kneeling in front of Agnes. "Can you feel your fingers?"

Agnes shook her head no.

"Is she having a heart attack?" Sutherland demanded. "She keeps grabbing her chest. I think she's having a heart attack!"

White attempted to calm Sutherland. "Please sit down on the end of the bench. I don't want you to have a problem too."

She turned her attention back to Agnes. "Do you have a history of heart problems?"

Agnes again shook her head no.

Another cop had a blood pressure gauge on her right arm. "Her blood pressure is way down!"

"Hyperventilating," White said. "You're okay. We're going to help you." Agnes nodded. "Cup your hands. Here let me help you. That's right, now put your face in your hands and breathe slow and deep. Breathe in to a count of four, one, two, three, four...good now breathe out again slowly...that's it."

Repeating this action several times, color began to return to Agnes' face. White noted color also returned to Sutherland's face. "Are you feeling better now?" she asked Agnes.

"Yes," Agnes said weakly. "Sorry."

"Nothing to be sorry about," White said. "How's her BP doing? Can someone get her some water?"

"BP is coming back up, almost normal," the cop with the blood pressure cuff said.

White looked at Rathkey. "What happened?"

"I don't know. I guess it's been a tough morning for her."

Agnes started to get up, but White eased her back down. "No, you need to sit here for at least ten more minutes." The water came and Agnes sipped it.

Gramm, hearing commotion in the lobby, was surprised to find White attending to Agnes. Before he could question anyone, Rathkey handed him the computer. "Here, hang on to this. It's her sister's computer."

Agnes tried to talk, "That man…"

"Don't try to talk yet," White told her.

"No, no…that man…"

"Ma'am you need to be quiet," White advised.

"No!" Agnes yelled in a sudden rage breathing in before her second word exploded, "Killer!"

Almost everyone seemed confused, but not Rathkey. "Let her talk. What man?"

"The yeller…the man…the killer!" Agnes blurted, her words coming out in gulps.

"Take a deep breath," White said. "Breathe and tell us again."

Agnes followed her direction and after a few seconds of breathing said in a whisper, "The man shouting was the man on the phone…"

Sutherland interrupted, "Oh my God! She must be talking about the man who threatened Bonner on the phone the night of the party. Milo and I were there when it happened."

Gramm sat on the other side of Agnes. "How do you know that man is the person on the phone?"

"Breathe slowly," White urged and got a nasty look from Gramm, which she returned.

"I know that voice," Agnes said. "He said the exact same words." She took a few seconds to breathe and then said quoting Stan, "Nobody does this to me, NO BODY. He was that man…I'm sure."

Gramm stood up and told Sutherland to watch Agnes until the EMT's arrived. He then told White and Rathkey to follow him into his office. On the way, White stopped to read the DMV report on Leroy's cars which had been put on her desk. Gramm veered left, handing off Agnes' computer to one of the techs who had been waiting for it.

Milo sat down in one of Gramm's office chairs waiting for the duo to arrive, digesting the events of the past few minutes. The situation was looking grim for Stan who was now tied to not only the scam but also the threatening phone call.

Stan as a murderer isn't going to surprise anyone.

White interrupted Milo's thoughts, waving the DMV report above her head as she strode into the office, followed by Gramm.

"Get a load of this!" she said, slapping the file on Gramm's desk.

"More blockbusters? How many are we going to have today?" Gramm said, picking up the file.

"Read it."

Gramm opened the file and shook his head. "I'll be. No wonder we couldn't find the cars, and there's that damn Whitehorse again."

"Care to share with the rest of the class?" Milo asked.

"Leroy's Hummer is licensed to the Whitehorse Company, and a second car—could be Stan's—also Whitehorse Company."

"Let me guess, a dark gray muscle car?"

"A brand-new Dodge Charger, dark gray in color."

"So, we've solved a murder—just the wrong murder." White stated the obvious.

Gramm took it a step further. "We may have solved them both. If Stan is our mystery voice on the phone threatening to kill Bonner, there's a good chance he carried out that threat. We need a search warrant for the Adult Emporium property."

Rathkey was quiet. The discovery of the muscle car triggered something in Milo's mind. He now saw what had bothered him in the original police report. "Son-of-a-bitch," he said to the empty room.

Gramm and White were already gone.

24

With warrants in hand, Gramm briefed the assembled team. "Stan Shultz has been implicated in the hit-and-run death of James Bonner's bookkeeper, Barbara Cook. He is volatile and dangerous. Leroy Thompson is considered to be an accessory to that murder. We want two things today. First, Stan Shultz and Leroy Thompson brought in with a minimum of trouble if possible; second, we need to find Shultz's car, a newer model Dodge Charger, dark gray in color."

Gramm continued, "Both Shultz and Thompson work and live at the Adult Emporium in the middle of the block. That's our first stop. Sgt. White, myself, Officers Stewart and Beady will go in the front door. Butler, and Hughes, you will cover the back. Young, position your K9 unit in the back in case one or the other does a runner. Everyone wears vests and helmets!"

After a few minor questions, Gramm called Roger Lund, told him to close his store as a precaution. The motorcade formed up and headed for the Emporium. On cue, the cars covering the back broke off and inched down the alley. The store was dark inside as Gramm and White pulled up. Being cautious, both took out their guns and proceeded to the front door. It was locked.

Alerting the officer in the back by radio, Gramm told them the front was locked with no sign of activity. His radio crackled in response, "This is Hughes. The back is locked too. There is activity in a garage next door. We hear at least two people inside."

Fast-pacing it back to the car, Gramm ordered his officers to hold tight. He instructed officer Steward to park her squad car at the far end of the alley, blocking it, while he and White proceeded into the alley from the opposite side. Officer Beady was to remain in front in case the two tried to escape in that direction. If the people in the garage were Stan and Leroy, they were boxed in.

Gramm parked his squad car blockading the near end of the alley. He and White proceeded on foot. As they approached the garage, they could see Young had her German Shepard, Taj, out and ready. Butler and Hughes were positioned on either side of the large, barn-like garage doors.

Gramm could hear angry shouting from the garage. White took Hughes' position on the left side of the garage, knowing that Gramm would take the lead. With his gun drawn, the lieutenant edged toward the garage door, standing a bit to the side.

Banging on the door, he yelled, "This is the police. Come out and keep your hands where we can see them!"

There was no answer.

Angry shouting inside the garage intensified. Gramm recognized the cursing of Stan Shultz. A powerful motor revved up and the door exploded, knocking both Gramm and White to the ground. Shards of wood came flying as large front wheels, with dangerous chrome spinners, careened forward at them and then veered left. The ricocheting icy rocks and cinders pinned both Gramm and White down.

Gramm rolled and jerked up to see the dark gray Dodge Charger lurching toward Officer Butler. He managed to get off two shots, but the car swerved again, fishtailing several times down the alley.

There was shouting for the car to stop, but it sped up, intending to ram Officer Stewart. In the midst of this chaos, she aimed her 9mm at the tinted driver-side windshield and squeezed the trigger, shattering the glass, sending the car sliding sideways into a huge snowbank. It recoiled once and then came to a dead stop.

White scrambled up and, with gun drawn, ran toward the car. It took Gramm a few more seconds to get to his feet. Cursing at his stiffness, he walked as fast as he could behind White.

Officer Hughes, noticing Leroy standing in the middle of the garage with his hands in the air, rushed to cuff him.

By the time Gramm got to Stan's car, the other officers had put their guns away and were calling for an ambulance. Looking at the hole in the front of Stan Shultz's head and the blood pouring onto the steering wheel Gramm added, "Call the medical examiner. Stan isn't gonna need an ambulance."

He checked for a pulse, but there was none. Gramm mumbled, "Nobody's going to screw with Stan anymore. NOBODY!"

White asked Officer Stewart if she was okay. Receiving an affirmative nod, White gave her space to collect her thoughts.

Gramm walked back to the garage and was glad to see that Officer Hughes had the presence of mind to deal with Leroy. Thompson was handcuffed, hands behind him, sitting on the ground bellowing his innocence. Upon seeing Gramm, he refocused his tirade to separate himself from his partner, "I tried to stop that son of a bitch. Stan's an idiot."

Without missing a beat, Gramm corrected. "Stan *was* an idiot."

"Damn." After a huff of derision, Leroy added, "He was too much trouble anyway."

Helping Leroy to his feet, Gramm admonished, "And you're not?"

Leroy's bluster was gone. "No, I didn't hurt anybody. Stan did."

Anticipating the flip he was hoping for earlier, Gramm wanted to make sure that all of Leroy's statements were on the record. "Officer Hughes have you read this man his rights?"

She nodded in the affirmative, "Yes sir."

"Leroy did you hear your rights and understand them?"

"Yeah, yeah, yeah! So, you guys really killed Stan? Really? Like he's dead?"

Ignoring the question, Gramm said, "Take him down to the station, and take his statement. I'll be there in a couple of hours."

Gramm walked back down the alley, calling on the radio for crowd control and for internal affairs. "We have an officer shooting a suspect."

"Do we have a problem?" Gramm recognized the voice of his boss, Deputy Chief Sanders.

"No."

By now, several television stations had arrived and were doing live shots from the scene. Gramm hated doing interviews on television. Stepping out beyond the crime tape, he winced at the blinding television lights. As he waited for the cameras to gather around, he watched White directing the forensic people. Gramm relaxed. She was young, but smart, and knew what to do.

White had hoped they would cuff Stan and Leroy in the Adult Emporium, and the entire operation would be over in less than hour. Staring at Stan's car still embedded in the snow bank, she realized there was going to be hours of work before anyone went back to the office let alone home tonight.

The forensic photographer was busy taking pictures. She instructed him to take special shots of the front-end damage that might have been caused by the hit-and-run murder of Barbara Cook. Stan might be dead, but they still had to prove he was the hit-and-run murderer before they could close that case.

Officer Stewart was talking with the internal affairs guy. An investigation was standard procedure. Having witnessed the event, White was sure there wouldn't be a problem. It was clean and justified.

Late afternoon shadows were lengthening. Several people from the technical side were already putting up work lights and setting up generators.

Gramm, finished with his interview, walked up to White, offering a cup of coffee. "Leroy is talking up a storm. He's fingered Stan for both murders."

White took a sip, "You know, looking at this whole case, Bonner was such an SOB. Creating that Decency League was part of his scam to make money. Who does that?"

"Even worse, he set up his own kid. That card game was run by Leroy who worked for him. He knew about Richard's debt, the poor kid's anxiety, and still put him through hell. I wonder if he did all that to use the name Whitehorse in front of his wife."

White pulled up her collar and shivered. It seemed a lot colder.

§

Shortly after Gramm and White left the police station, Rathkey headed back to Lakesong, and Sutherland drove Agnes home. Gramm indicated that Agnes would have to come back the next day to formally identify Shultz as the man she heard on the phone.

On the way home, Sutherland decided she needed food, his go-to remedy for all things Agnes. He couldn't do anything else for her, and she had a tendency to forget to eat. Agnes didn't refuse the offer of a meal, but she said she needed to be home.

Depositing Agnes on her couch, Sutherland called Martha, and arranged for delivery of two of her fabulous dinners with a couple of bottles of wine. He went back to the living room, lit a fire, and offered to make tea, an offer which Agnes was happy to accept as she curled up underneath a cozy throw.

§

Gramm called Rathkey around ten that evening. "I suppose you've heard about Stan Shultz."

"Yeah, I saw you on TV before dinner. It's not good for digestion."

After the long, tough day, Gramm ignored Rathkey's feeble attempt at humor. "I thought you'd like to know, Leroy cut a deal with the DA tonight by admitting Stan shot Bonner and ran over Barbara Cook."

"Two for one, not a bad day's work. What set Stan off on Bonner?" Milo asked.

"Leroy says Stan was furious about the car. Bonner wouldn't let Stan get it repaired. He knew we'd be looking for it. Stan insisted Bonner replace it. Bonner refused. Stan went nuts."

"So, he shot Bonner over a car?"

"I guess. I think once he got mad, Shultz could shoot anyone over anything. You saw him. Leroy claims he wasn't with Stan, so how Stan got to the house will remain a mystery. Leroy also admitted it was Bonner who ordered Stan to kill Barbara Cook."

Rathkey was quiet.

"This case is over. The late Stan Shultz was a double murderer."

"You've had a busy day," Milo said, "You should go home and get some sleep."

"Yeah, home and a cold one. Tomorrow begins a couple days of paperwork, my least favorite activity. Thanks for your help by the way. That tie-in with Barbara Cook made all the difference."

"No problem," Milo said, hanging up. To the empty room he said, "No problem at all."

25

Agnes gazed with wonder around the gallery, the high glass ceiling, and the living trees. A real cat stared down at her as if to say, "Who are you?" The summer park in the middle of winter was so much friendlier than the cold, sterile gallery of her former place of work. She started to laugh.

Sutherland looked puzzled. Agnes looked at him. "This room is so much fun!" she said, by way of explanation.

"There are bird houses, and birds! There's a parrot right next to the cat! That is a real cat, right?" she exclaimed, looking up and pointing in various directions.

"That would be Annie," Sutherland said looking up. "You know, I almost forgot these birds were here," he said, smiling. "I remember it as a point of contention between my parents. My mother wanted real birds, my father did not, so they settled on the fake variety. It sent the former Annie into a week-long frenzy, hunting birds that did not move."

Rathkey looked up and admitted to himself he had never noticed the birdhouses and the birds.

"Let's go over to what my father used to call, *The Thicket*," Sutherland said, leading Agnes to a wicker sitting area in the middle of a clump of small trees, causing her to giggle once again.

"It's like a jungle," she said, laughing.

Sutherland made a big deal out of trying to get through the trees, even though there was a tree-free path leading to the sitting area. "I must remember my machete next time," he joked. He liked seeing her happy.

Milo followed along. As he settled himself in one of the three comfortable armchairs surrounding the table, he looked up to see if there were more birds, or papier-mache monkeys.

Sutherland motioned for Agnes to sit as he poured coffee for all three of them.

"I want to thank you both for all the help and kindness you two have shown me through all of this. I now have some peace. I know who killed my sister, though I still don't know why."

Leaning back in the chair, she continued. "Hopefully, after I do the lineup thing at the police station today, someone can tell me."

Milo cleared his throat. "About that. I don't think the lineup is going to happen, in fact I know it is not going to happen."

"Why?" Agnes blurted out. "He did it!"

"Well, he's dead."

Both Agnes and Sutherland were shocked. Watching television news had not been part of their plans last night.

Milo continued. "The man's name was Stan Shultz. I don't have the specifics, but he was shot by the police and died late yesterday afternoon. The police are convinced that he killed your sister and James Bonner."

"So the killer is dead?"

"Yes, as I said, it's over, but we didn't ask you here to discuss that. Sutherland, why don't you tell Agnes what we have in mind?"

Agnes looked from Rathkey to Sutherland who brightened up immediately. "Oh yes! I almost forgot. We have a problem we believe you can solve. We need a house manager. Wait, let me rephrase that. We desperately need a house manager and are offering you the position."

"What? I've never been a house manager."

"True, but you are an over-qualified administrative assistant. You can organize, schedule, and deal with accounts payable. That's what we need."

The more they discussed the responsibilities—as well as the salary and benefits—the more the offer intrigued her. It sounded like fun, and she could use a little fun.

Sutherland looked at his watch and said, "I hate to break this up, but I have to get going. I have a meeting; work has kind of slipped in the last few days."

"I'll take Agnes home," Milo offered.

Before leaving for his meeting, Sutherland sweetened the pot for Agnes by indicating all the art in the house needed cataloging.

After Sutherland left, Agnes sipped her coffee and said almost to herself, "It would be a complete change of pace. Cataloging the art would be a dream. Also, this place is so close to my old office, the cost of going back and forth would be about the same."

"Why don't you just drive?" asked Milo.

Agnes seemed surprised at the question. "I don't have a car. I think I mentioned that."

"But you do. You have your sister's car."

The statement rattled her. "I…I…do, but…I never use it."

Milo took a deep breath. "Except that one time."

Agnes said nothing, but her face flushed and her eyes filled with tears. There was a long pause while Rathkey waited for her to speak. Finally, she whispered, "You know…how long have you known?"

"It took me a while to see it in the police report—just a mention. Your sister parked her car in the ramp. You must have gotten that car back. You made a point of saying you didn't have a car—no way to get back to the Bonner house—but you did."

"Why would you offer me this job if you knew?"

"Because the case is closed. Stan Shultz murdered James Bonner. Neither of us needs to take it any further."

Agnes looked at him, trying to decide if he was a monster like Bonner, playing with her, or did he mean it was over.

"Look, you can trust me. The police have no evidence. Stan was a murderer. He murdered your sister, and the cops have closed the Bonner case. Even if you confessed, I could get you an attorney that would get you off, but why bother? Look at it this way, I'm saving the city the price of a trial."

"Why would you do this for me?"

"A bad man is accused of killing another bad man. Both are dead. That's justice."

They sat in silence until Agnes whispered, "Would you like to know what happened?"

"I think I know most of it, but I've always wondered what you really heard on the phone."

Agnes sighed. "I don't ever remember saying Mr. Bonner was being threatened."

"That's because you didn't. You said *Bonner…murder*, and Sutherland made up his own story from there."

Agnes smiled, "Sutherland is such a dear." The smile faded as she began to revisit the phone call. "The man, Barbara's killer, was screaming at Mr. Bonner about how killing my sister damaged his car. It was clear that my boss ordered it. I couldn't believe what I was hearing."

"No wonder you looked so shocked."

"I didn't go there to kill him. I needed to know why. I drove back there in Barbara's car. He told me to go away."

Rathkey said to himself, "The fourth tire print."

Agnes not understanding, continued. "Bonner said it was over and not important. The next thing I remember, the gun was in my hand and his blood was on the wall. I couldn't believe it happened. I stood there for what seemed forever. No one came. I don't remember leaving."

"That gun has a hair trigger. Touching the trigger could cause it to go off. It was an accident, and if anyone was at fault, it was Bonner. With his personality, that gun laying on the desk was an attractive nuisance."

Agnes stood up straight. "I've tried, but I can't be sorry."

"Neither is anyone else who knew him," Milo assured her.

"Are you going to tell Sutherland?"

"No. There's no reason to."

"I must tell you, if anyone other than that man had been accused, I would have come forward."

§

Leroy Thompson sat in his cell in the county jail, awaiting trial on one count of fraud, and one count of obstruction of justice. He smiled. Offering up Stan had its rewards. At most he was looking at eighteen months, less with good behavior. Unlike Stan, Leroy knew how to behave.

The door to the cell block opened. A new prisoner was shouting on his trip down the cell block to his new home. "Piss on you people! You got the wrong guy!" The guards forced him into the cell next to Leroy.

The man immediately began to pace, taking a long time to assess his surroundings. In time his gaze settled on Leroy Thompson. "Hey, you're the guy who killed my brother."

Oh damn! David Bonner! What the hell!

Leroy's stomach began to churn. He had met Bonner once and knew him by reputation.

Stay cool Leroy…stay cool.

"It wasn't me. That was Stan Shultz, a guy your brother made me work with. I hated him…a real psycho." Leroy attempted to change the subject. "What are you in for?"

"What's it to you?" Bonner spat back.

Undeterred, Leroy jabbered, "Trying to make conversation. That Shultz guy helped me in the end…you know… work a deal, fingering him for the death of your brother. I gave them what they wanted, and had my charges reduced."

"So, did that Shultz guy kill my brother or what?" Bonner demanded.

"Damned if I know. He might've."

Bonner laughed. The little rat wasn't stupid. "You worked the angles."

"I have to. I gotta get out of here and make some money. I owe Morrie Wolf big time."

Bonner looked at the little guy, sure he was looking at a dead man. "Sucks for you."

"Yeah, I know, but I got some great ideas. I can pay off Morrie and make a lot of money. I gotta find a partner. Got any plans?"

§

Milo and Gramm stood back, away from the Bonner gravesite. The funeral was packed with curiosity seekers, and people who wanted to be sure Bonner was dead. Only a handful of them bothered to take the trip to the cemetery.

Richard stood beside his mother. Brad Nelson was absent as was David Bonner. There were a few employees trying to make points with their new boss, Mary Alice. Sutherland and Agnes stood side by side, a fact noticed by Gramm.

"What's with Sutherland and that Larson woman?"

Milo shrugged. "They seem to be friends."

Gramm's eyebrows went up. "It's good to have friends. Speaking of friends, I could wonder why my friend, the great detective Milo Rathkey decided to look into an all-but-forgotten hit-and-run."

"The great detective. I like that. I could put that on my cards, if I had cards, or a reason to have cards. But to answer your question, Agnes told me about Barbara at the Bonner's New Year's Eve party. At the time, I thought it was unfortunate, but once Bonner was murdered, it bothered me. Two murders, one office. I wanted to know why."

"You know, between you and me, the murder of Barbara Cook gives a strong motive to a person we never seriously considered. But I wonder." He tilted his head toward Agnes and Sutherland. "Did you ever suspect her?"

The service was ending. Milo and Gramm turned to walk back to their cars. Milo stated the obvious. "The case is closed. Stan Shultz killed Bonner. Leroy Thompson got a sweet deal admitting to that fact."

"That's true. It's a done deal, all tied up in a nice little bow. Everybody upstairs is happy, and I don't have to waste any more time or resources on the murder of James Bonner. Yet, I still wonder…is there anything you need to tell me?"

"Yeah, I think we need to go to Gustafson's. There's a meat loaf sandwich calling my name," Milo said.

"Only if the check also calls your name." Gramm laughed.

"I think I can afford it."

§

Taking refuge in his sitting room on the second floor of Lakesong, Sutherland removed the picture of the children from the art deco frame. It was as he thought, a picture of his father as a boy. Childish print on the back identified

Benny, Susan, me, and Annie. Under Annie's name John had written, *Where is Annie?*

Sutherland looked at the black and white photo that had captured four young smiles on a bright summer's day here at Lakesong. He knew the question was asked for a reason. A succession of cats and codes, plus his dad's buying this house, meant John had never stopped thinking of the smiling little girl at the end of the wall.

Whatever happened to Annie?

GREAT PARTY! SORRY ABOUT THE MURDER

If you wish to contact the authors, email us at authors@dbelrogg.com or leave a message at www.dbelrogg.com.

If you enjoyed this book please leave a review on Amazon.

BOOKS BY D.B. ELROGG

GREAT PARTY! SORRY ABOUT THE MURDER

FUN REUNION! MEET, GREET, MURDER

MISSED THE MURDER. WENT TO YOGA

Made in the USA
Monee, IL
10 June 2022

bad7e510-47f9-453e-abe0-43935bb7a33eR01